Thug-A-Licious

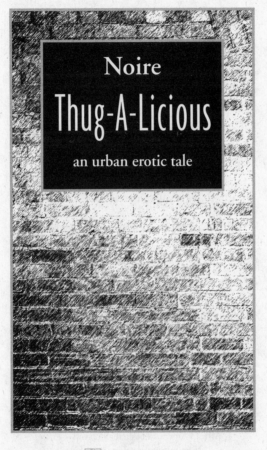

Noire

Thug-A-Licious

an urban erotic tale

one world ballantine books new york

A One World Books Trade Paperback Original

Copyright © 2006 by Noire
Excerpt from *Candy Licker* copyright © 2005 by Noire

Published in the United States by One World Books, an imprint of The Random House Publishing Group, a division of Random House, Inc., New York.

Song lyrics written by Reem Raw. Used with permission.

ONE WORLD is a registered trademark and the One World colophon is a trademark of Random House, Inc.

LIBRARY OF CONGRESS CATALOGING-IN-PUBLICATION DATA

Noire.
Thug-a-licious : an urban erotic tale / Noire.
p.   cm.
ISBN 0-345-48691-9 (trade pbk.)
1. African American basketball players—Fiction.
2. Rap musicians—Fiction.   I. Title.
PS3614.O45T47 2006
813'.6—dc22   2006043798

Printed in the United States of America

www.oneworldbooks.net

This book is dedicated to Reem Raw
and the rappers down with
N.J.S. Entertainment (Not Just Songs).

Keep doin the damn thang!

Acknowledgments

Father, thank you.

Missy, Jay, Nisaa, Man.

Bad-ass Tyrone, I love you.

My man Reem Raw, your lyrics are on fiyah.

Readers and music lovers, check out Reem's performance
on the *Thug-A-Licious* promotional soundtrack mixtape
available free at www.asknoire.com,
and hit Reem up at *Raw@asknoire.com*
and show him your love.

STAY BLACK

NOIRE

A Thug's Story

This here ain't no romance
It's an urban erotic tale
Hood life, gats, stacked papers
Set a thugsta up to fail

The 'Licious Lovers
Known for the closed lips
Letting the 'dro drift/whole click, boat trips/Pocono slope shit
Running our own shit

But life is more than riddles and rap
Check it while I draw you a visual map
Thru the ghetto where the criminals at, doing criminal acts
Between the present and the past, Thug is bridging the gap

Poseurs can't step in the same booth as I'm in
Blunts, Glocks, and diamonds
I'm hooping every day like I'm one shot from dying
These hoods give a fuck about jump shots and rhyming
They rather pump rock till the sun stops from shining

'Cause this here ain't no romance
We 'bout to thug it in this story
So grab a forty, flip the page, and live the pain and glory

In the beginning . . .

Have you ever wanted something so bad you was willing to crawl over bodies to get it? I mean, feened for it so hard it didn't matter who you hurt, how low you had to scrape, it was gonna be yours? That's what music and balling did for me. They were the fundamentals behind my rise . . . and the perpetrators of my fall. Check it. I came up in T.C.'s Place, a big-money pool hall over on St. Nick. The baddest gambling joint in Harlem. Me, Pimp, and Smoove. Dawgs-4-Lyfe and thugs to da bone. Sexing all the hottest freaks. Dominating niggahs with a roll of the dice. Spittin' gangsta rap on the mic every night. They called me Harlem's black prince. A rising star who carried street dreams on my back. But the streets, ya know. They got a way of coming for theirs. A habit of sneaking up on you when you ain't looking and snatching retribution straight outta your ass. And the night the streets rolled up on me to collect what was due . . . Dig. They call me Thug-A-Licious. I got so blinded by loyalty that I betrayed the ones I loved . . . and this is what it cost me.

NEW YORK—Baller, rapper, and NBA marquee rookie, Andre Williams, a.k.a. "Thug-A-Licious," was brutally knifed last night in front of thousands of fans during a heated NBA Finals game between the New York Knicks and the Los Angeles Lakers. Williams, a first-round draft pick and the league's leading rookie scorer, averaging 27 points per game, nine assists, and five steals, also dominates the street music scene with club-banging hits like "Just the Head, Please" and "How Deep U Want It?"

According to eyewitnesses, the charismatic six-foot-four-inch point guard had just left the court after scoring the final 3 of his 32 points, and giving the Knicks a slim third-quarter lead, when an unidentified young man made his way to the edge of the court and plunged an ice pick into the back of Williams's neck. Early reports detailing the extent of Williams's injuries have been conflicting, but at press time his condition was listed as extremely critical.

Five years ago Williams and two childhood friends were implicated in a vicious pool-hall robbery and massacre that claimed three lives. However, the immensely popular 25-year-old, whose court skills have been favorably compared to basketball legend Michael Jordan and is rumored to have fathered nine children with eight different women, was never formally charged.

All of this comes at a time when the sports world is being inundated by influences of rap music and hip-hop culture. And in an entertainment industry where sex, money, and power rule, it seems the fine line between the good life and the criminal life may forever be blurred.

Chapter 1

It was the night before our critical championship game against the Lakers and I was chilling in the G-Spot, watching some fine-ass stripper work the stage.

"Do that shit, Honey Dew! Show these niggahs how you can work them pliers you got stuck up in your pussy!"

The girl was built with perfect proportions and every dick in the Spot was hard, including mine. The G-Spot was a gentlemen's club for celebrities and hustlers deep in the game. I was a successful rapper and a rising baller with long paper, so I got a lot of nods of awe and recognition, and a few lame niggahs even stared at me, wishing they had my skills.

I'd had some beef with niggahs in the Spot a few years earlier, so after glancing around to make sure everthang was straight, I put my hand over the rock growing in my lap and sat back to enjoy the show.

The lights went dim, and suddenly a single spotlight flashed over Honey Dew's outrageous body. She gave us a few slow, nasty moves, and niggahs clapped and broke out the dollars as she bent over and spread her fine ass cheeks. She laughed and winked over her shoulder at niggahs in the audience, then squatted down and sucked a full bottle of Coke off the floor, gripping the neck with nothing but her tight-ass pussy.

"Dat ain't *shit*! Dat ain't about *shit*!" some drunk poseur standing beside me with gold fronts on his teeth yelled. "Dey got dat dere shit beat in the dirty souf! I know a ho down at Club Magic who can puff a cigarette with her pussy. And dat pussy be blowing perfect *O*s too!"

I prolly shoulda been resting at the crib on the night before a big game, but G had sent me a personal invitation, and I wasn't about to turn him down. Some major shit had gone down between G and my cousins a few years back that coulda got bloody. By showing up alone tonight I was sending him and his boys a clear message that Thug Williams was just as gangsta as ever. Don't let that NBA shit fool you. There wasn't a drop of bitch in my blood. Not a dime's worth of fear was in my pockets when it came time to roll up in G's Spot.

I stood up and clapped hard for Honey Dew, then tossed her a bill that fluttered to the floor at her feet. She scooped up all her cash and gyrated her juicy ass off the stage, and I stayed on my feet as the DJ introduced a dancer called Money-Making Monique.

"Goddamn!" I leaned forward so I could see better. This jawn was rocking her hips like a motherfucker. Her long skinny fingers was rubbing and squeezing her firm breasts, and from where I was standing it looked like she mighta had three nipples.

Monique was a true freak. She did some damage to that pole that had my collar choking real tight, but when the music changed and a bunch of big niggahs in tiny drawers came out shaking their dicks for the ladies, I knew it was time for me to bounce. I walked over to the bar and gave a hustler named Moonie some respect. He was real loyal to G, but T.C. had dug him back in the day so I knew he was solid.

"Whattup," Moonie said, showing me love.

I stayed cool. "Handling my shit, man. You know how it be."

"Your album is hot, man. You been hooping like a mother-fucker, too. The Knicks needed you, man. They ain't been this hot in years. Keep 'em lifted, yo."

Even though G had sent me a personal invitation, nothing in his Spot came free. I'd dropped a grand to get in the door, and another one to cover my drinks and a piece of pussy too. I was cool with it tho' cause I knew I'd get more than my money's worth in one of them back rooms. Some wild, funky sex always helped me get focused before a big game.

Juicy-Mo from 136th Street walked past and grinned at me real quick like she was scared to open her mouth and speak. It was hard to believe a dime piece like her was fucking with cold-hearted G, and even though she was still fine as hell, it was only a matter of time before that niggah crossed her out.

I'd sat down with G in his office and exchanged a few cool words earlier, and I could see why he was so strong in the game. That old niggah was smooth and crafty. He had absolutely no scruples and didn't give a fuck about nothing except runnin' his dirty money game.

An image of T.C. flashed through my mind and I leaned against the bar. T.C. had warned me about fuckin' with a OG like G.

"Look, Thug. That cat G took my brother Sonny out. If your cousins Pimp and Smoove wanna get shit all over their hands fucking with that motherfuckah, let 'em. But you carrying street dreams on your back, son. Me and Miss Lady got all our faith and hope riding on you. Besides, you too smart to get sucked into any pot that dirty niggah got cooking. Work your talent, man. Keep your hoop game tight. Pimp some broads. Cut all the rap music you can cut. But stay away from Granite McKay. Fuckin' with him can be dangerous."

"Yo, Moonie." I signaled my man. "Lemme get some Moët, man. Two bottles."

I took the bottles over to the cashier and got me a chip to room number nine. I'd already picked out the girl I wanted to get with, and when I got to the room she was ready and waiting.

Her name was Saucy and she was holding a full physical package.

"Whassup," I said and closed the door behind me.

She smiled and I couldn't believe how gorgeous she was. Her caramel-toned body was ripe and curved everywhere. Nice hips, big thighs, small waist. And at least five mouthfuls of big firm titties.

"Hey, Playa," she greeted me with a big hug. She had on some slinky shit that was clinging tightly to her curves and felt good when she rubbed up against me. She reached over and pressed a button on the nightstand that let the cashier know I was officially on the clock. "You feeling good tonight?"

I kissed her lightly, then rubbed her bottom lip with my thumb. "I'm feeling a little better. Now that I'm with you."

Saucy laughed, then walked over to the small table and got me a small glass. She held out the glass and motioned toward my Moët. "Well pour me a little bit of that, Daddy, and I'll have you feeling grand in no time."

I poured and passed. She accepted.

"I know who you are, but I ain't seen you in here before."

"Yeah," I nodded. "It's been a minute. But it's good to be back."

We drank together for a few and shot the shit. Saucy mighta been a ho, but I liked her. She had an upbeat attitude and a sexy, playful personality. She recognized me and knew who I was too, and that gave me a big lift.

"All right now," she joked. She was giving me a lap dance and I told her to turn around so I could watch her from the back. I couldn't believe how she was holding it. She was slim in all the right places and phat where it was needed. She also had one of the biggest, roundest asses I'd ever seen on a slim girl. I couldn't take my eyes off of it. She tossed her hands in the air and jiggled her perfect ass cheeks until my eyes got crossed.

"The Knicks got a big game tomorrow, right? You ain't pumping out none of that supersperm tonight though, are you?"

"Umm," I hummed, gripping her waist and palming her ass like it was a basketball. The way she moved, I knew she had some good pussy. I could just tell. "I don't know what you mean, baby."

She laughed and bent over at the waist. I caught a whiff of her nook-nook and licked my lips and moaned.

"I heard all about your ass," she said over her shoulder. "I re-member when you used to hold the mic down with your two cousins, the 'Licious Lovers. They was just talking shit about you the other day on MTV and BET. Talking about how hard you rap and all them damn kids you got. Mama's babies and daddy's maybes! Just don't leave no babies in this room with me tonight, 'kay, big boy?"

I was the one laughing now. "You ain't gotta worry about that, sweetie. Trust me."

She started laughing so hard she had to stop dancing and turn around to roll her eyes at me. "Trust you? Niggah, please! That's probably what you tell all your baby mamas! But I can see why a bitch would wanna reproduce with you. You fine," she grabbed my hard dick, "you heavy. And best of all, your bank is long and you paid."

She gave me a crazy look and slapped herself on the forehead.

"Then what the hell am I talking about? I must be sleepin'! Who *wouldn't* wanna have your baby!"

I laughed with her, but it messed with my head when people talked shit about my kids. Not because I was ashamed of having so many of them, but because for the longest time I hadn't done enough for any of them. A playa had four sons and five daughters. I'd been real young when my first kid was born, and then the rest of them came so close together that I got paralyzed by all that responsibility. But my girl Muddah had corrected my vision on all that, and I was grinding hard for mine now. Had bank accounts and college funds and ere'thang for my babies. Life insurance too. It was the only way I coulda convinced Muddah to marry my ass. I had to be doing right.

"What else they be saying about me on MTV?" I said, changing the subject. I pulled her back onto my lap until she was straddling my legs.

"Well," she grinned, looking hot and sexy. "They say you doing some real nasty shit in the NBA, but on the mic you a little too competitive. They say you a gaming niggah who likes to keep up all kinds of go-to-war gangsta friction between rappers. That shit must work for you though, huh? You stickin' all over the charts when other artists are fallin' off. They rotating your cuts on the radio like mad too."

And every fuckin' word they said was true too. I was the baddest NBA rookie in the league, and had a club-banging album with triple platinum potential. *Let them hatin' motherfuckers keep talking,* I thought as I pulled Saucy's slinky little top down with my teeth. Especially them weak-ass rappers who was getting scorched by my shine. Crunchy-skinned, burnt-up motherfuckahs. Pourin' sunblock all over my flow cause they couldn't handle the heat. I heard all the shit they said about me when they thought they was safely under the umbrella. I just laughed and said fuck 'em. My life was a hustle. So just fuck 'em if they didn't have the stomach for my high-powered game.

Saucy was still straddling my lap and I started licking her big titties like I was a new puppy. Her nipples was rock hard and stood out like little bullets. I swirled my tongue around them and sucked the tips gently between my lips.

She was nibbling on my neck as my hand slipped under her skirt and rubbed her baby-soft ass. I pressed my thumb against her clit and slid my long middle finger between her lips, inserting it deeply. I moved in and out of her tightness. The more I fingered her, the wetter she got. The harder my dick got too.

I got up from the chair without disturbing a damn thing. With my tongue still going to work on her nipples, I carried her over to the bed and lay her down on the thick satin spread. I wanted to eat me some pussy but I knew better. Her shit smelled delicious and looked like caramel candy, but *hell* no. She wasn't my woman. She was a ho.

Saucy started grinding her hips real fast, spiking up the heat. First little circles, and then bigger ones. I felt her insides grabbing and clenching on my probing finger and I slipped another one deep inside of her and fucked her like that. Her eyes was closed tight and she sucked air between her teeth. This wasn't no ho-show, I could tell. Baby girl was feeling this shit and so was I. A minute later she started shaking like she was having spasms. Her slit was so wet her juices were squirting out. Her eyes were closed tight and she pulled her knees up so I could admire her pussy. I massaged her clit gently and she thrust that whole thing into my hand, fucking up on my fingers like they were a dick.

"You like that shit, huh," I asked her when her shaking had finally stopped. "Well wait till I hit you with some of this."

I unbuckled my belt as her manicured fingers went to work on my zipper.

Her lips slid over my joint like wet silk and I started breathing harder. She sucked and slurped me down like a real pro. I clenched my ass cheeks tight and moaned, then cursed because it felt so good. She was giving up the best head I'd ever had in my life. Her throat didn't have no back to it because my dick was pushing all the way down in her neck. There was a hot pussy down in there, I just knew it. The harder I mouth-fucked her trying to reach it, the longer her neck grew, and the deeper my dick slid down inside her throat.

"You . . ." I shivered, pleasure rolling through me like never before. This was some super head she was putting on me. Smoking my blunt, trying to steal my nut. Saucy's whole throat was vibrating. She was swallowing my shit so good that if she wasn't a ho I woulda rolled with her all night, based on her neck action alone. "You . . ." I tried again, "gonna make me . . . bust real quick, baby. I'ma have to . . . go out there and get me . . . another chip."

Saucy didn't miss a lick. She reached behind her with one hand and hit the timer button on her nightstand, which bought me some extra time and lightened my pockets by a couple hundred too.

"Good, then," I said, my joint about to skeet like a water pistol. I was surprised too. I was known for having supreme dick control, and I could usually last a lot longer than this. But Saucy had me caught in the grip of her pump-action throat, and I promised myself I'd get some redemption on our second go 'round.

She had me on lip-lock. Her fingers was stroking my ass cheeks and milking my balls at the same time. I opened my eyes and saw her cheeks puffing and collapsing, and my last bit of control went out the window. I screamed like a cherry-popped bitch and grabbed the back of her head and gave her about ten long, hard strokes. Then I busted so hard my knees sagged and I lost my balance. Sucking hard to get every drop, Saucy vibrated that tight neck pussy until I snatched my dick out her mouth and fell across the bed in surrender.

"Damn," I whispered, trying to catch my breath. "That shit was good, girl. You a fuckin' professional. I'ma have to leave you a real phat tip."

She laughed and crawled up my body until her wet pussy was resting on my stomach. "You do that, Playa. In fact, hold on to that phat tip until we get through with round number two. I got some new tricks to show you. I'm gone freak you out so good I guarantee that you'll be doubling that offer."

Chapter 2

So when I say THUGGA
Y'all say LICIOUS!
Thugga . . .
LICIOUS!
Thugga . . .
LICIOUS!

The next night was game night and the house was vibrating from all the noise.

The noise!

The *NOISE*!

I got high off that shit, ya know.

Didn't matter if I was out there spittin' on the mic or breaking ankles on the court, the best feeling in the world was performing in front of thousands of fans who couldn't stop screaming my name.

Thug-A-LICIOUS! Thug-A-LICIOUS! Thug-A-LICIOUS!

They were calling for me. Screaming for *me*. New Yorkers knew how to keep a baller stroked just right. And I was lovin' that shit. The noise was my crack, and I just had to have it. My latest cut was blasting outta the speakers. The fans were on their feet. They were stomping and screaming and waving banners that sported my name in big bold letters. They wanted me, yo! They adored me. Pumped a niggah up to the sky.

I was running game in triple-double land. The ball was like hot velvet in my hand. We were down by three, and I hit a three-pointer and got fouled. *And one!* Yeah, motherfuckers! That's how you get back on top.

Thug-A-LICIOUS! Thug-A-LICIOUS! Thug-A-LICIOUS!

Coach signaled me over, and I dapped Marbury on my way to the bench. Somebody passed me a water jug. I swigged a mouthful, pushed my face into a towel, and then suddenly blinding heat sliced into the back of my neck and I was falling. Falling . . . FALLING!

Thug-A-LICIOUS! Thug-A-LICIOUS! Thug-A-LICIOUS!

The crowd was going crazy, and even as I slipped into the blackness I could still hear them screaming my name.

"Dre! Yo, Andre! Can you hear me? Open your eyes! Oh, shit! Say something, motherfucker!"

The noise was fading. I struggled to hear it as I moved into a foggy tunnel.

Some half-naked freak with a killer ass ran over to the bench and threw her sexy black panties in my face. I took a deep sniff then tried to snatch them off.

"It's okay, Mr. Williams," a voice above me said as my hand was restrained at my side. "We're just giving you a little oxygen.

Try and settle down, we'll be arriving at the emergency room in less than a minute."

I shivered and struggled to get some focus. I was on a bed in what looked like a hospital room. Suddenly I felt easy. Light. Like I had smoked some high-grade chronic and was relaxing in a deep, bubbly Jacuzzi. Every chick I'd ever boned in my life was up in there with me too. Bodies tight and crucial as they gathered around me smiling and rubbing suds all over my arms and legs. Massaging my big nuts. Sucking my earlobes. Laughing my name.

Thug-A-LICIOUS! Thug-A-LICIOUS! Thug-A-LICIOUS!

Yeah! I laughed and reached out and flicked a hard nipple. A niggah like me was a freak to my heart. All the honeys knew what time it was when they got with me. I'd make 'em cum until they cried. Lick 'em, stick 'em, do all the nasty shit they loved until they begged me to stop. I couldn't even bust me one unless a chick vibrated on my dick a couple of times first. And even then, I keep sexing her until she threatened to call the po-po and have me locked up.

I turned to my right and saw Muddah sitting next to me looking finer than ever. I broke out in a grin. My ride-or-die baby. Carmiesha "Lil' Muddah" Vernoy had been with me since back in the day. She was more than a dime piece. She was drop-dead gorgeous and had the best pussy in the world. Her bronze skin was hot in that tight-ass bikini. Nipples poking out on them big, firm titties. Luscious ass high and round, with that one little stretch mark shaped like a lightning bolt on her left ass cheek. My dick stood straight up as I remembered all the wild shit we used to do. I blew her a kiss. No matter how many other bitches there had been, nobody would ever come before her. There could only be one Muddah. She was my down-for-whatever queen. The only girl who'd ever gotten close to my heart.

Thug-A-LICIOUS! Thug-A-LICIOUS! Thug-A-LICIOUS!

I heard giggling and that's when I noticed there was kids up in there with us too. Little Precious! Shonee and Duqeesa. Even Kathy and the twins were up in there rubbing soapy water all over me. Their hands was soft and warm, and they massaged my shoulder muscles until they felt like pudding.

But it only took a second for all that shit to change.

Suddenly my whole body was on fire and the heat was coming outta their fingers. Massage, my ass! I tried to knock their hands away but I couldn't move. Them bitches was pinching. Every last one of them. The kids too. Standing over me scratching and scuffing. Digging their fingernails into my flesh like bird claws. Those whispers of love started smelling real nasty coming out their mouths.

Bastard! Lying mothafuckah. No-good playa! Ho-ass deadbeat bitch.

"Mr. Williams! Open your eyes. Try to stay with us, please! Okay . . . he's fading. Call a code. Everybody stand back."

Punches started rocking down on me. Female hands balled into man-sized fists, thumping into my chest, my arms. My lip got busted. Somebody grabbed me by the throat. One of them bitches punched me in the dick.

Stop! I tried to yell but they stuffed a pair of panties in my mouth.

None of them was adoring me now. Instead, they was spitting in my face and calling me all kinds of low-down niggahs.

Those jawns was beefing so loud they were drowning out the roar of the crowd. Shit, I could barely hear the noise.

Would y'all shut the fuck up so I can hear the noise!?

I was surrounded by a bunch of hateful black women calling me all kinds of motherfuckahs. Earrings was dangling. Necks swiveling, fingers pointing. Cursing my ass out from twenty different directions.

Where the fuck is my money? I want my goddamn child support! Your fuckin' baby needs Pampers, you sorry mothafuckah! I know your lying ass been fuckin' around! Niggah your dick is dirty! You gave me herpes!

Vikki, Rasheena, Remy, Breezy, Lani—they were all standing over me, jabbing me, hurting me, fouling my name. And the kids was getting some too. *Slap that mothafuckah! Bite him! Harder! That's right! Knock the shit outta your no-good ass Daddy!*

One of them snatched off a shitty Pamper and mushed it in my face. The rest of them bust out laughing. That crazy-ass Passion leaned over and laid our dead baby on my chest. *Who the fuck had let her out the joint?* The baby had on the same little white dress they had buried her in, and all kinds of maggots and flies were crawling outta her nose.

I screamed out loud and turned my head, and that's when I saw him.

Trust Chambers. Better known as Harlem's T.C. His killer eyes was full of disappointment as he watched me from a chair in the corner. He was smoking a cigar and pressed out in some deep, expensive gear. He had his arm around Miss Lady, his main squeeze, but she was half-dressed and so hurt she wouldn't even look at me. Vyreen was standing right next to them with her nose blown away. Her red skirt was bunched up around her thick hips, and she was staring at me with disgust in her dead eyes.

I was paralyzed and couldn't move. I knew this day would come. This was what they called payback time. The period for atonement. The credo of the streets dictated it, and you could take that shit to the motherfuckin' bank. Niggahs don't slide forever. Whatever the fuck goes around, you could look for it to come back around. But only harder.

I coulda rolled over and put the blame on Pimp, but T.C. had taught me better than that. Every man gotta hold his own nuts. My crimes belonged to me, and sooner or later if you played the game you had to pay the dues.

Pay up, pay back!

But before you throw that rope around my neck, slide up a chair so I can put you down on how I ended up with a front-row seat in baller hell. Check my shit before you wreck my shit. A life like mine don't grow outta no fairy tale. I was just a hungry ghetto kid coming up with nothing but talent and ambition. Skills on the mic and moves on the court. But this is Harlem, yo, and the rules of the game was already written when I came on the scene. I mean, you gots to live dirty if you wanna survive on these grimy urban streets. So I didn't do nothing a whole lotta other heads didn't do. Fought. Stole. Schemed. Played a little ball, shot a little dice, fucked a whole lot of honeys.

Shit on a few friends.

Take or be taken. Get yours or get got. It was the code of the streets and I'd lived by it. The way things was looking, I was prolly gone die by it too.

Chapter 3

Five years earlier . . .

"**Y**o, motherfucker." Pimp was sweating, leaning on me hard. "Smoove is *family,* man. Anything and everything for the family, remember? Plus, you owe me."

Thug-A-licious! Pimp-A-licious! Smoove-A-licious!

We were standing in the lobby of Harlem Hospital. Fear was some shit I'd never seen on Pimp before, and it took me by surprise. Vyreen had just finished braiding my hair, and his call had caught me coming out of her crib with my 'rows looking tight. I knew shit was bad when he told me Smoove was in trouble and to meet him at the hospital.

Thug-A-licious! Pimp-A-licious! Smoove-A-licious!

Me, Pimp and Smoove, better known as the 'Licious Lovers, were recognized on the streets of New York as the baddest rap trio since Run-DMC and Jam Master Jay. We had battled and rapped on just about every hip-hop stage between Brooklyn and the Bronx, but I didn't even wanna think about the kind of fire the three of us were facing right now.

"Did you hear what the fuck I said?" Pimp elbowed me hard,

spinning me around until I was facing him. "Rico's joint got popped. Them fools dipped with the whole package! When G didn't get paid he sent Pluto and his niggahs out to scoop up Smoove, and I just got the call. They gone smoke him, Thug. Them bitch motherfuckers is holding my brother in the G-Spot. Down in that motherfuckin' Dungeon. And unless you and me make G's package good, Smoove's shit is done."

I didn't wanna believe that shit.

"How you know it's really G who got him, Pimp? Rico and his boys is tryin' to come up too, man. They coulda set all this shit up and be sitting on the package so Smoove can take the fall."

"Nah," Pimp said, shaking his head and talking real fast. "I know the call was real 'cause Juicy seen Smoove. You know. Juicy from 136th Street. Jimmy's fine-ass sister. She's G's piece of ass now, and one of my boys overheard her telling Jimmy what she saw. She said that big niggah Pluto was kicking the shit outta Smoove. G was too. Juicy said they stomped him down until he was bleeding, and then they threw him down the Dungeon steps."

"Slow the fuck down, man," I told Pimp, trying to stall for time. I was feeling crazy rage behind Smoove getting snatched, but at the same time I was fighting the dread I felt rising in my stomach.

"Let's go somewhere and think this shit through. Cause that shit you talking is crazy, man. G knows Smoove is a straight soldier, and T.C. and Miss Lady treated me right all my life. They treated you and Smoove right too. Besides. That weight Smoove was holding was fat. T.C. and them ain't got that kinda cheese laying around."

"They will later on tonight. Think, niggah. It's Harlem Week. T.C.'s *Sweep or Weep* gambling spree kicks off tonight. The cash will be there, Thug, I'm telling you. We just gotta slide up in that joint and get it."

Thug-A-Licious! Pimp-A-Licious! Smoove-A-Licious!

You know how they say that at the moment of your death your entire life flashes past your eyes? Well I wasn't dying yet, but my past and my future was damn sure about to collide.

What Pimp was asking me to do was crazy. Off the fuckin' chain. Insane. He was scheming to stick up T.C. and Miss Lady's pool hall so we could pay off G, but a playa like me was getting ready to go to college and put all that two-bit robbing and stealing shit behind me. And besides, how could a niggah betray T.C.? The realest cat in Harlem? A man who had fed me and put clothes on my back and spent his whole life elevating street kids like me?

"Man, there's gotta be another way, dawg. I know we gotta get Smoove back. That's real. I'm down with that. But we gotta come up with a better plan."

Pimp looked at me coldly. "What, niggah? How long you been a bitch without me knowing it? Them motherfuckers up in T.C.'s Place carry more weight than your own blood? Who took care of that shooter for Precious? I did a bid for your bitch ass, remember? It was me your punk ass came crying to. Not no fuckin' T.C.! You owe me, Thug. And we both owe Smoove. Everything for the *family*, motherfucker!"

Everything for the family. . . . Everything for the family. . . . Everything for the family. . . .

My little sister Precious took a bullet the summer she turned ten.

After all the pain and suffering that little girl had been through. After all the doctors and the hospitals and the chemotherapy and the sickness. A cute little girl who had just grew all of her hair back got erased in the blink of an eye.

And that's when Pimp proved what kind of cold-blooded street gangsta he *really* was. . . .

That bullet hit our family where it really hurt.

I'd just won a "Battle of the MCs" contest and gave Noojie every dime I had so she could hook Precious's shit up lovely, cause if anybody deserved a big-ass party, it was my little sister.

Precious was happy as hell that day too. The doctors had just told us that all the cancer was gone out of her blood. She was in complete remission, and Noojie had invited all Precious's little girlfriends from fifth grade over to celebrate her good news.

"I'm gone live, y'all!" Precious went around dancing and yelling. "Hey, Dre! Guess what? I'm gonna live! Pimp! I'm gone live, man!"

Me, Pimp, and Smoove were sitting outside on the stoop with Miss Carrie and her bony-ass mutt dog. When it was time for the kids to start leaving, Precious ran outside to tell all her friends good-bye.

"Okay," Noojie said when the last little girl was gone. "You had a good day, Precious, and you got a lotta nice friends. Come inside and wash all that cake off your face so you can go to bed. You ain't sick no more so you gone be in school every day from now on."

"It's not even late," Precious had complained. "Look." She pointed. "The streetlights ain't even on yet!"

Pimp had motioned for Noojie to leave her alone. He had a soft spot for Precious. We all did. She could twist every one of our gangsta asses around her little finger like a worm.

"She cool, Aunt Noojie. Let her chill out here for a minute. She still feeling her good news. I'll bring her inside when we get ready to bounce."

But life is flaky in the hood.

It didn't take long for good news to go bad.

We kicked it on the stoop for a minute and Precious bounced a handball near the curb. She was singing one of them little-girl songs and her barrettes was bouncing around all over her head.

"Have you ever-ever-ever in ya long-legged life, seen a long-legged sailor with a long-legged wife . . ."

A black Jetta slipped up outta nowhere, crawling down the street like a snake.

Shots rang out.

Niggahs up and down the street started screaming and scattering in all directions.

"Precious!"

The skinny dog fell over first. His whole head was blown open.

Old Miss Carrie got hit too. She was wiggling all over the ground holding her arm. Her dress was up, and her big white Fruit of the Loom panties was showing.

More shots, and more screams.

"Precious!" I hollered again and again. Me and Pimp both dove to get to her.

My baby sister was on her knees. Staring at me with the ball in her hands. Her face was a big question mark when she said, "What, Dre?"

Then her eyes rolled up, and she fell backwards.

Pimp got to her first.

"Oh shit!" he yelled, and carried her limp body over to the stoop.

"Oh, shit! Thug! Oh motherfuckin' shit! We need a fuckin' ambulance, quick!"

I bent over my little sister and looked at her closely. There was nothing wrong with Precious's face. Her eyes was wide open, and she looked like she was trying to smile. But her dress. Her little light blue party dress was getting all fucked up cause she was bleeding real bad from her stomach.

"Noooooooooo!" I heard Noojie scream as she came running back out the building. She pushed me and Pimp out the way and fell to her knees beside Precious, yanking up her dress. She screamed even louder when she saw Precious's blue and white polka-dot panties that was now soaked in red.

"Y'all niggahs got my baby shot!" Noojie cried. She started scooping up the flowing blood with her hands, trying to push it back into Precious's body.

"All that fuckin' cancer," Noojie muttered as she worked like crazy. "All that fuckin' cancer we just got outta my baby's blood . . ."

She scooped handfuls of blood in her palms and tried to pour it back into the bullet hole. "And now her blood just gone run out in the streets?"

Everybody knew exactly who that bullet had been meant for.

Pimp had been fuckin' with them small-time hustlers downtown and stirring up hard feelings for months. Plus, some kid on the Lower East Side had accused him of taking some pussy from his thirteen-year-old sister, and them niggahs had sworn they were gonna get theirs back.

"I got this, Thug," Pimp had told me on the morning of Precious's funeral. Noojie had gotten five hundred dollars from the Crime Victims Fund to bury her, and T.C. and Miss Lady had put *up the rest. "I know the pussies who did it, and I know how to make 'em pay too."*

The next night we rode over to a playground in the projects over on FDR Drive and lit that motherfucker up. Niggahs was crowded all around the benches and seesaws and shit conducting their business. Pimp led us up the walkway strapped like a motherfucker.

With me and Smoove holding the cover, Pimp walked right up on a low-level fool they called Evil and popped him in the neck.

Niggahs ran for cover and Pimp stood over Evil as he lay gurgling on the pavement. "Everything," Pimp said, and looked at me. "For the motherfuckin' family."

He looked around the playground at niggahs hiding behind all kinds of shit.

"Y'all motherfuckers betta listen," he hollered, holding out his gun. "Y'all don't step up in my yard no more, and I won't have to step back in yours. Y'all don't hurt my fuckin' brother or my cousin, and I won't spray y'all whole motherfuckin' families. Your mamas and your kids too."

Pimp whirled and fired two quick rounds into Evil's head, then spit down on that niggah as he laying bleeding on a bed of empty crack vials.

Smoove stepped up next and busted a cap in Evil's chest.

And I popped that niggah right where he'd popped Precious.

In his stomach.

— — —

I wish I could tell you that the shit was settled right there. But c'mon, yo. My life ain't no fuckin' fairy tale and what you bring to the streets you gotta be able to carry back with you. My little sister was dead. Noojie copped her some crack and went straight out on a mission. Two weeks later, a ho named Remy I was grinding dropped it on me that she was pregnant with my kid. The next day all three of us got knocked and Pimp got hit with a mandatory one-year sentence for a piece I'd carried into the crib months earlier. We'd gotten rid of the tools we used to smoke that fool, so when 5-0 came busting up in the apartment with a search warrant they couldn't find nothing dirty, but they did find something clean stashed in a plastic bag underneath my bed.

The cops hauled all three of us down to the 32nd Precinct, and within hours they came and hustled me and Smoove back outta the bull pen and told us we was free to go. A street narc I knew from T.C.'s place told me that Pimp had confessed to the charge, and as a result, he'd also be handling the mandatory one-year bid.

"Closed lips! Anything for the motherfuckin' *family!*" Pimp hollered as they led him out in handcuffs, and he proved without a doubt that he meant that shit.

And so did Smoove. That niggah had saved both of us from a bullet back in the day, and G snatching him up had caught me between a promise and a vow. See, my future had finally opened up wide, and realizing my dreams was almost at hand. I'd just signed on with Ruthless Rap to cut my first solo album, and Syracuse had offered me a full scholarship to play ball at their university in the fall.

But this was some for-real shit. The 'Licious Lovers were Dawgs-4-Lyfe. Yeah, I loved T.C. and Miss Lady deep like that, but I'd lay down and die for my blood. Pimp was on point. Anything and everything for the family. The three of us were a triangle and I owed him. And with a killer like G holding Smoove in that Dungeon . . . finding his dead body was only a matter of time.

So no matter how I tossed it, I was in a box with no way out.

Thug-A-Licious! Pimp-A-Licious! Smoove-A-Licious!

People rolled in and out of the front door of the hospital. They gave me and Pimp crazy looks as they passed by.

"Look, man," I said, putting my hand on Pimp's shoulder. He had punched his hand through a wall when he found out about Smoove, and his right fist was busted wide open. Meat was showing from between his knuckles and blood dripped to the floor in a steady flow. "You bleeding all over this joint. Let's roll on in the emergency room and make these motherfuckers stitch your shit up. We'll figure out how to get Smoove back. I promise, man. But let's get your shit straight first."

Pimp knocked my hand back and stepped to me hard, speaking in a cold whisper. "My shit *is* straight, niggah." We stood nose to nose, locking eyes. "The only one who need to come up on they game is *you*. You musta forgot what that fool G did to Big Sonny and his boys. I can't let my brother go out like that, man. I'ma take T.C.'s shit down tonight, Thug. With or without your bitch ass. I'ma go in and come right back out. I ain't planning on hurting nobody, but I'm getting that money. Cause if I don't get it, Smoove is dead."

— — —

I was just a kid when I shot that dopehead up in T.C.'s Place.

It was summertime in Harlem. The air-conditioning was broke, and it was hot and sticky in the little kitchen where Miss Lady had me standing at the counter wrapping dinner plates.

"Quit wasting my foil," she scolded me. She was smoking a cigarette and flipping pieces of hot fish around in a frying pan. T.C. had gone to Brooklyn to handle some last-minute business, and Miss Lady had sent all the workers home early so they could get ready for the biggest gambling night of the year. Normally she woulda been upstairs in her apartment getting ready too, but instead she was cooking me and Noojie some dinner so I could get home before the *Sweep or Weep* gambling spree got started.

Fanning herself, she put her spatula down and unlocked the door leading to the alley. She opened it wide and propped a big can of cling peaches against the door.

"Do it like this, Andre," she said, coming over to me. She tore a small piece of foil off the roll and spread it over the food. "You seven years old, boy. That's big enough to know how to cover a plate and tuck it under the edge."

I'd been "working" for T.C. and Miss Lady for over a month. I lived in the baddest tenement slum in all of Harlem and was the biggest thief on the block. My moms, Noojie, had told me that the two little stumps on the sides of my hands came from being born with six fingers, and that's why I was always stealing something. But Miss Lady was getting real tired of seeing me get chased past her window by whomever it was I had stolen from that day.

One morning I'd played hooky and was speeding past T.C.'s Place as fast as I could run. I had a basketball under one arm and a bunch of bananas I'd snatched from the Korean fruit stand under the other when Miss Lady stepped out of her doorway and snatched me inside the pool hall and started beating the shit outta me with her house shoe.

"You thievin'-ass little thug!" she hollered as the Korean owner stood in the doorway laughing like a motherfucker as he watched me get my ass whipped. She slapped me all upside my head with that dirty pink shoe. "If you ain't fightin', you stealin'! Ain't no damn good gone never come of your black ass until you learn to fight only for right and work like a man for what you want!"

Miss Lady was fine and had a shape on her. I liked the way she smelled when she sat me up on a pool table and used the edge of her shirt to wipe my crying eyes. "And stop hollerin' like somebody killing you. I don't give a damn how little you is. I can't stand no damn thief. Besides, you wasn't crying when you was up there stealing other people's shit, now was you?"

I didn't answer cause now she was digging a tissue all up my nose. Cleaning out snot and shaking her head at my nasty boogers. "Boy!" She pulled down on my bottom lip until it touched my chin. "When's the last time these teeth seen a damn toothbrush?"

I jerked away and shrugged. Noojie ain't buy no damn toothbrushes. I was lucky if she remembered to throw me toward a bathtub every few months.

Miss Lady pointed her long finger in my face. Her nail was polished bright pink, and I thought it looked slick. "You gone march your little ass out there and give that Chinaman back his damn bananas, you hear me? And from now on I want your tail standing at my door every day soon as you get outta school. I know who your mama is boy, and just cause she ain't shit don't mean you can't be shit." She grabbed my arm and slung me down off her pool table. "You show up every day at three o'clock, you hear? I need some help round here, and your little ass needs a job. You gone shine my front windows, empty the ashtrays, and sweep out from under every last pool table we got. And when you through, I'll feed you and send you home with enough food for your baby sister too. But the next time I catch you putting your hands on something you ain't worked for I'ma bend ya damn fingers back till they pop off. One by one."

She handed me back my ball. "Let's see how good you fight and steal and how much damn basketball you can play then."

I didn't care what she threatened me with. Miss Lady was the classiest woman I'd ever seen in Harlem. Her and her man T.C. were real good people. Their pool hall was a gathering spot for hustlers and big-time gamblers who were looking for good times and had money to burn.

T.C.'s brother, Big Sonny, was Harlem's number-one drug kingpin and had a black-hearted rep for pushing dope and pulling triggers. But T.C. and his woman wasn't into Big Sonny's shitty game. Him and Miss Lady believed in building their community up. They hired local kids to work for them, sponsored youth programs, and turned their profits around and put a lot of cash back into the Harlem they loved and lived for.

I'd been working in the pool hall every day for over a month but Miss Lady still didn't trust me. Sometimes she'd fix me a baloney sandwich, and I'd sneak behind her back and steal me a piece of fried chicken. I was more than a fighter and a thief. I was slick and smart. Especially with numbers. It didn't take me long to figure out that sweeping up in a gambling joint was even better than stealing on the avenue. Miss Lady paid me five dollars a day and pushed me out the front door when the night crowd showed up. As soon as she turned her back I'd sneak in through the back door and gamble them five dollars over and over until my pockets was swole.

But on this Friday afternoon Miss Lady had me with her in the kitchen. It was Harlem Week and T.C. was hosting hustlers and gamblers from all over New York City, Connecticut, Philly, and D.C., who were rolling through looking to make a cash killing at his annual *Summer Sweep or Weep*.

I tried real hard to tear the foil off like Miss Lady wanted, and I guess I was doing it right. "That's better," she said, nodding. I liked Miss Lady and couldn't wait to get big enough to get me a woman just like her. I could sit there and stare at her wiggly hips and round ass all day. She was real feminine and sexy, and I dug that shit. I also liked the way she grinned and gave me a hug every afternoon when I showed up at her door after school. Her and T.C. was doing more for me than my own moms did. Not only did they feed me and my little sister Precious and make sure I had clean clothes for school, they supported my talent for basketball by signing me up for a youth league. They even sponsored jerseys for the whole team.

"Goddamn! It's hotter than hell in here," Miss Lady complained. She smoothed her blouse and started fanning herself again. Miss Lady stayed looking right in her clothes and makeup, and even now she was wrapped real tight just to be frying some fish.

"And it's gonna get even hotter tonight when all them out-of-town niggahs start piling up in here." She looked up at the air-conditioning vent and frowned. "We gotta get that thing fixed, Dre. Run in the back room and bring me that telephone book off of T.C.'s desk."

"Yes, Miss Lady," I blurted. I almost dropped the plate I was holding I was so eager to get back there in T.C.'s office and see what I could get into.

I ran out the kitchen and down the narrow hallway. I passed a staircase on my right that led to the apartment upstairs where T.C. and Miss Lady lived. I'd never been invited up there but I had a colorful picture in my little head about how grand it musta been.

I hurried past the stairs and stood outside of T.C.'s office. The door was closed, but I opened it and went inside. I looked around with big, greedy eyes. T.C.'s office was just as sharp as he was. He had a huge brown wall unit off in one corner, a big fish tank with all kinds of colorful weeds in it, and a huge color television up in there too. The phone book was right on his grand Maplewood desk where Miss Lady said it would be. A big fat New York City Yellow Pages. You couldn't miss it. I glanced at it, and my eyes kept right on traveling. Before I knew it my sticky little fingers were pulling open T.C.'s top drawer, and I was feeling around inside.

I rambled through the stacks of envelopes and what looked like a bunch of receipts until I got to the back of the drawer. I was hoping to snag me a few dollars 'cause I knew T.C. was paid. But cash ain't what I stumbled on as my greedy hands searched the back of his drawer, though. I was already holding the weight in my hand when I heard Miss Lady yell out in alarm.

"What the hell you think you doing, Greek? You better get your stank ass up outta my kitchen and hope to God I don't tell T.C. about this shit!"

I heard her moving in my direction, and I dropped to the floor and scooted under T.C.'s desk until my back touched the wall. Holding my breath, I put the weight between my legs, then pulled my knees up to my chest as footsteps came barreling down the hall.

"Shut up and get your ass in there," a man's rough voice said as the office door opened, and their legs came into view. "Don't fuck with me, Miss Lady. Just gimme whatever cash you got and everythang'll be cool."

"Stupid ass, you come at the wrong hour," Miss Lady sassed him as he pushed her into the room. "What kinda thief is you? Shit, we don't even start waking up around here until way after dark. You see any motherfuckers gambling up in here? Where you think I'ma get some money from in the middle of the day?"

"Bitch, I told you don't fuck with me," the man warned her in a crackhead's whine, but Miss Lady kept right on talking shit.

"Naw, niggah! Don't you fuck with *me*! Now I hired you once before, and if you need another day job I might be able to help you out again. But I ain't got shit for you up in here for *free*, and you can believe that. Now take your fuckin' hands off me before you make me mad."

Miss Lady could fight like a man, but a niggah on dope was a dangerous thing. I'd seen Noojie get fucked up by enough crackhead boyfriends to know.

"Black bitch! Gimme your motherfuckin' money!"

Miss Lady's voice was full of scorn. "I ain't giving you *shit*!"

I heard fist sounds, and Miss Lady grunted in pain. The dopehead knocked her to the ground and blood shot out of her mouth when she fell.

I gasped out loud. A long moan came outta me at the sight of her laid out on the floor. Miss Lady heard me and turned her head, meeting my wide eyes.

"Bitch," the crackhead she'd called Greek said slowly. "I will kill your ass up in here—"

I was trembling as I stared into Miss Lady's brown eyes. The sight of her swollen lips made the inside of my stomach feel tight.

"Ohhh . . . ," I heard the man say, then a scraggly head appeared as he bent down and looked under the desk. He followed Miss Lady's gaze straight to me.

"What the fuck we got down here?"

I was trembling down to my bones. The pounding of my heart was making my whole body spasm. He reached out and grabbed at my foot, and I kicked his hand away.

"Little motherfucker," the crackhead said. "Look at ya. Shaking like a girl. You got any goddamn money? Little niggah so damn scared he 'bout to piss all over hisself."

He was right. I was shaking like a fiend. But it wasn't outta fear though. This pipe-smoking motherfucker had punched out my Miss Lady! He had her fine self laid out on the floor! A rage filled me so deep that I almost stopped breathing.

I waited until he bent down again. When he tried to grab my foot this time I gathered the weight in my hand and pointed it.

"Niggah," I muttered, "don't you hit my Miss Lady."

The gun boomed once. Twice. Three times.

The crackhead screamed in agony and rolled on the floor holding his leg. A bright splash of blood darkened his pants where one of my bullets had caught him, halfway between his knee and his ankle.

I looked over at Miss Lady. She was smiling through her busted mouth.

"That's my baby!" she said, beaming. She glanced at the howling junkie, then crawled to her feet and reached for me under the desk.

"Come on out from under there, baby boy. And gimme that gun. Let this dirty motherfucker lay here and bleed. T.C.'ll finish him off when he gets back, but I gots to get you home." She hugged me to her, but I kept my eyes on the crying junkie who was holding his leg and rolling all over the floor. Miss Lady took the gun from my hand. She hugged my shoulder and led me out the office. She closed the door and took a key out of her pocket. "I oughta shoot Greek's dumb ass in the other damn leg. But how 'bout we just lock him up in there until T.C. gets back instead? You probably *real* hungry now, huh? Want Miss Lady to whip you up a pan of corn bread to go along with your fish?"

Chapter 4

Growing up I used to wet the bed almost every night, but when Pimp and Smoove came to live with us all that shit stopped in a hurry. Pimp and Smoove were my cousins from the Bronx. Their mother, Druzetta, was my mother's little sister. Pimp was two years older than me, and his brother Smoove was about a year younger. The three of us slept together on a raggedy sofa in the hallway of our one-bedroom apartment.

"Piss on me again," Pimp warned me after his second night of waking up itching, soaked in my warm piss. "Just do it again, bitch. And see don't I get me a rubber band and wrap it around your dick."

I shoulda known better than to fuck with Pimp, but I went to sleep the next night and pissed just like I usually did. But this time I woke up doubled over. Moaning in pain. My joint was on fire and it felt like somebody was squeezing the tip of it with a wrench. I looked down and almost screamed. A fat rubber band was twisted tightly around the head of my dick, cutting off my piss and my circulation. Pimp stood over me with ice in his black eyes. "Can't no fuckin' babies be sleeping wit' me. Next time you piss on me I'ma get me a knife."

Pimp's mother, Aunt Dru, was one of those stinky-ass crack fiends who rode the number four train back and forth all day holding out a cup and pretending to be blind. She would get on at Fordham Road in the Bronx, beg all the way down to Brooklyn, and then beg back uptown and start all over again.

My grandmother was a Puerto Rican wino from Spanish Harlem named Migdalia, but everybody called her Mimi. My moms and Aunt Dru were her only kids. Mimi was a tall, light-skinned woman with long wavy hair and high cheekbones. She drank cheap wine and laughed all day long. She'd been married to a black man from Queens, and people used to joke that she had drank her husband straight under the table and that was what had killed him.

Pimp's real name was Carl Williams and Smoove's name was Todd. Mimi had given each of us a nickname when we were just babies, and I guess she called it right because the names fit us like a glove.

"Look at him," Noojie told us Mimi had grinned over Smoove showing her gums. "This one has skin just like my people! He so pretty he look smoove. And this one over here"—she'd laugh and kiss Pimp dead in the mouth—"this handsome *negrito* is Mimi's sugar pimp. Just watch. He's cold, but women like that. They'll bring him lots of money." When it was time to give me a nickname Mimi got serious. "This little red, badass hellion of Noojie's? He ain't nothing but a thug. His hair is curly and he looks like an angel in the face, but watch my words. This roguish little bastard is a thug at heart."

Wino or not, Mimi was still a fine Puerto Rican mama, and

people were always telling her how good-looking her little grand-sons were. My moms used to be real pretty too, before she started fuckin' with drugs, but you could tell from their old photos that it was Aunt Dru who had been superfine. But Aunt Dru was a chaser who swung both ways. She feened for both cocaine and heroin too, and she'd almost died when a dealer beat her down for getting tight with his supplier and trying to dip on his product.

Aunt Dru wasn't right no more after that, and when she fo-cused on the pipe and started riding the trains, that crack had her out there selling pussy for two dollars a shot. She even got so grimy that she broke into Mimi's apartment and tried to rob her own mother in the middle of the night. But when Mimi woke up and found Aunt Dru sneaking out the window carrying a frozen pork roast, they got to fighting over that meat and Mimi pulled out a knife. Aunt Dru was so high she grabbed a hammer and beat Mimi in the head until she wasn't nothing but a lump of blood. Mimi died, Aunt Dru got sent upstate for life, and Pimp and Smoove came to live with us.

My moms was a crackhead just like her sister, but unlike Aunt Dru, Noojie had a baby with cancer so she knew how to slow her roll. Whenever my little sister Precious got sick and them nosey caseworkers from social services started sniffing around, Noojie would get right and handle her business in a hurry.

Still, Harlem was a gangsta town, and the three of us boys rolling together wasn't nothing but some trouble looking to get started. We grew up fast and hard, running the streets day and night. Digging music, hooping on the neighborhood courts, chasing girls, and stealing anything that wasn't bolted or chained down. I did all kinds of shit just to keep my rep up and get re-spect in the streets, and Smoove was just a fast-mouthed, Vin Diesel wannabe who followed behind me and Pimp trying to be hard. But Pimp was a for-real motherfucker who didn't give a fuck about nothing except making money. He was one of them pretty niggahs too. Black and shiny and had a tough jaw and hard eyes. He was cold and evil-hearted, and there wasn't no boundaries on the kind of crazy shit he would do. Pimp would sneak into a dirty alley, bang on a few garbage cans, then corner the biggest rat he could find and stomp him dead. He'd walk up to one a them little church girls, steal him a kiss, then hit her in the chest like she was a man. One time Smoove came running home from 125th Street hollering at the top of his lungs.

"Aunt Noojie! Aunt Noojie! The cops is out there chasing Pimp! They say he poured gasoline on somebody's dog and tried to set it on fire!"

The only person Pimp gave any kind of respect to was my moms. Noojie felt sorry for Pimp and Smoove cause their mother was in jail and they didn't have nobody else. As bad as Pimp was, and as much trouble as he brought to her doorstep, Noojie saw something she loved in Pimp and so did I. In fact, I loved Pimp more than anybody else in the world. We was more than friends and cousins. We was blood brothers. Down in the dirt for each other. Loyal no matter what. We shared everything. Clothes, money, ass. If Pimp ate, I ate. If I fought, Pimp fought. Smoove was all the way down too. We was like a triangle. Three strong points. And as hard as Pimp was, Smoove had already proved he was a hard little niggah too.

When I was nine Noojie let some raggedy niggah move in with us. He was an ex-pro boxer named Kelvin, but he made us call him Killer. Killer was a psycho dude who had taken a lot of head blows when he was fighting in the ring. He got a crazy check every month from being hurt in the service, and Noojie said he had earned that shit.

Me, Pimp, and Smoove used to laugh and run from his ass cause his nose was always running and he blew snot and boogers right into his shirt like it was a handkerchief or a tissue. The only reason Noojie liked him was cause he was a duji-head and she could dip in his pockets whenever he got to nodding out and didn't know what the fuck was going on.

But Killer couldn't stand little kids, and whenever one of us boys so much as walked past his ass in the crib he would reach out and bust our lip or punch us in the chest so hard we dropped straight to the floor. Killer called that his one-punch lunch, and he hit us like that so many times I don't know how one of us didn't mess around and fall over dead from a heart attack.

One time Noojie had to spend a weekend in jail for boosting and the four of us was left at the crib with Killer. Me and Smoove was scared as shit. Killer had been fucking Pimp up, prolly worse than he did me and Smoove, cause Pimp never cried when he got hit. Scared just wasn't on Pimp the way it was on me and Smoove. All Pimp ever got was mad, and he whispered to us that he would take Killer out if he ever got the chance. Well, Pimp never did get where he could do nothing to that niggah, but Smoove sure did.

Killer started drinking that Friday night and the more he drank, the meaner he got. He sat on the couch smelling like liquor and piss. Mumbling and cursing with his double-barrel slung across his lap. He had on some brown shorts and a dingy wifebeater that was ripped at the neck and had food and dried snot and crusty boogers caked all over the front.

Killer cursed and squinted through one yellow eye, drinking vodka straight out the bottle and muttering to himself as we played on the floor and laughed at the cartoons on television. Every now and then he would scratch his balls, then dig his fingers into his nappy head of wild-ass hair, like bugs and shit was biting him everywhere.

A crash exploded in the air and got our attention. We turned around and saw Killer staring down at one of Noojie's glass ashtrays. That fool had thrown it down on the floor on purpose. It had shattered and cracked in a million pieces, and cigarette butts and glass and ashes were all over the floor.

Killer stared at us with mad, drunken eyes. "What y'all looking at? Huh?" And then, "You!" He pointed to Pimp. "I said what the hell you looking at, you ugly motherfucker! C'mere, you ugly-ass little niggah you!"

Killer grilled Pimp like he was a grown man instead of a ten-year-old kid. "You been walkin' round here like you the motherfuckin' killer up in this house." He motioned at me then snapped his fingers. "You too, ugly. Bring your ugly red ass over here right fuckin' now too."

Me and Pimp stood up and walked over to him, and I got punched to the floor first. Boom! His junkie fist almost caved my chest in. I rolled around on the floor in all those ashes and pieces of sharp glass, wheezing in pain and trying not to cry.

Pimp was next.

Boom!

Killer hit Pimp even harder, and his knees straight buckled. He dropped to the floor beside me, and we both lay there moaning, getting stuck with glass, and trying not to throw up.

But Killer wasn't finished yet. That niggah started kicking the shit out of us, doing his best to get to our little nuts.

"Y'all ugly little motherfuckers ain't no grown men up in here! I'm the man! I'm the man! I'm the man!" He put his foot in our asses as deep as he could get it. After getting our balls crushed, we got smart real fast and rolled over on our stomachs with our knees up to our chests, and let him kick us like that.

Killer took turns on us. He beat me, then he beat Pimp. He punched us all in our heads and backs, stomped us with his stank-ass feet, and then that niggah took off his belt and started swinging that shit on us too. We was all sweating. Me and Pimp on the floor with glass splinters and sooty ashes sticking to us, and Killer wobbling on his feet and dripping wet funk.

Every time he left me for a second and got busy fucking up Pimp, I would hold on to my busted side and try and breathe and crawl toward the kitchen. But as soon as I got anywhere near out of the living room he would jump off Pimp and come running after me again.

I don't know how long that niggah fucked us up, but when he picked up his shotgun and cocked that shit I squeezed my eyes closed tight and prayed that somehow Noojie would bust up in the house and save us.

"Look outta that goddamn winder!" he ordered us. I peeped open one eye and got slapped in the face with a fat drop of hot sweat. His was showing all of his rotted-out teeth, and his chest was heaving up and down from beating us so good. "Ya see all that goddamn sunshine, you ugly-ass little niggahs? Ya see it?!

Well take a good look, goddamn it, cause it's gonna be the last piece of sun ya ugly asses see in this world!"

Killer made me and Pimp get up off the floor, then he pushed us into the coat closet and locked the door. We sat there in that hot dirty closet on top of old boots, sweaters, and turned-over shoes. Pimp didn't show no signs of being hurt, but I was sore and shaking and praying for Noojie to come home.

"Put your nose between the cracks," Pimp told me when I started breathing real hard, and I leaned forward and breathed through the dusty ventilation slats on the bottom part of the door.

When I lined my eyes up just right I could see straight out into the living room. Smoove was still on the floor holding on to Precious, while Killer was out there tearing shit up. I could see his feet as he stomped around throwing shit, cussing, and terrorizing us like crazy.

"I'll blow a hole straight in that motherfucka!" he threatened us, pointing his shotgun toward the closet door. "Shoot the ugly offa both a y'all asses. Blast y'all into the end of next damn week! Fuckin' with *me*!"

I was scared as hell as I looked down that barrel. That niggah was gonna kill us, and me and Pimp both knew it.

"Just watch," he promised. "I'ma shoot both a y'all right in ya head, just watch and see. Boom! Put a hole right between ya ugly-ass eyes. As soon as that goddamn sun comes up I'ma put both of y'all niggahs to sleep. You just watch!"

Me and Pimp spent the whole day in that closet. We could breathe all right and see into the living room through the slats, but we were hurting and hungry and by now both of us were scared of getting shot.

The day turned into night, and I peed on myself.

Pimp didn't say nothing. He didn't even move away from me and that scared me even more. I musta dozed off at some time in the night, because I remember waking up in the darkness of the closet wondering if we were already dead.

More time passed, and I opened my eyes and almost cried out loud when Pimp elbowed me in my sore side and told me to look between the slats. I saw Smoove and Precious on the floor by the television. They were laying next to each other asleep.

Killer was sitting on the couch again. His shotgun was across his lap.

A belt was tied around his arm, and he was cooking up his shit in a teaspoon. We watched as he got his works and squirted water out first, then stuck the tip of the needle into the dope and sucked it up before finding a vein and sticking it into his arm.

Just like always, he went into a nod almost right away. His head dropped down to his chest, then jerked back up, then dropped down again before his hands fell to his sides, the needle still stuck in his arm.

Seconds later, Smoove jumped up and ran over to the table.

"What he doing?" I whispered, and Pimp elbowed me again and told me to shut the hell up.

Smoove crept up and got the teaspoon off the table, then ran over and eased the needle outta Killer's arm. He knelt down at the coffee table and pumped the works liked we'd seen Killer do, then pulled the plunger back until the syringe was filled up with the rest of the cloudy dope.

I held my breath as Smoove tiptoed back over to Killer, who was so high he was slobbering down the front of his crusty shirt.

Smoove stared at Killer for a second, then stuck that needle in the side of his neck and pushed the plunger down as fast as he could.

Killer jerked on the sofa and sat up a little bit. His body got real stiff, and his spine curved all the way back like the letter *C*. The shotgun slid off his lap and fell to the floor, then Killer did too. Shaking and twitching, his whole body went stiff. He danced and jerked on the floor like a fish that had jumped out of a tank. I watched all this in total shock and fear, but Pimp was next to me clapping his hands and laughing out loud.

As soon as Killer had almost quit moving, Smoove bent over and dug in his pockets until he found the key. When he unlocked that closet door and let us out, Pimp jumped up and grabbed him, hugging his brother and swinging him around the room.

"You got that junkie motherfucker, Smoove! You killed his ass!"

Smoove just grinned his face off as the three of us watched Killer lay there and foam at the mouth until his eyes rolled backward in his head and stayed there.

"Everything for the family," Pimp said and hugged both of us again, and he was right. We was living that shit. Me, Pimp, and Smoove were united against the world, and on that day we made a vow that no matter who we had to put down, we'd be Dawgs-4-Lyfe.

■ ▬ ■

The years passed, and we grew up fast and hard. New York City was our whole world and Harlem was the center of the universe.

We was poor, but we had big dreams. Talent and skills. We put our heads together and decided that one day we was gonna be some paid niggahs. We saw the kind of life ballers and hustlers were living. The women, the flamboyant cars, the phat mansions, the mad platinum jewelry.

"You can't boost your way to the big time," Pimp told me one day as I limped up to the crib. The cops had busted me stealing for the third time, and they had kicked my ass around and put their sticks on me before pulling into a dirty alley and tossing me outta they car. The only reason they had let me go was because I was a minor and they couldn't reach Noojie. She was too busy chasing a high to come pick me up from the station, and they were too damn lazy to bother getting social services involved.

"There ain't shit people in Harlem got in their houses or in their pockets that's gonna make you rich, Thug."

He was right, but I had already figured that out. With Noojie being strung out on shit again wasn't no real money coming in the house. I wanted nice gear, but I wasn't trying to get busted no more cause jail would only interfere with my time on the basketball court and more than anything, I wanted to hoop. I was still working at T.C.'s, and I'd graduated from emptying ashtrays for Miss Lady to helping T.C. keep his books in the back office, but what he paid me still wasn't enough to live large. I could've asked him or Miss Lady for more money, but I was already working more than I wanted to, and they didn't believe in just handing shit over to nobody for doing nothing.

Everybody in Harlem knew T.C. stood for Trust Chambers, but I'd been a crowd-pleaser in the joint since I was a little kid, and since I was so good rolling the dice, hustlers started joking that T.C. really stood for Thug Central.

"Thug?" Miss Lady would say and roll her eyes. She always kept my most recent report card taped to the wall for everybody to see, and had recently placed a big pickle jar on the front counter with a sign on it that said Help Send Dre To The NBA! Every Friday she took the donations out and put them in a bank account she had opened for me.

"What kinda name is 'Thug' for a future NBA player? Boy, don't you know you Harlem's black prince? The one we pinning all our hopes and dreams on? Thug's the last thing you need to be round here calling yourself. Unless you wanna end up dead or in jail."

Miss Lady wouldn't call me nothing but Andre or Little Dre, but I was a wild niggah with a solid rep. I'd proven myself at an age when most cats was still drinking milk. That guy I'd shot in the leg worked for T.C. full-time these days. Instead of letting T.C. kill him, Miss Lady had given him a job, and when he limped his punk ass around the pool hall dragging his shattered leg, everybody knew it was me who was responsible. So yeah. I mighta been Dre to T.C. and Miss Lady, but every fuckin' body else called me Thug.

When I look back on those early days, it's obvious that getting my ass beat with Miss Lady's house shoe was probably the best thing that ever happened to me. Her and T.C. were dead against kids selling or using drugs, and they made me swear not to get involved with rock or ice or any of that hard shit at any cost.

"You can gamble, pimp bitches . . . shit, you can even steal cars if you want to," T.C. warned me. "But you fuck around and get involved with my brother Sonny and his corner action and you can kiss your future good-bye."

He didn't have to worry. Drugs could only slow me down on the court, and besides, working with T.C. on his books had taught me that I had a sharp mind for numbers. Miss Lady encouraged me to stay in school and get good grades.

"Dre, you gotta get through college before you can see the NBA, you know. Don't count on being picked up right outta high school like Kobe did. That would be stupid anyway. Study your math, baby boy. Get you a college degree first. Make sure you actually *graduate*. Then get your ass in the NBA!"

Miss Lady was down for me like a mother would be for her child. She helped keep my dreams alive and focused, and she made playing professional ball seem like a reality and not just a poor kid's fantasy. She signed me up for basketball programs like the NikeGO High Five Kids Club, and the Sprite Junior Knicks League. Every Sunday morning she drove me down to Basketball City to practice with the Youth Development League. She paid my team fees, bought my basketball shoes, went to parents' meetings, and told my coach to feel free to bust my ass if I showed up late for practice or gave him any shit.

But Pimp was right. Fuck all that stealing. All three of us was bringing top talent to the court. We was from the streets, had the skills, and definitely had the heart. We dominated local pickup games, busting niggahs' pockets and hustling street ball like professionals. I was the tallest and the fastest, but Smoove was a vicious outside shooter and Pimp had a mean defensive game and could shake a niggah back like a fly.

"I'm signing up for the Junior NBA Gatorade Championship," I told Pimp. "Just watch. I'm getting in the NBA. I'ma be bigger than Jordan, bigger than that niggah Kobe too. I want you and Smoove to be down with me."

Pimp just laughed.

"You do it, Thug. Go for it. And when you get on you can put me and Smoove down. You know how we do, niggah! Everything for the family. . . ."

Chapter 5

So what I'm trying to telling you is, I had history with T.C. and Miss Lady. I mighta been a cold niggah out on them streets, but I had real feelings in my heart for the good people Pimp wanted me to rob. Regardless, the clock was ticking down on my cousin Smoove, and Pimp's half-assed plan was pressing down on my mind. I left him getting his hand stitched up in the emergency room at Harlem Hospital, and walked down to the Flip It and Clip It Hair and Nail Salon, ignoring all the heads that turned my way.

I wasn't even through the door good before females started coming up out the sinks to check me out. Even them loud-ass hair dryers couldn't cover the sounds of my name being tossed around.

Thug-A-Licious, Pimp-A-Licious, Smoove-A-Licious!

The 'Licious Lovers were well-known all over the Harlem street set. Me, Pimp, and Smoove had performed as a trio in clubs from New York City to B-more, spitting bangers and hard gansta rhymes, and even some of Smoove's dirty crunk cuts that kept more thongs flying our way than we could handle.

But as much love as we got in other cities, it was the folks of Harlem who claimed us and kept us warm. Especially the honeys. They literally threw themselves on my dick cause I had a rep for knockin' it out real nasty. It wasn't unusual to find six or seven jawns waiting for me when I jumped off a stage, fighting each other to be the first piece of meat on my plate.

But right now Smoove's life was on the line and Muddah Vernoy was the only woman who could help me get my head right. Muddah worked in the salon part-time and went to school at night. I'd met her when I was fourteen . . . about a week after Noojie stabbed the rent man with a pair of scissors and got us all put out in the street in the middle of the winter.

Me and Pimp had rolled up to the crib one afternoon just in time to catch Noojie cussing and screaming out the window, and the rent man staggering outside holding his neck.

"You took pussy for rent last month, mothafuckah!" my moms hollered, throwing empty beer bottles down at him as he tried to run to his car. "Whut? Whut? I ain't suck your nasty dick the way you like it this month? Whut?"

We jumped dead on that fool. He was a Dominican cat with short gray hair. If he thought he was bleeding when Noojie stuck him, the snow was red with blood when me and Pimp got through with his ass.

We took turns kicking and stomping him. I wasn't sure where Pimp's rage was coming from, but I beat that motherfucker down out of shame. Hell yeah I was embarrassed. What down cat wanted their moms on her knees sucking dick to pay the fuckin' rent?

It took social services to get us out of our jam. And the only reason they rescued us is cause my baby sister Precious had cancer and they couldn't allow her to be living out in the cold. They gave Noojie an emergency rental assistance voucher and the five of us moved further uptown, deeper into Harlem where the buildings were even raggedier than the ones we had left.

Our new apartment building was much bigger. It had six floors and twenty-four apartments. Ours was on the top floor, right next to the stairwell that led to the roof. Like the young dawgs we were, me, Pimp, and Smoove went on an immediate pussy hunt. We started checking out all the females in the neighborhood to decide who would fuck who first. We weren't in our new building for more than two days before I got a hit from a girl who lived downstairs.

Her name was Yasmere and from the way she stepped to us I knew she was a chickenhead who knew exactly how to bring it.

"All a y'all niggahs fine as shit, but hell no," she said, pointing at Pimp. "Not him. I'll fuck you and the cute brown-skinned one over there, but this niggah here looks scary. I ain't fuckin' him."

"C'mon, now," I said, giving her my big smile that never failed to get the panties dropping. It wasn't working, though. A lot of females were hesitant about getting with Pimp. He had a hard edge to him that made it impossible not to peep his cruel nature.

She crossed her arms. "Hell, no. He can't fuck me."

"Damn, baby," I grinned some more. "What you got against my dawg? You don't even know him." I wanted to put Pimp down on some of this, but shawty had a nice body on her and a niggah like me loved to fuck. Pimp needed to learn how to approach a woman. He needed to stop banging them around and start treating them like I did. Like I appreciated that pussy.

She shook her head like she meant what she'd said. I didn't get pressed because I wasn't anxious to fuck behind Pimp no way. Wasn't no telling what woulda been left of this chick when he got through.

Yasmere stared into my eyes. "You," she said to me, then pointed at Smoove, "and you. But not him."

Pimp started laughing. "Fuck you, bitch. I ain't want none of your stank-ass pussy no way."

I shrugged and grabbed her hand, squeezing her fingers. Her breasts looked like water balloons under her sweater and her ass was nice and fat. She took me and Smoove into her dark apartment and told us to be quiet.

"Don't make no noise," she whispered. "My daddy is in the back sleeping. He works for Transit, and he gotta get up and go to work soon."

I pushed her up against a wall and slid my hands between her legs, feeling her plump pussy. She moaned, and I covered her lips with my mouth and started tonguing her down.

"Not out here," she whispered, even though she was squeezing her legs together and humping that pussy all over my hand. "We gotta go in my room."

Oh we was going to the room, all right. I just wanted her and Smoove both to know who was hitting that shit first.

The bedroom was small and almost empty. There was a narrow cot pushed against the wall and a turned-over box with a lamp sitting on it. I pushed her shoulders gently so she could lay back on the bed, then stood over her checking out her shape as I undid my belt.

"Yo, niggah!" Smoove spoke up in the background. "What the fuck I'm s'posed to do while you dig up in her belly? Watch you?"

I shrugged and kept my eyes on her. "Do what the fuck you do," I told him. "Just do that shit quietly."

Smoove walked out the room and closed the door, and I decided to take my time with this fine little dark-chocolate honey laying out before me. If she wasn't worried about her daddy waking up, then neither was I.

"I'm hot," she said and took off her sweater. Her chest was bare and full. My mouth got watery. I couldn't wait to suck her nipples. She leaned back on the bed as I buried my face between her mounds. I helped unfasten her pants, and she lifted up her ass so I could slide them down her thick, pretty legs.

When she was naked I got on my knees. The cot was weak and felt like it was on three legs. I had to balance myself or we woulda fell off and rolled to the floor. She helped me pull down my jeans and grabbed hold of my dick and I heard her grunt, surprised at what I was carrying. I smiled with pride. I had more than enough to impress any woman. My hands touched her everywhere, and I felt sweat forming on her body. I guided my throbbing dick toward her mouth, and she opened up wide, sucking me in deep.

Just watching her lips sliding over my joint had me making crazy faces. I let my hands roam over her shoulders and down her arms, enjoying myself. I loved women. I dug the way they smelled. I loved looking at their bodies and touching their soft skin. I enjoyed tasting them too. But that would come later.

Yasmere was sucking faster now and making slurping noises. She gripped my dick tightly with her lips and swirled her hot tongue around the head.

"Yeah!" she started whispering to it. Talking to that dick. She ran her tongue all the way down to my balls and back up again, rubbing my joint all over her face as she squeezed my balls.

I entered her mouth again and closed my eyes and concentrated on the rhythm she was creating. I hadn't gotten head like this in a long time, and I was excited. I balanced myself on my knees and held on to the wall. I was moving my hips and slamming into her mouth. She was bobbing so fast her lips made wet popping sounds on me.

"Oooh!" I moaned, holding the back of her head and stroking even harder. "You bout to get this shit girl!"

She pulled her lips off me and held up a condom. She laughed. "All this dick? Niggah you better not come till I get a chance to bounce on this shit for a good minute."

"We don't need that shit," I said, pushing her hand and the condom away.

She almost sat straight up. "You might not need it, but I damn sure do."

I was disappointed cause sex in a glove didn't do shit for me. I liked getting my joint nice and wet, but the way she was looking told me it was either wear the damn glove or get up and send Smoove in so he could get him a crack.

I knew what time it was. I nodded and she slid the hat down on me, then lay back with her nipples toward the ceiling and her legs spread wide.

"Open them wider," I said, tapping her inner thigh. "Hold them farther apart."

She slid one leg half off the bed and propped the other one up against the wall. I looked down into her wet pussy and sucked my breath in as she put her hand between her legs and inserted one finger deep in her tunnel, masturbating herself.

"Come get this pussy," she whispered, her snatch making wet sucking sounds as it gripped her moving finger. "You a thug motherfucker, right? So come rock it."

She arched her hips up in the air and I met her on the downstroke. Her ass was firm but fluffy in my hands as I thrust my dick straight into her and started stroking until she purred.

"Oh . . . yes . . . please . . . ssss . . . argh!" She wrapped her legs around my waist and whimpered in my ear, telling me how big my dick was and how good I fucked.

I drove into her gently, then harder. Hitting her spot and making her eyes roll up in her head. Her pussy was good, and I was ready to cum. Instead, I put one foot on the floor and turned her over on the stomach and started pounding her from behind.

She was yelling now. Singing a thug song. I slid my fingers between her ass cheeks and around to her clit and stroked it softly. Her body started trembling, and I reached between her legs and cupped her pussy. Humping hard, I spread two fingers into a V and pressed down on her clit with my palm as I felt my dick drilling in and out of her.

She backed that ass up into me, taking it all and urging me to go deeper. We were halfway off the broken-down little bed. The sheets was on the floor and we were both swirling our hips and moaning out loud.

"Ah! Ah! Ah!" she screamed, arching her back like a cat and coming hard. I was right behind her. I slapped her juicy ass, slamming my dick in deep and fast, then at the last minute I pulled out and snatched off the condom. Rubbing my dick all over her ass I came, coating her backside with hot slippery cream.

"Yeah," she panted, and to my surprise she reached back and ran her hand along her ass, then turned around and looked at me as she sucked my cum off her fingers. "That's the best dick I ever had," she swore, smiling with her big bright eyes. "How old is you? Forget it. It don't even matter cause your ass fucks like a grown man. I'm for real too. You the best."

I laughed and pulled her up to me. I kissed her, sucking on her bottom lip as she caught her breath.

"So what now?" I asked a few minutes later. I deliberately spoke in a cold voice as I put on my boxers and zipped up my jeans. I buckled my belt. "You ready for me to send my boy in here, or what?"

She was laying back on the rumpled bed, rubbing her nipples and squeezing one juicy tit in each hand.

"Your boy?" She laughed loudly. "Your boy? You think your boy can come in here and hit this pussy right behind you? I don't care what kinda weapon he might be holding, the only dick I wanna ride tonight is yours!"

I smiled as she grinned and licked her lips. Her stomach was flat and sexy and her hips curved and strong. I felt my dick getting hard again, and I shrugged.

"Whatever, then," I said and got on my knees. I stuck out my tongue and started licking all over her sweat-coated body, then buried my face between her thighs. "First let me get a little snack-snack. And then I'll let you go for a ride."

Thirty minutes later my second nut had been busted. Smoove was nowhere in sight and I had had enough of Yasmere to last me through the night. I'd handled her so right that she was hanging off of me, wanting to cuddle and shit like women always do after getting some prime dick. I slapped her firm ass. Sucked her neck. Balanced those firm titties in my hands. I gave her all the affection she needed on my way to the door.

I was definitely looking forward to getting me some more of Yasmere in the future, so I took a quick second to give her a last little bit of love before I bounced. We were standing in the open doorway kissing when the stairwell door slammed. Both of us looked up as a gorgeous sistah came around the corner holding a cup in her hand.

Yasmere laughed and started talking shit, but I just stood there staring. The girl was bad. Fine, classy, and had a body that made the one I'd just climbed off look like a bag of twigs. But it wasn't just the body that had my jaw dropped and some strange feelings tugging at a niggah's heart.

"What?" Yasmere said. My hand had slid off her titty and she grabbed my fingers and tried to put them back on there. "You around here begging again? Girl, when you gone get a damn job and handle your damn business?"

What the fuck? I thought. Everybody was poor in this joint. Niggahs in the hood borrowed shit all the time. Yasmere was foul to talk that kinda shit, and I decided she would never get a chance to bounce on my good dick again. I was still staring at the girl. I busted the shameful look that crossed her face and knew it would stay with me for a long time. *Don't worry, baby,* I promised her fine ass in my mind and in my heart. *Just wait till a niggah like me get on. I'ma make sure you ain't never gotta beg nobody for shit else again in life.*

— — —

Like I said, jawns was coming up out the sinks to get a good look at me, but the only woman I was studying was Muddah. I waited at the counter until a pretty young sistah with big eyes came out the back room and greeted me.

"Welcome to Flip It and Clip It. You need somebody to hook up your braids?"

"Nah," I answered, ignoring the undeniable interest coming from her eyes. "I'm looking for Carmiesha. She here?"

"Uhm, ain't you one of them 'Licious Lovers? I seen y'all cuttin up over at Harlem World."

"Yeah, I'm Thug. Carmiesha here?"

The girl smirked, seeing her opportunity to get with me go up in the air.

She popped her gum and looked over her shoulder. "Yeah, she here. She doing her homework in the back."

While she went to get Muddah I leaned on the counter, looking through the window at the Harlem streets outside. I loved these streets, and they'd been good to me. I'd been through the fire on these streets and had even thought I would die on them. But that was back in the day. I was twenty now and it was time to get with the rest of the program. Time to stop playing games and get my solo album cut. Time to start thinking about my kids who I never hardly saw and didn't do shit for when I did see 'em. Time to get my ass upstate to college and prove myself, and then get out there and bust some niggahs up wearing an official NBA jersey. Just thinking about all of that balanced against what Pimp wanted me to get down on was giving me heartburn.

But when I thought about Muddah everything inside me got comfortable. My heart felt like it had a home. We wasn't together full-time no more cause she couldn't get with the baby drama and all the other women. She had started seeing other dudes cause she said a niggah like me just couldn't do right. And no matter how much I tried to explain that sex with groupies and honeys was just for fun, and that what I felt for her was from the heart, Muddah just wasn't having it. I guess in a way that made me dig her even more.

Muddah came out the back room looking fresh and tight. Even the shit with Smoove didn't stop me from noticing how good she looked. She had the body of a freak but carried herself like a queen diva. Like she knew her pussy was good but wasn't advertising that shit. She'd gotten rid of her glasses and moved up to contact lenses years ago, and as I stared into her eyes I let my real, naked self show.

"Hey, Dre," she said, standing on her toes to kiss me. "How you doing?" Maybe she sensed something in me cause she looked deeper into my eyes. "Whassup? Something wrong?"

I pulled her close to my chest and breathed deeply. I knew a million nosy eyes was on us but I didn't give a fuck.

"Nah. I'm straight, baby. I just wanted to see you, you know? Maybe get wit' you if you got a little spare time for a niggah."

She looked at her watch. "I still have to do a lot of homework, and I'm supposed to clean up in here tonight, but maybe I can get Joy to cover for me. I'll be right back."

I watched her ass cheeks swinging under the sexy skirt she wore, and even though I'd busted a big nut with Vikki last night I still wanted me some Muddah. I couldn't wait until we got back to the crib. I was gonna push up in my girl and duck out on the world.

"I gotta be somewhere so I ain't got a lotta time," I told her when she came back out. Muddah nodded and I grabbed her hand as we walked out the door. Behind us, them sistahs was hating on her hard, talking shit cause Mami was rolling out with me instead of one of them.

Unlike most of these ghetto jawns who were wrapped up in all kinds of surface shit that didn't mean a damn thing, Muddah was like me in a lotta ways. She was from the streets but she had goals and dreams. She mighta been working in the beauty salon right now, but come six o'clock at night she took her ass cross town to study business at Hunter College. I couldn't wait until the day when she had her own damn joint. She would put her business training to work and shut all these frontin'-ass hoes down.

"That's cool," Muddah told me as I held her hand tight. "I can't hang out for long neither, but we can make the most of the little time we got."

Chapter 6

Carmiesha liked being seen out on the streets with Thug.

He was tall as hell, and fine too. It didn't hurt that he moved with an attitude about him that commanded total and immediate respect. All kinds of females stared him down like he didn't have a woman on his arm, but he knew not to let her bust him checking them out in return cause she was tired of bitches blowing up her spot and disrespecting her on account of his roaming dick. Andre had just turned twenty and he already had six kids. He'd gotten two females pregnant in the past year and one of them, a chick named Kathy, had the nerve to drop a set of twins.

"That Thug motherfucker need to get his dick laminated," one of the girls at the beauty salon had laughed when she found out Carmiesha was tight with her favorite rapper. Chickenheads was steady putting Dre on blast for having three babies in one year, when behind closed doors they were dying to get some of that infamous dick he was slinging. Carmiesha had ignored the nasty comment cause she wasn't trying to get in no fight and get her face sliced up behind no man who couldn't keep his dick in his pants.

Besides, she thought, remembering the night she had met him. It wasn't like she couldn't tell Dre was a ho right off the jump. . . .

She'd been sitting on the edge of her bed and squinting at the pages in front of her. She was trying hard to get the hang of eighth grade math, but the lone lightbulb in the room kept flickering on and off and her back hurt from bending over the desk she had made out of a milk crate.

"Muddah!" her grandmother had called from the kitchen. Carmiesha closed her heavy math book and sighed.

"I'm doing my homework, Mere'maw. What you need?"

"Come on in here and help me get some food on the table for your brothers, baby. It's getting late and I bet that narrow-ass Rome ain't put nothing in his stomach all day."

Carmiesha sucked her teeth under her breath but she stood up anyway. She didn't see why she had to do a damn thing for her trifling-ass brothers. Even though she was the youngest, Carmiesha was the only one of Mere'maw's grandkids who was gonna make it out of junior high school. Both Rome and her other brother Justice had quit going to school before the seventh grade just so they could run the streets and hang out full-time.

Carmiesha walked the few steps down the hall and into the small kitchen. Greasy pots and pans were stacked everywhere, and dirty dishes overflowed out the sink. She looked at the mess and wanted to cry. She loved Mere'maw like crazy, but she was tired of living in this slum. She busted her ass going to school every day and shampooing hair for tips at the beauty shop on the weekends, and the only thing Mere'maw had to do all day was keep the house clean. Instead she wasted all her energy worrying about what her grandsons were doing in the streets and let the household chores slip. That meant Carmiesha had to pick up her slack.

Carmiesha had blinked back tears and made herself go hard inside. Right now she was wearing her last pair of clean panties and there was no kind of soap whatsoever in the house. She would have to go downstairs and beg Yasmere for a cup of soap powder. She'd use most of it to wash the dirty dishes, and if there was any left over she'd run water in the sink and wash out her panties and bras and maybe a shirt or two. That was the only way she would have some clean clothes to wear to school the next day.

"Here," Mere'maw said, passing Carmiesha a chipped dinner plate. "Fix your own food first."

Carmiesha reached for the plate and missed. She cringed as it fell to the floor and slid under the table, and when she bent over and reached down to get it, she jerked her hand back and cursed.

"Shit!" She glanced over at Mere'maw, who had narrowed her lips in disapproval.

"Sorry bout that, Mere'maw. There's a dead mouse in that trap down there. I almost touched it."

"Them boys." Mere'maw shook her head as Carmiesha carefully retrieved the plate. It was cracked, but she was gonna eat out of it anyway otherwise she'd have to get a dirty one out the sink and rinse it off. "I told them to get that mouse outta there two days ago. Seem like I be talking to a brick wall when I ask them to do something round here."

Carmiesha shrugged. "Well maybe if you didn't let them get away with murder, Mere'maw, they'd listen to you better. Rome is almost fifteen and Justice is sixteen. They don't go to school and they don't work nowhere neither, unless you count all that scrambling they doing up there on that corner. The three of us should be taking care of you instead of you trying to feed us every day. You took us in raised us when Mama got killed, and that's enough."

Mere'maw took the top off a small pot of neck bones. There were a few grains of rice floating in the thin gravy and two long strips of onions. "That's what family do, Lil' Muddah. If I hadn'ta took y'all in, the state woulda got you and who knows where y'all would be right now."

After dividing the small pot of food into the four plates, Carmiesha covered her brothers' plates with a torn piece of paper bag and set them inside the stove. She handed a plate to Mere'maw, who took it and shuffled back into the living room so she could finish watching her talk show. Carmiesha ate her own food standing up in the kitchen. She was too scared to sit down at the table where that dead mouse was.

Carmeisha ate her food real slow, enjoying the few grains of rice and dipping the neck bone into the watery gravy and then sucking it dry. Hunger was something that was with her every day, and she felt lucky to get the small but tasty meal. She kept aligning the crack in the plate so the liquid wouldn't seep through, and when it did, she used her finger to wipe it from the bottom of her plate and scoop it into her mouth.

Life had always been hard for her. At the age of eight Carmiesha had been the only witness to a brutal crime. She had watched her father pull a .38 from a plastic bag, fire two blasts into her mother's chest, then raise the gun and shoot himself in the head.

Carmiesha and her brothers were sent to live with Mere'maw after their parents died. Carmiesha could understand why her brothers had turned to slinging rock and beating women. They got that shit from their father, and it ran in their blood. Carmiesha picked up her empty plate and dropped it on top of the pile already in the sink. She was still hungry and had been tempted to lick the last bit of gravy off the plate, but forced herself not to.

"I'll be right back," she called out to Mere'maw, taking a plastic cup from a cabinet.

Mere'maw didn't answer. She was too busy laughing at something somebody had said on television.

Carmiesha left the apartment and ran down the stairs to the first floor. She hated borrowing shit from Yasmere, but she was the only one in the building who ever had anything to loan. Yasmere had a nice mother in the house and a father who had a real job. Her gear stayed tight, and she never went hungry. Even though she fucked anything with a dick, including Justice and Rome, she usually gave Carmiesha whatever she came asking for. But only after she made sure she made her feel like a piece of shit for asking.

Carmiesha had exited the stairwell and was approaching Yasmere's door when she saw that it was already open. Yasmere was in the doorway wearing a thin robe. Carmiesha could tell she was butt-ass naked underneath. One of the new guys who had just moved in the building was standing there with her. He was tall and buff and had creamy light skin and long cornrows. He had on a wifebeater and some low-slung jeans, and he was sucking Yasmeen's neck and feeling all over her big titty like he was her man. Carmiesha saw Yasmere giggle and rub old boy's dick through his pants. She started to turn around and walk the other way, but they both looked up and saw her when the exit door slammed.

The guy, who was even finer up close, dropped Yasmere's titty and came up off her neck, and stared at Carmiesha.

"What?" Yasmere laughed, sliding his hand back to her big breast. "Your ass down here begging again? Girl, when you gone get a damn job and handle your damn business?"

Carmiesha just looked at her. She knew Yasmere was a minor ho, but she didn't have to put her on blast just to impress some niggah. Carmiesha had a job and Yasmere knew it. She came her frontin' ass into the shop and got her hair washed and wrapped every week. For free. And Carmiesha always hooked her up lovely without complaining.

"I just—," Carmiesha started, then stopped. This long-legged gangsta-looking niggah was staring her down like it was her titty he wished he was holding in his hand. He had a thick tattoo on his arm that said T.H.U.G., and a diamond earring glinting in his left ear. Carmiesha turned toward Yasmere, ignoring him. He was tall and real cute, but he looked just like the rest of the no-good crack-slanging niggahs who prowled the avenue with her brothers. "Damn, Yasmere. You ain't gotta go there like that. I just need to borrow a little bit of soap powder, that's all."

Yasmere laughed again. "Borrow? Bitch what the fuck you mean borrow? 'Borrow' mean you planning on paying something back, and you ain't *never* did that!"

Carmiesha knew what time it was. This bitch was acting extra cause she'd just got fucked.

"Cool," she said and walked back toward the stairwell. She'd wash her dirty drawers out with two drops of fuckin toothpaste before she gave that bitch the satisfaction of begging her in front of some stray niggah.

Back upstairs in her apartment Carmiesha went straight to the kitchen and started stacking the pots and dishes. When she had them in high piles, she ran cold water over them one by one and scraped off the crusted-up food the best she could. There was never more than a little bit of hot water in the pipes and she wanted to save it to wash her panties.

She was still scrubbing pots when somebody banged on the front door like they was trying to tear it down. Carmiesha froze. Nobody but the police knocked like that. She cut off the water and moved toward the door and met Mere'maw coming down the hall.

"Chile," Mere'maw said, her eyes wide. "A knock like that ain't nothing good."

Carmiesha got in front of her. "Let me open it, Mere'maw." Wasn't no need in the cops banging down the goddamn door. Justice and Rome were up on the avenue, right in plain sight.

She flung open the door with much attitude on her face.

"Whassup."

It was one of the new guys from next door. The one who had been downstairs fucking Yasmere. He was holding a big red box in his hands.

"You wanted some soap powder, right? Well here go some."

Carmiesha let him stand there holding it as she stared him down.

"Sorry. You got the wrong door. The cheap pussy is downstairs where you just came from," she told him. "I don't fuck for soap powder so you can take that shit back wherever you stole it from."

Instead of giving her the street attitude that she expected, the young brothah gave her a big pretty smile.

"I thought you'd prolly say some wild shit like that." He kept right on smiling as she slammed the door in his face, leaving him standing there with his big red box.

Backing away from the door, Carmiesha bumped right into Mere'maw, who'd overheard the short conversation.

"I don't fuck for soap powder neither," the old woman said, shocking Carmiesha and making her jaw drop, "but Lord knows we can use some."

Mere'maw nudged her granddaughter aside and opened the door again. The boy was gone, but the large box of soap powder was sitting right there on the floor.

Lightweight motherfucker, Carmiesha had thought. She'd known he was a poseur cause the box had been opened. His shit mighta looked tight, but he was straight fake. A paid niggah wouldn'ta brought her no soap powder that had already been opened and used. But at least it was Tide and not the weak store brand.

Carmiesha grabbed the box before her grandmother could reach for it, surprised to find that it was so heavy. Walking back into the apartment, Carmiesha set the soap powder on the counter and flipped the lid open. She stared at the contents, and her jaw dropped again.

Two one-hundred-dollar bills were sitting on top of the white flakes.

She picked up the money and felt it, then held each bill up to the light. As much as she hated to take that niggah's money, she wasn't a damn fool. Justice and Rome tricked out every dime they hustled on bitches and slum jewelry. It was hard to get two dollars out of either of them, and whatever chump change they gave Mere'maw they expected her to squeeze it until it hollered. Two hundred dollars would buy them some groceries and pay the light bill too.

Carmiesha folded the bills and stuck them in her pocket. She'd keep the money, but she still wasn't impressed. His pretty ass needed to stick to fuckin with hoes like Yasmere, and leave future business owners like her the hell alone. There wasn't shit about Mister T.H.U.G. that pressed her out. At least not on that night.

Chapter 7

"You want some Kool-Aid?" Carmiesha asked.

Thug nodded and sat down on Mere'maw's raggedy sofa. "Yeah. Y'all got some sugar in it, right?"

She slapped him on the back of his head. "Yeah we got sugar in it, fool. Don't play like we still so poor where we gotta drink colored water and make like it's Kool-Aid."

"C'mon, Muddah." Thug rubbed the back of his head. "What I tell you about putting your hands on me, girl?"

Carmiesha stood between his long legs with her hands on her hips. "What I tell you about calling me 'Muddah'? My name is Carmiesha, just so you know."

Thug pulled her down on the couch with him. Carmiesha let him slide her onto his lap, but she moved her head when he tried to kiss her.

"Let me hear you say that. Carmiesha. Car-mee-sha. Come on. You can do it."

Normally Thug would have cracked backed on her. He woulda called her some of everything except Carmiesha, just to make her laugh. But today he was quiet and Carmiesha saw the trouble that was in his eyes.

"C'mere, boy," she said, hugging him and laying her head on his big shoulder. She took his hand and instead of holding hers, his fingers stayed limp. "What's up, Andre? You ain't looked this shook since Kathy told you she was having twins."

Thug made a noise and tried to push her off his lap. "Stop playin. I ain't in the mood for that shit and besides. I don't even know if them babies are mine."

"Niggah, you the one need to stop!" Carmiesha said, smirking. "Them babies is yours for real. They both got your mark. Just like Little Precious, Dante, Shantay, and Duqueesa. Why you frontin'? One of them twins was born with six fingers on both hands, and the other one was born with six fingers *and* six toes. So don't even try it cause a judge ain't gone buy it."

Thug sighed. "Where Mere'maw at?"

Carmiesha nodded. "She's back there snoring. She was up all night talking about how bad her stomach hurt. I keep telling her she need to leave all them sweets she be eating alone."

"Cool," Thug said and put his arm around her.

Carmiesha laid against him, enjoying the feeling as he rubbed her shoulders and ran his fingers down her bare arm.

"You hear anything more from the college yet?"

Thug shrugged. "Same old shit. They gone give me a full ride and pay for my room and books and shit. Coach tried to talk me out of majoring in engineering, though. He thinks I should prolly study something more low-key like basket-weaving or some stupid shit." He shrugged again. "Them motherfuckers don't give a damn what I do. Long as I play good ball and put some *W*s in their column they could give a fuck about what kinda learning skills I got."

Carmiesha was proud of Thug for getting accepted at a top university like Syracuse. Even though she was a year younger, he'd fallen behind two grades so she had graduated a year ahead of him. She'd already finished beauty school and had just enrolled in college, but instead of going on to a big university she'd had to be satisfied with a CUNY scholarship that would let her go to community college for free.

She put her arms around his neck and kissed his bottom lip. "So you letting that shit bother you? Is that why you walking around here looking like you lost your last damn dollar? Tonight's the *Sweep or Weep* over at T.C.'s, right? Take your ass over there and win you some green boys if you broke."

Thug pulled away and sat up straight. The look on his face was ice cold. "Who the fuck said I was broke, Muddah? Don't never let me catch you talking no shit about me and money, girl. I ain't broke, and I ain't looking for no damn money."

Carmiesha got quiet. She knew for a fact that something was wrong. Thug never went off on her. Never. She could call him all kinds of lying, cheating, dick-slinging ho-ass motherfuckers. She could slap him upside his head and tell him to kiss her funky ass, and he never raised his voice to her. Never.

"Cool. Stay your ass home tonight then. You still want that cup of Kool-Aid?"

"Nah," Thug said quietly. His arm went back around her shoulder and his fingers started massaging the curve of her hip. "I don't want no fuckin' Kool-Aid, Muddah. I want me some a you."

Thug slipped his tongue into her mouth and licked it around in greedy circles. His need was thick and heavy in his lap, and he kissed her with so much heat that Carmiesha felt her panties getting wet.

"I need you," Thug whispered, pressing his lips forcefully to hers, his tongue snaking around the inside of her mouth. "I need you, Muddah. I need some of your pussy."

Carmiesha didn't resist him when his hands started roaming, even though they hadn't fucked in a long time on account of the guy Ya-Yo she was seeing, and all of Thug's baby-mama drama. He had really hurt her by messing around with chickenheads like Rasheena and Kathy and Paula, and being stupid enough to run up in all them bitches raw at that. The only reason she was still speaking to him was because her conscience fucked with her to the point where she had no choice but to forgive him. Thug wasn't the only one who had made a baby. It's just that his shit was out there on blast for the world to see and hers wasn't.

She leaned back and accepted the sucking he was giving to her neck and tried to control her breathing as his tongue swirled around her earlobe and his teeth started nibbling.

Carmiesha had her own little secret that she'd been keeping for six long years, and no matter how much she loved Thug, she could never bring herself to tell him. She loved him so much she couldn't tell him. He'd wanna kill some fuckin body if she told.

Shame and anger came down heavy on her as she thought about that hot August night when she'd been violated in every kind of way. There had been so many times when she wanted to just fess up and tell Thug what had happened. To come clean and let whatever was gonna go down, go down. But each time she tried, just as she opened her mouth and got ready to say those words, something stopped her. Her throat straight clogged up and made her suck back those words just like she'd sucked . . .

Thug was running his fingers over her nipples, and Carmiesha fought to stay in the moment. As hard-core as he was, and as big of a gangsta rep that he had, when it came to pleasing a woman Thug was the most tender man in the world. She liked the way he took his time to turn her on, exploring every crease and curve he thought might hold some pleasure for her. Thug had mastered the art of licking and hot fucking, and there was nothing he wouldn't do to make her feel good.

Carmiesha moaned lightly as his fingers crawled up her shirt and loosened her bra. She was laying in the crook of his arm, and while his lips and tongue were all over her face and neck, she thrust her ass out and humped around on his erection.

"I need you, Muddah," Thug whispered again between kisses, and just those four words got Carmiesha's pussy juices flowing like a stream. No matter how many other bitches he got with, Andre "Thug-A-Licious" Williams needed *her*. Not one of those gold-digging thug-a-holic hoes who shook their asses up in the club while he was spittin' on the mic, or one of them groupies who tried to spin on his dick after a basketball game. It was her. Thug needed *her*.

Carmiesha stood up and walked into her tiny bedroom. She didn't say a word, and she never looked back. She didn't need to. Thug had a thing for her phat booty, and she knew just the sight of it rolling around in her tight jeans would have him following her like a crackhead chases that white ghost.

They undressed eye to eye in her cramped bedroom. Staring each other down with sexual appreciation as each piece of clothing hit the floor. Mere'maw was snoring loudly in the next room, so Carmiesha wasn't worried about waking her up. She stood in front of Thug naked and smiling cause she knew he was crazy about what she had to offer.

"C'mere," he said, taking her hand. He had her lay out-stretched on her stomach with her arms over her head. Carmiesha trembled in hot anticipation of the dick down she was about to get.

He started out holding her hair up and kissing the back of her neck. Licking it actually, then trailing his tongue down to the middle of her back. Carmiesha squirmed in delight as he sucked and licked her back, arching upward as his tongue crept down lower until it approached the sexy split of her ass mounds.

"You still got that stretch mark on your ass, girl. A crazy ass lightning bolt on the top of your left booty cheek."

"Ooohh," Carmiesha sighed, ignoring him and grinding her pussy into the bed. Thug was taking small bites of her ass, nipping lightly as he covered both of her fine round, honey-colored lumps. Moments later he was pushing his whole face between her legs, sniffing and licking and sucking the insides of her thighs so hard he left hickeys.

"Eat it," Carmiesha whispered raising herself onto her knees. "Eat it, baby . . . please."

Thug went to lunch. He licked her pussy out from the back with long strokes. Starting at her clit he lapped backwards, catching a mouthful of juice on his tongue.

"I luh this pussy, Muddah," he whispered behind her. "You got the best fuckin pussy in the world, girl."

Carmiesha couldn't hold back. She came hard, bucking on her hands and knees and backing her ass up to meet his tongue.

Thug waited until she stopped shaking, then pushed down

gently on her back so she could lay flat. He laid on top of her and moved his super-erect dick along the moist valley between the back of her thighs. Carmiesha opened up for him, and he pushed into her gently, savoring the sensation of each rock-hard inch as it invaded her tightness.

He felt her shiver and grasped her by the hips and thrust down hard, hammering into the back of her pussy as deeply as he could. Carmiesha bit down on a howl as Thug pounded her forcefully from behind. He was fucking her like a maniac. Going to town in her pussy so hard that the bed was moaning and her head was slamming against the headboard hard enough to wake up Mere'maw.

"Th-th-thug . . ." Carmiesha tried to plead, but that dick was holding her hostage and before she could complete her sentence she came again, her pussy overflowing with hot juices. Thug was like a monster behind her. Slamming every thick inch of his dick into her until his balls almost slid up in her too.

Clenching her bedspread in her hands, Carmiesha turned her head to look at him and almost screamed when she saw his face. Thug's eyes were closed and he was biting his bottom lip. His whole face was twisted and contorted in what looked to her like pain and maybe even some guilt.

Before Carmiesha could say anything he came hard, slamming his dick deeply inside of her and making a mess on the bed as their combined liquids seeped from her and onto the spread.

It took them a long time to catch their breath, and Thug lay quietly on top of her without speaking. When he finally did move, he pulled his still-long dick out of her and moved back until he was kneeling between her legs.

Carmiesha lay there confused, waiting for some kind of an explanation for the way he had fucked her. But a second later she felt his weight shift off the bed and when she turned her head he was picking up his clothes and putting them back on.

She watched his face but didn't see a damn thing. It was solid like ice. Thug had shot all his emotions deep inside the folds of her pussy, and the look in his eyes scared her because it meant nothing and nobody could reach him.

He used his drawers to dry off his dick, then stepped back into them and put on his jeans. He had on his sneakers and was buckling his belt when Carmiesha spoke to him softly.

"Where you going, Andre?"

Thug laughed coldly, then looked at her with absolutely nothing in his eyes.

"To hell, Lil' Muddah. I'm going straight to hell."

Chapter 8

Carmiesha laid in the bed for a good fifteen minutes after Thug left. She stared at the ceiling and tried to figure out what could be so wrong that he'd had to fuck her like a wild animal. Maybe he was still grieving over his little sister. He felt real guilty behind Precious's murder, and sometimes he got down seemingly out of nowhere. Or maybe he had got another bitch pregnant, she thought, her temper rising.

Like a fool she'd let him do her without a raincoat, something she hadn't fallen for in years. He swore to God he had been tested for HIV and everything else as part of the physical he'd taken for his college admission, but that didn't mean shit cause that niggah just couldn't do right. Carmiesha was just as scared of getting pregnant as she was of catching a damn disease. If a girl didn't make Dre use a hoodie, then he damn sure wouldn't. She loved him, but she wasn't trying to catch nothing from him, and she wasn't having no more babies until she had her career going and was settled in with a man she could trust.

Just the thought of babies and getting pregnant was enough to make her curse at herself for being so damn stupid. All she could do was hope he didn't burn her or give her nothing to take back to her man, Ya-Yo. That shit would be dangerous and too damn foul.

She wrapped her bedspread around her naked body and went into the bathroom to wash up in the sink. The now-cold cum that was running down the inside of her legs reminded her of the night that had changed her life. The night when she'd caught such a bad one that not even a thug like Dre could protect her . . .

At the age of thirteen Carmiesha had had the body of a full-grown woman. No matter how hard she tried to hide her round breasts and plump, apple-bottom ass beneath baggy clothes, all kinds of men hit on her every day and it was distressing for a girl her age to receive all of that erotic attention.

Even though she had already started catching feelings for the opposite sex, Carmiesha wasn't even thinking about giving up no booty, even to Thug. She would drop her panties and let him eat her out any day of the week, and yeah, she'd pay him back by dipping her hand in a jar of Vaseline and jerking him off until he came. She'd even given him some serious head a few times and was surprised at how much she enjoyed the way his hard dick felt in her mouth and against her lips.

But Carmiesha wasn't nowhere near stupid. She saw how hard life was for Mere'maw trying to raise them, and how little respect Rome and Justice had for girls. She was too smart to let some boy stick his dick in her and leave her to deal with the consequences of his nut. She'd rather masturbate to a hot erotic

Emery book than let some wanksta get his thrills knocking her uterus up in her chest.

But no matter how careful Carmiesha tried to be, fate was not on her side. She was carrying a bag of goodies home for Mere'maw one hot summer night when it happened. Normally, she wouldn't have even thought about going out so late at night unless she was traveling with Thug or one of her brothers, but this night was different. Mere'maw had been craving something sweet all day, but Thug was out rapping at a club across town, and both of the boys had gotten locked up for thirty days for street gambling with some dudes from the Bronx.

Carmiesha had already washed up and put on a pair of tight gym shorts and a tiny T-shirt to sleep in, but she was tired of hearing Mere'maw complain about her sweet tooth, and the Spanish store right up the block stayed open all night.

Besides, it was hot and sticky in the house. There was no sign of a breeze coming from nowhere. A walk down the block would get her out of the sweatbox that slum tenements in the city became every summer, and plus she'd shut Mere'maw up so they could both get some sleep. Leaving her scarf tied around her head, Carmeisha had taken the house key and two dollars' worth of quarters from a drawer in her room, then told Mere'maw she'd be right back.

Carmiesha walked down the streets of Harlem with her ass bouncing and her breasts shaking. Eyes hit on her from every direction but she ignored them all. She knew how her body affected men, and there were plenty of dyke females who had tried to get with her too. The fact was, she was built. She had a mind-boggling shape on her and there was nothing she could do about what naturally showed. But she made it her business to look fly and decent at all times. She coulda walked around in stank-ho clothes, but her ass would've gotten her in a whole lot of trouble, and that's the last thing she was looking for.

Carmiesha had made it all the way to the store and was walking back to her building when she noticed footsteps coming up behind her. It was late but the hot streets of Harlem were still alive, and there were plenty of people either sitting on their stoops or lounging on parked cars drinking cold beer and getting high.

Carmiesha glanced back, glad to see a familiar face, even if it was one she couldn't stand. Both of her brothers had changed since this cutthroat niggah came on the scene. Before he moved in the building, Justice and Rome had been small-time scramblers who made just enough cash to trick it up the same night. But when this dude came around all that changed. Her brothers started following behind this fool, and he led them deeper into the world of slinging rock. So deep that now Justice and Rome both worked for him. They got out there risked themselves to the po-po to make the quick cash, and this crazy-looking niggah raked in the profits and threw them a little side chump to keep them quiet.

She walked a little faster, wishing her ass wasn't so damn big. She wasn't trying to give his creepy behind no show back there, but she could feel her booty bouncing from side to side.

She picked up her pace again when she got near the entrance to her building. A light was on in Yasmere's window, and for some crazy reason Carmiesha was overcome with a sense of dread. She almost started to knock on Yasmere's door and ask to use the phone or something, but she wasn't fucking with that crazy bitch no more, so she shook her dark feelings to the side and pressed the button for the elevator instead.

The elevator usually ran slow whenever it was actually working, but tonight it came pretty quick, like it had been waiting just a floor or two away. When the doors opened Carmiesha got on, clutching her bag and stepping over a big puddle of piss as she punched the button for the sixth floor real fast. The doors began creaking closed and Carmiesha was just about to feel safe when a big black hand shot through at the last moment, triggering the emergency mechanism and causing the doors to retract and slide back open.

The dude stepped into the elevator with a scowl on his face. He was fine, but to Carmiesha fine on his ass didn't matter. There was something off about this niggah. Something that gave her the creeps real bad.

"I *said* hold the fuckin' elevator," he beefed, looking her up and down.

Carmiesha stood her ground. His lying ass hadn't said shit. And even if he had, she damn sure wouldn'ta held it. There was no way she would have got in no elevator by herself with him if she had a choice.

"Well I didn't hear you," she replied sarcastically, staring him down in return. This niggah was like a bully-ass fuckin dog. Show him a lick of fear and he'd be all over your ass. Carmiesha couldn't figure out how the hell he got his nickname unless it came from his cold-ass heart, cause there wasn't a chick in Harlem who was crazy enough to fuck with him on that level.

The elevator doors closed and the car rose slowly toward the sixth floor. Carmiesha stood with her back in the corner and the small bag of chips and candy in front of her to block his view of her firm breasts.

He stared at her for a second, then said, "What's in the bag?"

Your mother, bitch, is what Carmiesha wanted to say, but instead she answered, "Candy. For Mere'maw."

The next thing she knew the bag of candy was flying through the air and she was flat on her back on the pissy elevator floor.

"Bitch, you think you a star, don't you?"

Carmiesha couldn't have answered if she wanted to. The motherfucker had knocked loose her tooth and blood was running from her nose.

"Get up, you stank-ass fuckin ho!" He kicked her in her ribs so hard with his Timbs that she slid all the way over to the other side of the elevator, cracking her knee against the wall.

Carmiesha was in shock as he grabbed her by the neck and dragged her back over to him. Her scarf slid over her face, blinding her, and he almost broke her head trying to snatch it off.

"Motherfuckah . . . ," Carmiesha managed to crawl to her feet and mumble when she saw what he was up to. He'd flipped the emergency stop switch, freezing the elevator between floors and was opening his pants.

"I'ma . . . tell Thu—," Carmiesha tried to say, but he slid his belt out the loops and swung it hard in her face. The buckle knocked the words right out of her mouth. It cracked her front tooth too.

"Tell that motherfucker what?" He choked her with both hands until she sank down to her knees gasping for air. Carmiesha tried to fight back but he was older, bigger, stronger, and much crazier.

He took one hand from around her neck and started messing

with his zipper, and that's when she knew what time it was. When his skinny little dick was sticking out the hole of his boxers, he punched her in the face again, then shoved it in her mouth and moved himself around.

"Yeah, bitch," he threw his head back, then moaned and laughed at the same time. "Suck this big-ass dick. You know you like it too. Suck my joint, bitch. And if you do it real good I'll stick it in your pussy and let you come when I'm through."

Carmiesha choked and gurgled as he held her by her hair and jerked her head around like it was her ass. She had no control over the situation as he pumped in and out of her mouth, tearing her lip on his zipper and poking her in the throat with a dick that wasn't much fatter than a pencil.

No! She screamed inside, and snapped her teeth together, biting down on his hard, wet flesh. Pain exploded in her cracked front tooth, and she quickly let go and yelped.

"Bitch!" he screamed and started punching her all over her head, in her eyes, her nose, his fist slamming into her mouth causing her injured tooth to ring with pain even more.

"Bite me again! Go 'head! I dare you, bitch. You gone suck this motherfuckin' dick and you better not bite me. Suck it! Suck it, bitch!"

He pumped into her mouth even more violently. Ignoring her cries and brutalizing her mouth. Just when Carmiesha thought it was almost over, he did what he said he was gonna do. He pushed her back down on the wet, filthy floor so he could fuck her.

Carmiesha found the strength to fight like hell as he ripped open her gym shorts and fell on top of her. She screamed with pain and rage as he penetrated her, but that didn't stop him. He thrust into her over and over again until he got his nut, and then he slobbered and panted in her ear trying to catch his breath.

"Yeah," he said, climbing off of her and pulling up his pants. "My cousin was right. That is some *ill ass na-na*." He looked around at the candy scattered on the dirty floor and picked up a few pieces, opening a wrapper and popping one in his mouth.

"Now, you wanna go running your mouth telling somebody? Go right the fuck ahead. Your punk-ass brothers think they got knocked for being stupid . . . them and any other motherfucker who thinks he's hard'll get straight popped if they come fuckin' with me."

He flipped the alarm switch and the rickety elevator started moving again. When the doors opened on the sixth floor Carmiesha was still laying there in a pool of cold piss. She was half-naked, bleeding, and crying softly.

"Get up, bitch," he said from the doorway. "And the next time I want me some pussy I better not have to fight you for it. Cause if I do, I might just have to go on in there and get me a little bit from Mere'maw instead."

He laughed loudly at the look of horror that crossed Carmeisha's face.

"Here, crybaby." He tossed a piece of candy down at her and laughed. "Have a peppermint. On second thought, have two. As good as that pussy is, your motherfuckin' breath stanks."

▬ ▬ ▬

He raped her any time he felt like it. And he beat her down each time too, spitting in her face as he called her the dirtiest kind of low-down bitches and hoes.

"Yeah, ya nasty shit-eater. Suck this big dick like you like it!

Turn that big stank ass over'n lemme stick this pole up in there. Fuckin' ho. Chickenhead! You know you been begging for this shit! You lucky I don't let a few of my boys get at this shit too. Maybe I'll bring 'em up here and let 'em run a train on you first, then hit Mere'maw next."

At thirteen Carmiesha was still just a child, and just the threat of somebody sexually hurting Mere'maw was enough to keep her quiet and compliant. She did whatever he forced her to do, retreating deeper inside herself more each day. She cut off all her little girlfriends and stayed locked up in her room. She stopped seeing Thug too.

"C'mon, Muddah," he would beg, promising to eat her pussy real good for her.

Carmiesha refused. It was just too hard to face him knowing that the cherry she wouldn't give to him had been stolen by somebody else. At one point she had thought about telling Justice and Rome, but the more she watched her brothers the more she saw how useless they were. Both of them were scared of that deranged niggah and acted ready to suck him off. Telling them how he had abused her would probably make them mad at her and tell Mere'maw that she asked for it.

Carmiesha didn't know where to turn. If she told Thug what was going on, she knew blood was gonna get spilled and she didn't want to put him in that position. Plus, she was too ashamed of what that crazy motherfucker had made her do. He'd stuck his skinny dick in every hole she had, and she felt nasty and violated and mad enough to kill his ass at the same time. He fucked her on the elevators, on the staircase, and even up on the roof where that hot concrete cut into her knees and burned the skin on her ass and her bare back.

By the time shit came to a head a couple of months later, Carmiesha was so sick and nervous that she'd lost fifteen pounds. Her hands shook all the time and her hair was breaking off in clumps. She didn't know what was gonna happen the next time he rolled up on her, but she had already decided he wasn't fuckin' her no more. She started carrying a knife with her at all times, ready to stab him or, better yet, slice his dick open if he touched her again.

As it turned out, Carmiesha had underestimated Mere'maw for real. She found out how much heat that old lady was packing one day when that niggah got so bold he thought he could come right up in her apartment and get him some pussy just because he felt like it.

She was stretched out on her bed reading when she looked up and saw him standing in her doorway.

"How the fuck did you get in here?" Carmiesha sat up quickly, her eyes darting across the room to the Reebok gym bag where she kept her knife.

His sick ass grinned. "My boy Rome let me in. We down like that. What you reading? Oh? *How to Sex a Baller?*" He moved into her small room, closing the door behind him. "I'm ya baller, baby girl. So why'ont you come over here and show me a little sumpin you done learned."

Carmiesha shot across the small room like a cannon. Her hand was inside her gym bag searching for her knife when he jumped on her.

"What I tell you about fighting me?" he said, laughing as he tried to grab her wrists and pin her down. Carmiesha twisted from side to side, grunting as she tried to find her knife. She brought her knee up between them and he leaned on her leg, opening them wide and pinning her with his weight.

"Bitch, don't make me—"

The door to her room flew open, and both of them turned their heads and froze.

"Boyyyyy," Mere'maw said real slow as she reached between her thick legs and pulled a small silver pistol out from under her housedress. "I don't know what you came in here to find, but I can sure tell you what you bout to get."

Carmiesha was stunned. *Where the hell did Mere'maw get a gat?*

The moment Pimp jumped up, Carmiesha got her hand around her knife and yanked it out the bag. She held it in front of her, but he wasn't even studying her no more. Carmiesha was just as shocked as he was, and watched his face go blank as he stared down the barrel of the small pistol Mere'maw was aiming with a fat, steady hand.

"What the hell was you doin to her, boy?"

Pimp laughed. "We was just playin', Mere'maw." He pointed toward the CD player, which wasn't even turned on. "We was dancin' and shit, and then she fell—"

"Oh?" the old woman said. "You wanna dance with my granddaughter?"

Carmiesha screamed as Mere'maw fired.

"Dance, durn you!" Mere'maw yelled, popping shots into the floor all around Pimp's feet. "Lemme see how good you can dance to this kinda music!"

It was almost funny watching as Pimp jumped in the air and hopped from foot to foot, stutter-stepping as he tried to dodge

Mere'maw's bullets. Not one of them came close to hitting him, and Carmiesha knew the old woman wasn't even trying to.

"Now get your no-good tail outta here." Mere'maw stopped shooting and waved the gun, motioning Pimp toward the door. "And leave my grandsons the hell alone too. Ain't nothing in you but trouble, and I'm old enough to shoot a no-good drug-dealing gangsta like you and get away with it."

She kept the gun locked on him as he rushed past her and out of the room, then said, "Next time I catch you anywhere near my door, ain't gone be no dancin'. I'ma shoot you clean dead. And if I ever find out you done something to Lil' Muddah here, I'ma shoot you twice."

"Yeah, motherfucker!" Carmiesha screamed, waving her knife and rejoicing that her nightmare was finally over. "Get the fuck outta here and don't bring your crazy ass back!"

But three weeks later Carmiesha couldn't find a damn thing to be happy about. Her breasts were sore and she'd been getting sick to her stomach a lot. Her period hadn't come yet, and she was worried. A few days later a cheap drugstore pregnancy test confirmed her worst fear. That nasty niggah had got her pregnant. All she could see was her dreams in the gutter and her world crashing in. How was she gonna take care of a baby when she was only thirteen? How could she bring Mere'maw another mouth to feed when they were barely eating already? And how could she tell Thug she'd already been fucked when he was still waiting to be the first one to slide his dick between her legs?

Carmiesha missed the next three days of school. She laid in bed with the covers over her head shaking. She refused to eat or drink, and would only close her eyes and tremble when Mere'maw begged her to tell her what was wrong.

When she was finally able to accept her situation she forced herself to come up with a plan. Aside from her deep shame at being raped, the last thing she wanted was a baby. Especially by a twisted motherfucker like him. But she knew getting an abortion was out. She didn't have the money or the insurance, and even if she could somehow come up with the cash, she didn't believe in killing babies. But there was also no way in hell she could bring nobody else's baby into her relationship with Thug.

On the fourth day Carmiesha got out of bed and walked into the kitchen to tell Mere'maw she was going to school.

"Bout time," her brother Rome said. He had folded the last slice of bread in half and was wiping it around the inside of an almost-empty jelly jar.

Ignoring him, Carmiesha slung her Reebok bag over her shoulder and headed out the door. She was actually hoping she would run into that motherfucker on her way out today. She'd stick her knife in his dick so deep . . .

Carmiesha wandered down the streets of Harlem like a black girl lost. She cried inside at all the shit that had been forced upon her her whole life. She wondered what her life mighta been like if her father hadn't murdered her mother right in front of her eyes and left her with that lasting image in her young mind. If her brothers hadn't been so damn useless and had gone to school and then worked together to move them out of Harlem. If she had had a knife or an ice pick on her that night in the elevator when that crazy niggah whipped out his pointy dick.

She walked around grieving until she found herself standing outside of the pool hall. It was too early in the morning for folks to be gambling, and the doors to T.C.'s Place were chained and locked. Carmiesha went over to a smaller doorway and rang a bell. Dre had told her that T.C. and Miss Lady lived in an apartment upstairs, and she hoped they wouldn't be mad at her for ringing their bell so early in the morning.

She rang the bell for a long time, and had almost changed her mind and turned away when suddenly a second-floor window was snatched open and a pretty, sleepy-looking lady with a bright red scarf around her head appeared.

"Don't be wearing my goddamn bell out!" the woman hollered, then looked closely at Carmiesha. Her voice changed when she realized that Carmiesha was just a child. "What's the matter, baby? What you doing down here on a school day?"

Carmiesha swallowed hard. "Uhm, Miss Lady? Uhm . . . I know Thug. I mean, Dre. I know Andre."

Miss Lady's whole face changed. "What's wrong?" she said, her voice rising with concern. "Don't tell me that boy done got his narrow ass into something. Is he okay?"

Carmisha nodded. "He-he's fine. But he told me how much you help people. People like him . . . and me."

Miss Lady pursed her lips and took a real hard look at Carmiesha.

"You in trouble?" she asked quietly in a no-nonsense voice.

Carmiesha nodded, trying her hardest not to start crying again.

"Well what you standing out there for then?" Miss Lady said, waving Carmiesha toward the door. A buzzer sounded and the lock slid back. "Come on upstairs, child. Miss Lady ain't no joke. I whip trouble's ass seven days a week."

Carmiesha went over to the window and looked down the street. So much had happened since that horrible day, and she felt blessed to have made it through without losing her young mind, thanks to her guardian angel. The night Carmiesha delivered her son it was Miss Lady who had been there beside her, soothing and encouraging her, and promising her everything would be okay.

She hadn't even looked pregnant, especially with her clothes on. She'd gotten only one stretch mark. A thin, jagged line on her left booty cheek. And the only things that had grown any bigger were her breasts and her ass. Her stomach was barely pooching out enough to be called a potbelly. Miss Lady had already taken her to a dentist and gotten her front tooth fixed, but there was nothing she could help Carmiesha do about the baby that was growing in her stomach except comfort her while she waited.

Carmiesha remembered being shocked because the baby hadn't been due for two and a half more months, but the pains had been unbearable for hours, doubling her over as they tore through her young body and drenched her in sweat.

She'd managed to stay away from Mere'maw for most of that day, scared to let on to her grandmother that she was in so much pain. Miss Lady had already made all the necessary arrangements and assured Carmiesha that nobody had to know about her shame, not even Mere'maw.

Around 7 P.M., Carmiesha had been forced to climb into her small closet and scream into her pillow against the sharp waves of pain drilling through her spine. She stayed there on her knees, panting and moaning as fire ripped across her back and lower stomach and the baby crept further down into her birth canal.

By 9:30 Mere'maw was snoring on the couch in front of the television and Carmiesha managed to stumble from the apartment. She wasn't worried about running into anyone because both of her brothers were locked up. And Thug was too. Him and both of his cousins had gotten caught riding in a stolen car, and while Pimp was old enough to get sent to Rikers Island, Thug and Smoove ended up with a six-month sentence at a youth correctional group home up in Glenmont, New York.

In the emergency room at Harlem Hospital, she leaned heavily on Miss Lady.

"Treat her right," Miss Lady instructed the nurses as they handled Carmiesha. "She ain't nothing but a baby herself, and she's been through a lot."

At one minute after ten Carmiesha gave birth to a three-pound baby boy. She barely got a chance to look at him and could only stroke his little finger before he was whisked away in an incubator to neonatal intensive care.

"He gone be all right," Miss Lady assured her, rubbing her cheek.

"Them people still gonna take him, right?" Carmiesha had asked in a trembling voice.

Miss Lady nodded. "Yeah, baby. They still want him. But they gone let you see him sometimes too, okay? I've known the Washingtons for a long time and they good people. Your son gone have the best of everything. And even though Bert and Jessie gone be his mama and daddy, you gonna be a part of his life too."

When they brought her the legal papers to sign Carmiesha quickly scribbled her name over and over. In the space where she had to name the father of the child, Carmiesha hesitated for a second, then carefully printed a name in the box. After the staff had collected the stack of papers, Carmiesha closed her eyes and slept. And in the hour before dawn she slipped from the hospital room with the help of Miss Lady, and silently let herself into the apartment she shared with Mere'maw.

No matter how hard she fronted in the coming years, Carmiesha could never forget that she had given birth and had a child in this world. Even when she tried not to remember, she still couldn't forget.

Chapter 9

As good as Muddah had handled me in bed, sexing her hadn't done a damn thing to take my mind off my cousin Smoove. It was almost midnight and time was running out. Granite McKay's word didn't mean shit when it came to bitches, drugs, or dollars. Me and Pimp could bust up in T.C.'s safe and steal every dime he had, but handing the cash over to G didn't guarantee that we'd be getting Smoove back alive.

The thought of going to jail behind this shit crossed my mind real quick, and made me feel even worse. I'd been in lock up a lot, and me and Smoove had done six months in a group home for youth offenders after getting caught riding in a stolen car, so while it wouldn't be my first bit of contact with the penal system, prison and the NBA didn't mix and I wasn't anxious to do no time.

Besides. I was already two years late getting to college. I was twenty, not eighteen like most people who were about to graduate. All that hooky playing, stealing, and getting sent to juvenile jails had set me way back. There was younger cats coming up hard and hungry every day, and I was gonna be an old head compared to the other freshmen hoop stars. My music career was looking up too. I wasn't performing with Pimp and Smoove that much no more, but I had a solo deal with Ruthless Rap and a brand new mixtape that was creating a big buzz. I wasn't ready to gamble with all my potential success like that.

And what if some shit went wrong? Pimp was known to get crazy over minor shit. I didn't know if I could trust him to pull off a job like this without nutting up in the middle of the mix.

I mean, I'd always known Pimp was cold and didn't give a fuck about nobody, but about a year ago something had gone down that made me question what kinda black shit was really living in my cousin's heart. Especially when it came to females.

The three of us were hanging out rapping in Hamilton projects with some niggahs Pimp had got tight with on Rikers Island. Them fools had done a push-in and took over some old lady's apartment, and they were in there cutting crack and mixing weight. They told us they was waiting for a connect to show so they could handle a little business, so we stepped out to let them do their thing. Pimp had been kicking it with one of the young jawns hanging around the apartment. She was real young and had bumpy skin and slum rings on every finger. She told us she was living next door with her grandmother while her mother was in jail, and she took us up to the roof to smoke some chronic. We was up there getting nice and plottin' to run us a game on some herbs, when Pimp decided he wanted to bang the girl.

She was young, but she was down for it. She had on a real short Baby Phat dress, and it rose up over her cute yellow butt when she stood on her toes and started kissing all over Pimp's neck. Pimp put his head back and laughed, and it wasn't long before he had her on her knees pulling his dick outta his pants. Smoove went over there and got in on it too, but I just leaned against a pillar and smoked up all the chronic, watching them groove.

Smoove was just trying to get him some pussy, but Pimp was rough-handling the damn girl. She started saying ooch, ouch, and shit like that as he squeezed her little titties and twisted her nipples. He gripped her ass real hard and then started slapping it like he was a jockey and she was his horse.

The two of them got that girl butt-ass naked, and it tripped me out when Pimp snatched her by the hips and spun her around. He bent her over and rammed his dick in her so hard she screamed like she had gotten stabbed.

"Ow, motherfucker! You in my *ass*!"

Pimp held her by the hips, dicking her furiously. "Shut the fuck up and handle it bitch! Get up in that pussy, Smoove."

They fucked her together like that. Hard and cruel. Thighs touching. Knees bumping. Smoove in her pussy, Pimp in her ass. She was moaning and crying but they was steady fucking. Them niggahs almost blew my high. I turned my back on that shit and smoked the rest of the blunt. When I turned back around I saw blood running down her skinny yellow legs. I didn't know if it was coming from the front of her or the back, but I felt sick and didn't want no part of that shit.

"Yo," I said, walking toward the stairs. "I'm out. I'll meet y'all downstairs."

Pimp laughed. "What? You don't want next on none a this?"

I pushed on the door that led to the stairs. "Nah, dawg. I don't hurt females, man. They got what I need."

I was downstairs on the porch for about fifteen minutes when the elevator came, and Smoove got out. That niggah's whole head was sweaty and he was breathing real hard.

"Where's Pimp?"

He looked up. "Still up there. He can't get him no nut, so he prolly gone be a little while."

I left Smoove standing on the porch and walked up to the avenue and ordered me some chicken fried rice and a Pepsi from the take-out Chinese joint. That chronic had me munched out, and I ate that shit right there standing up in the store. When I got back to the building a crowd of people was standing outside staring at something.

At first I thought some shit had gone down with Pimp and his boys up in that drug spot, but when I asked a little kid what happened I found out it was much worse than that.

"Somebody died," he said. "They think she got pushed off the roof."

I walked around the edge of the crowd and pushed through until I could see what everybody was looking at. It was a body, all right. Laying on the side of the building not far from the back stairs. Somebody had thrown a blanket over it, but the arms was showing and I could tell the hands belonged to a young chick. She had cheap rings on every finger too.

I turned right around and stepped. Got the fuck outta there without looking back. I didn't need nobody to pull the blanket off to figure out who the young girl was. And I didn't have to be standing there when she sailed off that roof to know who had tossed her ass neither.

There was a subway station not far away, and I calmly walked my ass toward it and got on the train. I didn't even worry about where Pimp and Smoove was, because I knew the deal. Both of them niggahs was long gone. Pimp prolly jetted before the girl hit the ground good, and if Smoove was still standing on the porch when his brother got downstairs, he'd taken off with him.

I was walking down 125th Street shaking my head as I remembered all that shit when my cell phone rang. The ring tone told me who was calling, and I already knew why.

"Whaddup?"

"We need to be about some business, son. Where you at?"

"On the avenue."

"Meet me at the crib."

I didn't rush to the building, but I didn't take my time neither. When I got there Pimp was smoking a blunt with Muddah's brother, Rome, and just by the way them niggahs was vibing I knew Pimp had put him down.

"Don't tell me you bringing this cat in?" I said, staring Rome down.

Pimp nodded. "Yeah. We need a lookout, man. You got a key, and you know how to get in the safe. I'ma have your back on the inside and both of us can carry the package out. Rome ain't gotta do shit but watch the fuckin' door. That's all."

"Motherfucker, is you crazy?" I grilled Pimp. "Can't no base-head niggah be depended on to watch nothing!" I paced the room shaking my head. "This ain't gone work, man. You gone fuck around and get Smoove killed. Shouldn't nobody be down with this shit but you and me. Cutting a deal with Rome's stupid ass is like calling the fuckin' po-po and telling them to come lock us up."

We argued for hours, cursing and almost throwing up blows over that shit. Pimp swore we needed Rome. I said he wasn't nothing but a fuckin' leech. Always trying to skim somebody's game after they had already stacked it. I wanted to leave that grimy motherfucker up on the roof sucking on his hot pipe.

"It don't even matter now," Pimp pointed out. "The niggah know everything so he might as well be there. Believe me, man. This is my brother's life we going after. I wouldn't do nothing to fuck with that."

"But what if something goes fuckin—"

He cut me off.

"If something goes wrong," Pimp said, taking a shooter from his pants and making sure it was loaded. He looked over at Rome, who just sat there like it wasn't no thing. "Just let something go fuckin' wrong. I'll blast me a motherfucker myself."

■ ■ ■

It's just a day in the life
I'm doing wrong/all along/tried making it right
Pay the cost to be the boss/it's the ultimate price
We in the dark/look how easy we can stray from the light
God strengthen my sight
It's just a day in the life

We stayed up arguing over our plan all night long, and by the time we left the building at 4:00 A.M. both of our tempers were on boil. Pimp was taking shit too far. He wanted us to roll with like two gats each, and I said hell the fuck no. For one thing, we was just gone slide in and glide right back out. Nobody was gone be downstairs in the pool hall so it wasn't necessary to carry no guns anyway. I tried to tell his hot-headed ass how stupid that shit was.

"Ain't gone be no Rikers Island for you next time," I warned him. "You get tapped on another gun charge and you looking at some upstate time."

"Don't worry about me, you soft motherfucker."

I shook my head, wondering if I was gonna have to knock Pimp on his ass. "I don't know where," I flexed on him with my height advantage, "you getting all this 'soft' bullshit from, dawg, but you just keep fuckin around. I can show you gangsta better than I can tell you."

He pushed past me on the way out the door with a killer look in his eyes. I made sure that all that motherfucker saw in my eyes was some cold killer too, because showing an ounce of weakness with a niggah like Pimp was just like copping your own death warrant.

Pimp had wanted to walk up in T.C.'s Place earlier and just hang out and gamble the way we usually did, but I refused. I was a hard niggah, but not twisted enough to eat and socialize with my peeps knowing I was planning on robbing them before the night was over.

So we waited on the rooftop of a tenement building across the street, watching high-rolling hustlers swing in and out of T.C.'s Place and listening to the music pumping each time the door popped open.

I had a lot of time to think while we was waiting for 6:00 A.M. to come, when T.C. would lock up his joint and head upstairs to his apartment for the night. I had time to think, to change my mind, to figure out some other way of getting that money for Smoove, and time to try and talk Pimp out of what we was about to do, but I didn't. I wasn't normally the type of cat to just roll with a situation and let it handle me, but this time my black ass was getting swept along with the program and as hard as I tried, I didn't see no way out.

"Let's bounce," Pimp said about fifteen minutes after we watched T.C. lock the front door. Rome was sitting with his knees bent and his back against the ledge, snoring like wasn't shit in this world weighing on his mind.

I kicked that niggah's foot out and shook my head when his leg hit the ground.

"Get the fuck up." Yeah, I knew I was taking my frustration out on him, but so what. I was swole up with a mad amount of anxiety and guilt, and I had to put that shit somewhere.

The sun was just about to come up and St. Nick was mostly quiet. We crept across the street and Pimp and Rome stood to the side as I used my key to unlock the front door, then used the back of a pen to quickly punch in the security code that would turn off the ten-second alarm. Pimp didn't know it, but the alarm wasn't nothing but a front. All it did was make a lot of noise. T.C. wasn't running the kind of business where he wanted his shit connected to no precinct. That was real obvious.

It was dark in the foyer. Quiet too.

I glanced over my shoulder. Rome had come inside behind us.

Get that motherfucker outta here! I mouthed to Pimp, who shrugged and mouthed back for me to just chill.

Already shit was deviating from the program, and I didn't like it.

We crept through the main poolroom without making a sound.

I knew every inch of this joint. I had come of age up in here, and it was more of a home to me than the crib where I rested my head each night.

I led them in the back past the kitchen and motioned for them to wait there.

The plan was for me to get into T.C.'s office and pop his safe, then pass whatever cash that was in there out to Pimp. If shit went right, we would go back out the same way we had come in, and I'd reset the alarm and lock the door behind us. But if we fucked around and heard somebody coming down the stairs, we'd hit the kitchen door and disappear down the alley right outside.

I started toward T.C.'s office and Pimp moved with me.

"Wait here, motherfucker!" I barked through my teeth. I wasn't about to let him get up in T.C.'s office and start sticking shit in his pockets. Or worse, start scoping it out so he could hit it again without me being there to regulate shit the next time.

That motherfucker Rome was up on me too. Closer than Pimp. Lookin' all happy with his fuckin teeth showing in his face.

Both of them breathed down my neck as I rolled up on the office.

But the second I opened the door shit changed in a hurry and I froze.

T.C. was in there. Standing up, facing his desk.

His pants was down on the floor around his ankles, and his naked ass was pumping pussy. He moved hard, growling and slamming his dick up in Vyreen, who was sprawled on his desk with her red skirt pushed all the way up around her stomach and her thick thighs wrapped around T.C.'s waist.

I prolly coulda backed up and eased the fuck outta there without being seen if it wasn't for Rome.

That niggah was dead on my ass, and before he could move

Vyreen busted us, staring up at me with confusion in her green eyes.

"Dre?"

Life got wild.

T.C. whirled around, and the second he spotted Rome he went for his shit.

A boom rang out near my right ear and I almost went deaf.

"Rome!" I screamed. "You stupid motherfucker!"

But it wasn't that grinning niggah Rome who had fired. It was Pimp. He was standing there looking murderous as T.C. stumbled forward, then tripped over his own pants and fell to the floor.

My mind went on automatic.

T.C. was hurt real bad, I could tell. The bullet had hit him in his chest, and he lay on his back half-naked with his dick wet with pussy juice and his feet twisted up in his drawers.

Somebody screamed behind us, and I turned around like I was in a dream.

Miss Lady musta heard the shot, cause she'd run down the stairs in just a bra and a half-slip. She had a scarf tied around her hair, and I noticed how smooth her face looked without all that makeup.

"T.C.!" she screamed and tried to push past Rome and Pimp to get to her man, but Pimp grabbed her and yoked her up before she could reach him.

"WHAT THE FUCK YOU DOIN' MAN?" I jumped at Pimp, but Rome checked me with his piece.

"Back up, Thug," he said, and his grin was gone. "We puttin' in work, motherfucker, so do your fuckin' part."

I looked over at Pimp.

Miss Lady was trying to scream, but he was choking the shit outta her. Vyreen was still sitting on T.C.'s desk with her legs open. She had on that same red skirt she was wearing when she braided my hair earlier in the day. She was staring down at T.C.'s body as he bled out all over the fuckin' floor.

"Go 'head and get what the fuck we came for, man," Pimp said, looking down at Miss Lady.

She was bent over at the waist with her knees sagging, and it was worse than seeing my own mama with her ass hanging out in front of a bunch of black-hearted fools.

"Okay, okay," I said, moving toward T.C.'s safe. Miss Lady was gurgling now. Whispering too. She was saying my name. Over and over and over again. *"Dre . . . Little Dre . . . help us, baby boy. Little Dre . . ."*

I didn't have a gat on me and wasn't nothing gonna stop Pimp except money, so I jumped on opening that safe. I wouldn't even *let* my motherfuckin' hand slip. Wasn't no time for that.

I cracked that bitch on the first try, and it was full too.

"Here!" I passed out stacks of money. T.C. hadn't had time to batch it up, so some of it was just laying loose in money bags and I passed all that shit out to Rome while Pimp muscled Miss Lady around.

When I had the safe empty I turned around to face Pimp, still on my knees.

"You might as well let her go now. Ain't no fuckin more. Just let Miss Lady go."

That niggah glared at me, and I knew I'd just made a grand mistake. Never, never let a killer like Pimp look down on you. I jumped to my feet real fast and stepped toward him. I knew better than to show too much emotion over Miss Lady, though. Pimp fed on shit like that and wouldn't hesitate to use it against me.

"Come on, man. Just let her go. You ain't got shit on your hands, dawg," I said, making my voice stay cool. "Neither one of us do. We can swing by the G-Spot and pick up Smoove, then walk away from this the same fuckin' way we walked into it."

Pimp shook his head and nodded toward T.C., who was laying there stiller than a motherfucker and not even moaning no more.

"We got a body on us, man. We still got shit to handle."

I shrugged. "Naw, dawg. *We* ain't got shit. This niggah here"— I swung my head toward Rome—"got him a fuckin' body. This his fuckin' fault! If he hadn't been right up on me like that then they never woulda seen us! Me and you is straight. We can rise and fly out this motherfucker and be good all the way around."

"Niggah, don't be so fuckin' stupid," Pimp said, shaking his head and gripping Miss Lady even harder. "This bitch here ain't never liked me. Even when I was just a fuckin' kid. She always said I had hell in my eyes."

"That's crazy, man! Miss Lady fed you, man. She fed all of our asses. While Noojie was out there getting high left and right, we was eating outta Miss Lady's fuckin' kitchen!"

Putting Noojie in it was a bad move. I busted that right away. Pimp's face got even harder, and I knew he'd fight me for talking about my own mother.

"She's a fuckin' witness, Thug. And if we leave her here, she's damn sure gonna talk. On me and on your stupid ass too. I ain't gone back to jail cause of this bitch."

"She ain't gone *say* nothing, man! Trust me. I know her. We straight."

Pimp stared at me, and I could tell he didn't buy it. But he surprised me though. He uncurled his arm from around Miss Lady's neck, and let her go.

Miss Lady gasped and stumbled, then fell against Rome, who yoked her right back up again.

"What the fuck you doing!" I yelled, lunging toward him, but it was too late.

Rome had reached in his pocket and came out with a knife.

Miss Lady was smart. Unlike me, she saw the writing on the wall. With her last bit of breath she tried to spit on Pimp. "Hell *is* in your eyes, motherfuckah, cause that's where your evil ass is going!"

Rome tighted his arm and jerked Miss Lady up until her legs was almost straight, then swiped the knife across her throat and slung her body to the floor.

"No . . . ," I whispered and dropped down to my knees beside her. Miss Lady grabbed her neck and tried to scream, but no sound came out and blood shot through her fingers instead.

"Oh, no . . . ," I whispered again. I held her in my arms and pressed my hand over her throat, like the love in my fingers could somehow stop the bleeding. "Call a fuckin' ambulance!" I screamed over my shoulder. "We gotta get her to the fuckin' hospital right NOW!"

Nobody moved. It was too late anyway. Miss Lady was almost gone. All I could do was hold her and grieve as she wiggled weakly in my arms without making a sound. The only noise in the whole joint was of gurgling and bubbling blood coming out the deep gash across her throat and the sound of our breathing.

I knew Miss Lady was dying, and I couldn't think shit and didn't wanna let myself feel shit either. It just hurt too damn bad. I just moaned and held her real close to me. The same way she used to hold me when I was a hungry little boy who needed somebody to love me and take care of my raggedy ass.

Pimp broke my trance.

"It's your turn, niggah. And don't be slow."

I didn't move. Miss Lady's movements were fading, but her eyes were still clear. They stayed locked on mine until the second she passed away.

Vyreen moaned when Miss Lady's body shuddered, and I finally looked up. I had forgotten all about her, and when Pimp spoke again I felt sorry for her because she had to know what time it was.

"It's your turn, Thug. Do this bitch real quick so we can bounce."

I looked at my cousin and shook my head.

"What? You crazy, man."

"Dawgs-4-Lyfe, remember motherfucker? We all gotta be down on this shit."

Pimp pulled out his gat and let it hang in his hand. His message was clear.

Rome laughed and just put it right out there.

"C'mon, Thug. Do it, or get done. Ain't nobody got time for no soft niggahs. If two of us in it, we all in it."

Pimp nodded and brought his gun up. Just enough.

I stared at my cousin, and in his eyes I saw some shit I'd been trying to deny for years. Pimp was soulless. The niggah's heart wasn't nothing but a black piece of rock.

The scene flashed in my head like a snapshot, and I knew it would stay with me forever.

T.C. . . . Trust Chambers. A motherfuckin' *man*. The realest gangsta on the planet. It was a crying shame. A baller like him was gonna get found dead with his dick hanging out. They'd see Vyreen laying there with her fine legs cocked open. Them same legs I'd sat between less than twenty-four hours earlier as she scratched my scalp and braided my hair. She was about to be laid the fuck out. Blasted on T.C.'s desk with a pair of red panties hanging from her right ankle. And Miss Lady. My Miss Lady on the floor! And with her slip pushed up and her business out in the open. Her butter-cream thighs gaped open in her violent struggle with death.

Pimp stared back at me too, and his next words came out cold, but also sad.

"I luh you, Thug. You family. You my niggah to the bone. But I ain't doin' no murder time. Not even for you. So if they gotta find four cold bodies up in this joint tonight, then that might just be how it gotta be."

I'm ashamed to even tell you what ran through me at that minute.

It wasn't fear, and it wasn't guilt or grief either.

It was survival, motherfucker!

It was do or be done. Get or get gotten. It was self-preservation like I'd never felt before, and when Rome passed me his piece I didn't even hesitate as I raised that bitch in the air and aimed it at Vyreen.

I'm sorry, Reeny, I told her with my eyes. Then the air split with a boom and a bloody hole appeared in Reeny's forehead.

Cold laughter rang out behind me, and when I looked over my shoulder Pimp was still holding out the piece he had just fired over my head.

"Bitch-ass niggah," he said, then laughed again. "You ain't no killer. You ain't even got the heart."

I stared at the unfired pistol gripped in my hand. Deep inside I was glad he had beat me to pulling that trigger. And nah, I wasn't no bitch-ass woman-killer. But I had just come real close to becoming one. But what Pimp did next was just fuckin' unbelievable. He grabbed Rome's knife and walked around by Miss Lady's head. Then he bent over and stuck her twice. Once in each of her dead eyeballs.

"What you see in my eyes now, bitch?"

Rome laughed like a motherfucker as blood streamed down Miss Lady's face, but a big piece of my soul had just cracked off and died.

A minute later Pimp had all the money in a duffle bag, and we bust out the kitchen door and ran down the side alley. Pimp and Rome ran toward 125th Street, but I headed east to the Harlem River Drive.

Walking. Grieving. Wrapped up in cold guilt. Rapping.

> It's just a day in the life
> I'm doing wrong/all along/tried making it right
> Pay the cost to be the boss/it's the ultimate price
> We in the dark/look how easy we can stray from the light
> God strengthen my sight
> It's just a day in the life

I stripped off the shirt that was wet with Miss Lady's blood, and walked out of Manhattan and all the way to the Bronx, going downtown to cross the Third Avenue Bridge, and hitting the Boogie Down just as the borough started coming alive. The streets was waking up. Winos was staggering out of foyers as crackheads came out of drug houses squinting into the sunshine like they were zombies who'd been hiding underground all night.

By the time I made it up to Fordham Road I'd walked into a serious mental zone and come to a cold, hard decision.

I had to lose T.C. and Miss Lady.

Wipe 'em outta my mind and outta my heart. Cause the only way I was gonna survive what I'd just seen was to put it away. To bury that shit. To dig it so fuckin' deep that I didn't even remember it. Put it away like it never even happened.

And that's exactly what I did.

■ ■ ■

They say what goes around comes around, and that shit ain't no lie.

We'd gotten Smoove back, but Pimp ended getting served, and that stupid niggah Rome definitely got his too. I hadn't gotten mine yet, but I knew it was coming.

They found T.C. and them that same afternoon, when Vyreen's husband rolled up looking for her. Word of the robbery and killings was all over the streets when I got back to Harlem later that night, and I stayed balled up in Muddah's bed as people all over town mourned for T.C. and Miss Lady.

Over the next few days the cops half-ass questioned a couple of people, including me and Pimp, but they wasn't able to put nothing on us. They sweated Vyreen's husband pretty hard for a while, though. They figured he'd prolly walked in on his woman getting fucked, and then nutted up and started shooting, but Razz had worked an overnight shift for Transit and was able to prove he wasn't nowhere around.

Two weeks after the funerals, Pimp got knocked.

You must be crazy if you think all that money we stole from T.C. went to G.

Pimp held on to a bucketload for self, and he'd torn Rome off a few decent slices of cheese too. I didn't want a penny of it, and I told him that when he tried to slide me some.

But retribution is a funny thang, yo, and when it was all said and done, Pimp ended up getting sent upstate for some shit he didn't even do. What was even worse, they locked him down in the same joint where his mother Dru was doing hard time for life.

You see, a few months earlier Pimp had started fuckin with this jawn from the Bronx. Her name was Nayesha, and she was one of them weak-minded females, the only kind that Pimp could hold on to for longer than a minute. Nayesha had a baby though, and after all that shit went down up in T.C.'s Place, Pimp decided to lay low at her Jerome Avenue crib until life cooled off in Harlem. But Pimp had hand problems, and Nayesha got tired of that niggah beating on her and busting up her face. When she told Pimp she was gonna call the cops on him, that niggah snatched her baby up and hung him over the balcony and told her he was gonna fly his little ass down to the ground.

Nayesha fought like a madwoman for her son, and that niggah dropped the baby on the floor and pulled out his knife, then fucked around and cut off Nayesha's finger trying to get to her throat.

Nayesha and her baby survived, but she got her a little get-back on Pimp's ass too.

That sneaky girl testified against Pimp at a trial they held on the side of her hospital bed, and not only did she tell the po-po it was Pimp who had cut her, she told them he'd stuck up a low-level drug dealer over on Jackson Avenue, and told them where they could find his stash at her crib. So Pimp ended up losing all his money and getting served, even though he didn't even know no drug dealers out on Jackson Avenue, and the only person he had stuck up recently was T.C.

So there you got it. Pimp got a robbery charge hung around his neck, and Rome? That sherm fucked around and tried to buy some dope from an undercover cop. A whole lotta dope. Me? My retribution was a lot slower in coming. But I took my ass upstate too. Not to the joint, but to college, man. Late August found me wearing the orange at Syracuse University. Running ball and humping ass. I left my demons and my past right on St. Nicholas Avenue in Harlem where they belonged, and did my damnedest not to look back.

Chapter 10

"So where are we gone go today, little man?" Carmiesha asked the boy walking next to her. She'd been picking him up one weekend a month for just about his entire life, and each time she saw him she felt something different. He was tall for his age, and he looked just like her. Except for his skin tone. It was dark and smooth. Much prettier than hers. "You wanna check out the Science Center or the Botanical Gardens?"

"I don't wanna go see no flowers and gardens!" he said, looking at her like she was crazy. "I wanna go to the movies. I wanna see that new hood movie that got a pimp in it. *Hustle & Flow.*"

Carmiesha wiped some crumbs off the And 1 shirt she had just bought him and checked to make sure his jeans were pulled all the way up on his ass.

"I know you know me better than that, Jahlil. You know I ain't taking you to see no garbage like that when that's the same kinda madness going on here in Harlem every single day."

Jahlil made a dissing noise. "All a my friends done seen that movie except me. I can't wait till I'm big enough to go where I wanna go."

Carmiesha ignored his noise. Jahlil was only seven, and he had a long way to go before he was old enough to do whatever he wanted. But that was something he needed to get inside that hard head of his.

She had a lot of love for him, but something hurt deep in Carmiesha's heart whenever she looked at the child. He was so restless and frustrated. He had always been that way, even as a baby. There were times when she could tell the Washingtons were overwhelmed by Jahlil's difficult ways, and one time Jessie even had the nerve to ask Carmiesha if she had smoked anything like crack or ice while she was pregnant with him.

"We're gonna go someplace that stimulates your mind in the right way, Jahlil. Just like we usually do. It ain't gotta be the Botanical Gardens but it will be somewhere where you can see that life is more than just what goes on out here on the streets every day."

They ended up at the New York Hall of Science out in Queens. Jahlil liked riding the trains, and Carmiesha liked taking him all the places she had never gotten a chance to go when she was a kid. Sometimes she wondered how different their lives mighta turned out if they'd lived differently. Her brother Rome had recently gotten stabbed to death in prison, and Justice had disappeared one night with some dudes from Brooklyn and never come back. Poor Mere'maw was racked with grief and worry over those boys, even though she should have seen it coming.

Carmiesha looked at Jahlil and smiled. She could see how

smart the child was. Even if he did show his ass and cut up in school almost every day. She still wrestled with herself over the way she got pregnant, and after signing those adoption papers she knew she could never be a real mother to Jahlil. But even still, all she wanted was for him to have a better life than the one she and her brothers had.

So many times Carmiesha wished she had stayed her ass in the house that hot summer night. And if she had to get pregnant, she wished she had given her virginity up to Dre and gotten pregnant by him, instead of getting raped on a pissy elevator floor by his cousin.

But a lot had happened since those days and Carmiesha gave herself props for coming up from all that. Miss Lady had supported her and paid her way through beauty school, and afterwards Carmiesha had gotten grants and scholarships that would take her through community college. She worked all day, but took as many classes as she could at night, and in a few years she would graduate with her degree in business.

Carmiesha owed so much to Miss Lady. She'd been dead for a few months, but to Carmiesha it felt like it had happped just an hour ago. She didn't know how Dre had sat through that funeral without breaking down, as much as Miss Lady and T.C. had done for him. The whole world seemed like it turned out to put those two away. People were busting down the walls of the church, screaming and wailing out their grief, but not Dre. He never shed a single tear. He'd left for college without talking a whole lot about it either, and when she'd looked in his eyes to see what was in his heart, all she found was a brick wall.

They stayed at the Hall of Science until late in the afternoon, and Jahlil waited until they had taken the train back to Harlem and were walking towards the Washingtons' house before he started asking all his questions again.

"So, Carmiesha. You gone tell me about my father or what? Last time you said you would tell me more when I turned eight, right?"

Carmiesha took his hand, surprised that he didn't get embarrassed and pull away. She had always felt boxed in by that whole father issue. The Washingtons had never lied to Jahlil about her being his mother. She'd been a part of his life since the day she gave him up. Miss Lady had made sure of that. But Jahlil had been wanting to know who his father was for years, and Carmiesha knew she couldn't just keep telling him Jesus and brushing him off.

Swinging his hand, Carmiesha sighed. "Well you won't be eight for a couple of weeks, Jahlil, but still. Mr. Washington has been a real good father to you, right?"

He nodded.

"So what are you missing out on, man? You have everything you need right there with them. Don't you think it might hurt Mr. Washington's feelings if you keep asking about some other daddy?"

Jahlil thought for a few seconds. "I don't be trying to hurt his feelings. But I still wanna know, Carmiesha. How you know my real daddy ain't looking for me? How you know he don't miss me and want me to come live with him?"

Oh that shit ain't gone never happen, Carmiesha thought.

"Your real father is in college," she lied. "He's from Harlem, but he's far, far away and doing a lot of things right now. So you can't just go live with him, Jahlil. Even if he wanted you to. They don't let little kids live at college."

"Then he should be here living with me!" Jahlil said, sticking his little lip out.

Carmiesha wondered. "Jahlil, do you ever get mad at me? You know I'm your real mother, but you don't live with me. I gave you up to Mr. and Mrs. Washington. Does that make you feel mad sometimes?"

He shrugged, then put his little arm around her waist. "No, Carmiesha, I don't get mad at you. You're my real mother because you had me. But you feel like my auntie. I like you being my aunt."

Carmiesha felt reassured, but she couldn't help noticing how quiet Jahlil was when she dropped him off at the Washingtons' and he told her good-bye. He didn't give her a kiss like he usually did, and she hoped he would just forget about all that father shit and be grateful for the family God had blessed him with.

But daddy or no daddy, the boy was bad as hell. Jessie had told her that if Jahlil got into one more fight in school they was gone put him out, and he'd have to go into a different school district. Carmiesha hated that he was so hard for them to handle but wondered if she could have done any better with him herself. As much as she hated to think it, she could definitely see some signs of Jahlil's real father in him, and out of all the shit that hurt her in life, that was the worst hurt of all.

▬   ▬   ▬

Carmiesha could hear the babies crying when she got off the elevator. It sounded like Noojie had at least two or three of them in there with her and she hoped she'd get to see Kathy's cute little twins. She knocked on the door.

"It's me, Noojie. Carmiesha."

Noojie came to the door wearing a linty black sweater and a pair of men's boxers.

"Muddah. Girl, I'm glad to see you. Dre up there in college, Pimp up there locked up, Smoove out there doing who the hell knows what. Here. Take one of these damn babies."

She passed Carmiesha one of the two babies she was trying to hold on to. Carmiesha took the baby and noticed how skinny Noojie was. Both of those babies put together probably weighed more than their grandmother did.

"How long they been here?" she asked.

She followed Noojie into the living room where a baby was in a walker and another one was laying on a towel spread out on the floor.

"Since this morning. I thought I was only gonna have Little Precious today, but Vikki got a temporary job and they called her. She can't pay nobody to watch Shantay since she ain't working every day, so I said I would keep her." Noojie picked up a Nuk pacifier off the table and stuck it in the baby's mouth.

"Kathy had to drop the twins off because she been spotting all day. I don't know why that stupid girl went and got herself pregnant again so soon when neither she nor Andre can take care of these two they already got."

"I hear that," Carmiesha said and kissed T-Roy's fat little cheek. "But the guy she's with now seems decent and besides, she would have to get pregnant about three more times just to catch up with Dre. So how's Duqueesa? What's Rasheena's story?"

Noojie put the baby down and lit a cigarette. She walked into the kitchen, stepping over toys and baby clothes and came back with two beers. She passed one to Muddah.

"Rasheena is just sorry as all hell. I might end up keeping Duqueesa for good. If it wasn't for you that little girl would been done starved, Muddah. You must love the shit outta Dre the way you help all his bitches take care of they kids."

Carmiesha just rubbed the baby's head. His little cornrows was so ashy and caked up with dust it was a shame. She was willing to take his braids out and re-do them, but she'd probably comb out all his hair trying to ungunk it.

But Noojie was right. She did love Dre. She had probably loved him from the day he brought her that soap powder to wash out her dirty clothes. But the first time she found out that he had gotten somebody pregnant Carmiesha had been tore up. Here she had snuck around and hid her pregnancy from him and then given her baby up, and he messed around and stuck a baby up in somebody else's ass.

But when Little Precious was born Carmiesha had fallen in love with her. And yeah. She loved every last one of them six-fingered babies Andre had made. She knew all of their mamas too. Most of them either lived nearby, or had gone to school with her in the hood, and almost all of them came by Flip It and Clip It to get their hair done.

So whenever Carmiesha had a few extra dollars she would help Noojie buy Pampers and snowsuits and stuff for the babies. Not because she was rich or crazy, but because those chicks needed help and wasn't nobody else available to give them none. The Washingtons would never let her give them a dollar for Jahlil, so Carmiesha considered what she did for these babies a small thing.

Except for Rasheena, the rest of the baby mamas was at least struggling to live halfway right. They used to clown and act shitty whenever they came by Noojie's and saw Carmiesha there. But every last one of them ended up being grateful to her for the things she did for their kids. She gave them babies baths, washed and braided their hair, rocked them when they was teething, and changed their shitty asses when they had diarrhea. And whenever Dre tore her off some money, she always split it up between his kids. She would've felt real minor taking all his cash and spending it on herself, knowing how needy his babies were. So in a way, whether Dre knew it or not, he did pay a little bit of child support.

But just because she loved Dre and loved his kids didn't mean she was stupid enough to put up with his bullshit. It was better for both of them that he was off in college upstate because Carmiesha couldn't see herself spending the rest of her life with a deadbeat dick-slinger who dropped babies all over the place and then forgot about them. That shit was just plain crazy.

So Carmiesha had started seeing other guys. She made sure anybody she fucked was as different from Dre and his crew as possible. Right now she was hooked up with a cool dude named Ya-Yo from 116th Street, and although he couldn't put that dick on her like Dre did, he had a real job with UPS and he treated her right. Things were really starting to get serious between them, and what she liked the most about Ya-Yo, aside from the way he ate her pussy, was that he knew how to tell the damn truth. Carmiesha had never once busted him in a lie, and she never had no kinda drama with him and no other chick. She damn sure couldn't say that for Dre.

"Yep," Carmiesha finally said to Noojie. "I love me some babies. And you gotta admit Dre's fine ass makes some real pretty ones."

Noojie waved her hand, then turned her beer bottle up and nodded. "Yeah. They pretty all right. But that don't stop 'em from pissing and shitting and hollering for food. I just don't see why that boy don't wrap his damn dick up before he goes sticking it in every goddamn body. Tie a knot in that shit or something. Or shit, better yet, get his cum-string clipped and be done with all the drama. Don't make no sense to keep making babies you know your ass don't take care of."

Carmiesha didn't say a word because Noojie was right. She knew how much Dre hated using condoms. He loved everything about female flesh, and he complained he didn't get no real satisfaction from fucking into a glove.

Carmiesha pulled a comb outta her handbag and started opening the braids in T-Roy's hair. Lil' Man probably needed his done too. She would have to shampoo both of their heads before she could comb through them, so she slipped out of her shoes and sat on the floor with Dre's baby boy between her legs and went to work.

Chapter 11

College was wild. I was like a happy little white kid playing in a sandbox full of toys. Honeys, basketball, music, I indulged in all of that shit to the max. And oh yeah. I went to a couple of classes too. I wasn't totally ass-out stupid.

Ruthless Rap hooked me up with a local studio so I could still record for them, but they were grimy when it came to paying on time so I had started stealing again almost as soon as I hit the campus. How else was I gonna keep my pockets swole? One of my boys from Harlem hooked me up with this white dude who had a chop shop outside of town. I would roll out late at night, hot-wire a couple of Hondas, and stash 'em in his garage where he stored them until he could chop 'em up.

One night when I was out there looking for a car to roll, I found out just how crazy some jawns can be. I had just busted out the back window of this Accord and unlocked the door, and as I leaned into the car to get to the wiring system I got busted.

"Get up, niggah. And get your ass outta my damn car."

I turned around slow, cause this chick didn't sound scared at all. Matter of fact, she sounded like she had control of the situation and was running things. As soon as I sat up I saw why.

She was holding her piece on me. It looked like a .32, but I couldn't be sure.

"Hey, baby," I said, looking down the barrel of that shit. Her hand was steady as hell. Not a shake in it. I looked up in her face and couldn't help but grin. She had busted me, she had my ass on lock, *and* she was fine as hell. "Girl, put that shit down," I said. "You got me, okay? And I'm sorry. But you ain't gotta shoot a niggah. The only thing outta order here is your window, and I can fix that. I promise."

"You damn right you gone fix it, cause you picked the wrong damn car to steal tonight."

I mighta picked the wrong car, but she ended up being the right girl. I talked so much game to that evil chick until I ended up going inside her crib and boning her all night long.

"Who's Precious?" she beefed when she saw the big tattoo running down my inner arm.

"My little sister," I said and reached for her.

"That's the stupidest lie I ever heard!"

She twisted her lips and gave me the evil eye. I was starting to think this girl was crazy. She was wild too. She rode me like she hadn't been fucked in ten years. Made me eat her pussy for two hours! The chick was into whips and chains. Some dominatrix type of shit. She got on her knees and tooted it up, begging me to spank that ass. First with her hairbrush, and then with my Timb!

"Beat me! Yeah! Yeah! *Yeah!* Now pull my hair, master! Harder!

Wrap that shit around your fist, niggah, like you gone yank it the fuck out!"

I drew the fuckin' line when she asked me to bang her head on the floor. I kept telling her that I wasn't into hurting females, yo. That just wasn't my thang. By the time she let me outta her house my dick was sore, and I was wondering if I prolly shoulda just let her call the cops on me, or shoot me in the back with her gun.

Getting caught by a jawn didn't even make me wanna stop stealing cars, but just to be safe I put my gambling skills to work too. I bet on all kinds of games, knowing in my nuts exactly when some points was gonna get shaved. Somebody in the athletics department got wind of my luck with the bookies and started hating on me, so I had to do that shit on a low level for real. Playing ball was my whole reason for being there, and I wasn't stupid enough to put my scholarship on the line by getting caught stealing or gambling or failing my classes or some bullshit. I got around that by using whatever jawn I was boning to place my bets for me, and I studied just enough to keep my grades just out of the danger zone. And when chemistry and calculus started getting in the way of my groove and I couldn't find a chick to write my papers or do my homework, I changed my major to physical fitness and sports, which was a whole lot easier to handle. Especially for a wild-ass hooper like me.

I didn't think about Harlem too much that year, except when I was in the city rapping or shooting music videos or giving interviews with *Vibe* or *Source*. Muddah called every now and then, and I dialed her digits a few times too, but shit just felt funny when I talked to her. We'd sat together at the funeral they had for T.C. and Miss Lady, and all I could do was stare at a spot on the floor while folks went crazy with the hollering and the music and Muddah broke down and cried over Miss Lady like it was her own mama laying up there.

Both caskets were closed, and that was a good thing cause I couldn'ta made it through the services if I had to look down on their bodies again. As it was, I had to hold on to Muddah and let her cry for the both of us while I concentrated on making that cold hard spot inside of me even colder and harder.

So I kept my mind in Syracuse. Pimp was locked up not too far away up in Watertown, and every time I stole a car or won a hot bet, I made sure I tore him off a few greenboys and sent them in the mail. I even went to see him a few times that first year, and I hated to say it, but I was glad it was him locked up and not me. A niggah like me had to have room to run. The penitentiary had too fuckin' many hardheaded convicts in one damn place for me. And no pussy in sight. Nope. It wasn't for me. Them niggahs just didn't make my kind of noise.

But Pimp seemed to be chill with it. He was always cool and relaxed when I rolled up on him. He walked around with a smile on his face and got mad respect from the inmates like he was the king hustler of the joint.

One time when I was visiting him he told me they had pulled him down for questioning about an old case.

"What case was that?" I asked. We was walking through the picnic area and Pimp was checking out other niggah's visiting bitches like it was an open meat market.

He laughed. "Man, you know what fuckin' case. They know I was there, but they can't prove that shit. They tried to cut a deal with me, though. Said I could prolly get probation if I gave 'em a name. They wanted me to tell 'em who was down with me. And who pulled the trigger."

My mouth got dry as shit. Pimp mighta been cool with spending the night in a joint with fifty thousand other niggahs, but I was counting on going home to some hot pussy and real food tonight.

"So what you tell them?"

He laughed like a motherfucker. "C'mon, man! Closed lips! You know me! I ain't no bitch-ass snitch. I ain't tell them a motherfuckin' thang. But your boy Rome got shanked cold over in Greenhaven for having a big fuckin' mouth. That niggah got his tongue took and his eyes poked too. So he can't tell nobody shit neither. Besides, I'm gettin outta this joint in a year regardless. So I got this, baby. You keep shootin' them videos, man, and posin' on them magazines. I don't need nobody to keep me company while I do my time.

"Yo, man," he said, grinning. "Remember them hooks we busted that time we got locked up in Brooklyn? *If you trapped doin' time in the back of your mind and you feeling like you just ain't shit, join the click!*"

I laughed. "Hell yeah!"

"If you trapped in the grind in the back of your mind and you feeling like you don't exist, join the click!"

Years back we'd gotten locked up in a pissy-ass jail cell at Brooklyn's central booking. The cops had busted us for selling hot designer bags up on Utica Avenue for some cat who figured we was too young to get knocked if we got caught, but two fat white po-pos said fuck how young we was, and threw us in a cell for damn near three days until they could contact Noojie to come get us out. We was just kids, but we spent the whole two days and nights freestyle rapping and entertaining grown-ass in-mates with our lyrics, and when Pimp started spittin' that old shit I smiled at the memory and I went ahead and joined in with him like we'd just got down on that shit yesterday.

Come get acquainted with niggahs who never fake it
We 'bout to be paid in full for the perfect pictures we
    painting
So before you get ta hatin' just know these blickers is banging
I'm a beast/All beast
This is more than just entertainment!
This is
My pain/my pleasure/my fury and my frustration
This my life these motherfuckers be puttin' up in these cages,
    homey!
Yeah I'm a boss/You a bitch/Ain't no relation, homey!
That shit just not addin' up into this equation, homey!
Yeah I done held 9's/did a little jail time
No niggahs/no money
Couldn't holla at the bailbonds
But never bitch/never snitch/cuz I held mine
Do I feel as though they competition?
Niggah hell nah!
So if you trapped doin' time in the back of your mind and you
    feeling like you just ain't shit, join the click!
If you trapped in the grind in the back of your mind and
    you feeling like you don't exist, join the click!

By now convicts and their visitors was watching us and feel-ing us. COs too. Trying not to nod their heads to our beat, but knowing they was digging our flow. I dapped my cuz out, showing him mad love. I didn't have shit to worry about. I was down with the 'Licious Lovers. Known for the closed lips.

Besides, Pimp was a for-real niggah. He'd had my back my whole life. And I was grateful for that shit too.

"But you can do something for ya cuz while he up in here," he said, grinning.

"Something like what?"

"Damn niggah!" he laughed. "You act like I'ma ask you to go on a trailer visit and toss Fat Freddy's salad! Since you so concerned about how quiet I do my time, I thought you might wanna help me stay chill while I'm here."

I nodded. I heard the clock ticking, and I knew what time it was. "What you need, ak?"

Pimp stopped and elbowed me. "Y'all got a lot of them dumb-ass white girls in that college, right?"

"Hell, yeah. Them hoes working harder to get some black dick then they working to get that diploma. Why?"

"I got me a little side hustle goin' but I'm running outta fresh faces, nah mean? You help me get a few of them stupid white chicks on my visitors list, and I can keep my weight up."

"What they gotta do, man?"

"Use that white pussy!" Pimp said like I shoulda known. "This the fuckin' pen, Thug. They gotta carry a package through inside that white pussy and come give Sugar Pimp some motherfuckin' sugar!"

I got it. Pimp was runnin' a powder game on these convicts for good money, cause he sure wasn't using nothing other than weed himself.

"I'll hook you up with a little somethin'," I told him.

"Do that. You heard anything from Smoove?" he asked, changing the subject as we walked past a corrections officer, who nodded, giving him silent respect.

"Yeah. He still chillin' at the crib with Noojie. Last time I spoke to him he was complaining about the game. He said it wasn't fun no more without us. He's thinking about joining the military, though. I think he said the Marines."

After checking Pimp out I went back to school. I tried not to think about the cops digging around in what we'd done in T.C.'s Place. Without Pimp, they didn't have shit on me. And he wasn't telling. Especially after I rounded up six dumb-ass white chicks who'd been flossing up in my face for months, trying to get me to fuck 'em.

Pimp had shit hooked up with his connect where the dude met the girls in different spots all over Syracuse. They'd stuff their pussies with ballons full of product, and go in to see Pimp like they was just another silly upstate white girl who was wide open on black dick. They'd wait for the right time to go in the bathroom and dig up their pussies, then stick the balloons in their mouths and come out and give Pimp a real good kiss.

At first I had to lay pipe on them. White girls tripped me out. They'd curse and clown and turn their backs on their own parents over some black dick in a minute. It wasn't long before I had them strung out on my pipe action, and ready to do anything I told them to. I fucked 'em, but I didn't suck 'em. I couldn't get with that raw pink fish market action. I liked my fish fried. The hardest part was keeping my game outta the sistahs' faces. If one of them even suspected me of having a thing for white chicks, they'd all turn against me and my game would run bone dry. There'd be no more chocolate cookies for me, and I just couldn't risk that.

But Pimp was so good with his white-girl game that after a while they didn't need me no more. They was doing that shit strictly for Pimp, and for what he promised to lay on them when the state cut him loose in just under a year.

By the time my first school year was over and the summer rolled around, I was itching for a break and ready to get out of Syracuse. I'd been making runs back and forth to the studio to lay my Ruthless tracks, but wasn't nothing really pulling me toward Harlem on a personal level, though. Matter fact, if it wasn't for Muddah and Noojie I prolly wouldn'ta gone nowhere other than the studio for a long time. The streets held too many memories and the most recent ones coulda killed me if I let them.

So when it came time to clear out of the dorms, I hopped in a black Acura with this cute little honey named Passion I'd been boning, and burned concrete down to Albany where she shared a house with her older sister.

Passion was wild. She was the first chick I'd been with who liked to fuck in strange places. I'd tapped that ass in the girl's bathroom in every fast food restaurant we could find. I waxed it in dressing rooms at department stores at the mall too. She'd take a bunch a clothes in there to try on, and we'd be in there getting our funk on. I did her in the library and at a roller-skating rink.

I found out by mistake that Passion was into group sex too.

We'd gone to a Fourth of July barbecue with some of her girls, and later on that night we jetted across town with two other couples to keep the party rolling at one of their apartments. The niggah on the CD player was going back and forth between a few Game cuts, some Lil' Wayne, and even threw some Pac in the mix too. We danced and smoked a little chronic, and I was sucking on some Thug Passion when the heat started rising.

The apartment wasn't no more than a studio. A plain room with a queen bed and a lumpy little couch, and a half-assed kitchen across the way. I was sitting on the bed with Passion when she started getting frisky. She took the smoke out my hand and started kissing me, pushing me backward until I was stretched out flat.

"Uhm," she said, smacking her lips and running her tongue all over my chin. "You ain't hardly even looked at this pussy today, Thug! What? You too wore out to keep your girl satisfied?"

I chuckled. This jawn was giving me a run for my money. She stayed so hot I was gonna have to start walking behind her to mop up all that nookie-juice she was dripping all over the floor.

I sucked her tongue into my mouth and played with it. She started grinding on my dick, waking it up, and my hands automatically slid up her firm brown thighs and slipped under her skirt, cupping her soft ass.

"Yeah," she whispered in my ear laughing. "That's what I'm talking about. Show this ass some love up in here tonight."

Other people was in the room with us, but since she didn't care I didn't either. She reached back and lifted the back of her skirt all the way up. Her light-brown mounds rose like soft mountains in the air, and I slid my finger under the strap of her thong and moved it to the side.

I dug my fingers all up in her wet pussy. I entered her from the back as she worked that ass like we was all by ourselves. She was sucking on my ears, sticking her hot tongue inside them and wiggling it to the same beat my fingers was moving to inside her.

She sat up a little and lifted her arms, taking her shirt off in the darkness. Her titties were small but firm, and her nipples were jet-black little knobs that had my mouth watering. I pulled her down to me and grabbed one with my lips, sucking it until she squirmed. I was loving it cause her nipples was so different than any other nipples I'd sucked. I liked that about women. I could spend days and nights touching and licking and sucking their bodies. All of them were holding basically the same thing, but it was always packaged in a unique way.

A few minutes later me and Passion were rolling on the bed. She'd unbuckled my belt and took my dick out, and her soft little hand was jerking my thang like a pro. She had a perfect rhythm going and I played in her pussy as we masturbated each other.

I was surprised when I felt something soft cuddling up beside me on the bed. Passion's friend Tyra giggled and turned her back to me. I'd been checking her ass out in those Tommy Hilfiger shorts all day, and now she turned away from me on her side, and pressed her juicy ass against me and made room for the niggah she was rolling with to get next to her on the bed.

I wasn't into crowds, and there was about one niggah too many on the bed for me, but Passion had stopped jerking my dick and had covered the head with the wet heat of her lips.

"Ahhh," I moaned. She was sucking that shit just right. "Hold up, girl. Let's go get on the couch."

"Can't," she said between slurps. She was bobbing her head up and down like a motherfucker, and my legs was starting to shake. "Sheniqua and her man already on there."

I glanced over and saw a pair of long legs in the air, feet pointing toward the ceiling.

"Damn. Then let's get on the floor."

She sucked her teeth like I had insulted her for real.

"I ain't fuckin on no damn floor, Andre. What kinda ho do you think I am?"

What kind of ho was she? I shrugged and turned my back on the two humping bodies on the bed beside me. The kind of ho who had begged me to fuck her everywhere except a church pew, and who I wanted to be sucking my dick right about now.

"You ain't gotta go nowhere," Tyra turned her head and said. We were laying back to back, and she pressed that booty on me and rolled it around, teasing her man from the front and me from the back at the same time.

It wasn't long before both of them jawns was ass-out naked.

I got in the mix and was cool with shit as long as that other niggah stayed on the other edge of the bed. I didn't look his way and he better not'a been looking my way neither. I tried to forget he was there and concentrated on that head Passion was putting on me.

"Damn, this dick is big!" she slurped all in the back of her throat, her mouth nice and juicy as she slobbed my joint down, and I moaned out loud as I stroked into her neck and felt Tyra moving next to me on the bed.

Tyra got on her knees to blow her niggah. I put one hand on the back of Passion's head, and stuck the other one up inside of Tyra's hot pussy. I rolled her sticky clit between my fingers as

Passion sucked me off, and right when I was about to come, Tyra pulled her lips off her man and spun around, and both of them licked my dick and balls like little kittens until they were sharing the hot cum that squirted out of me.

Even though I was done, they weren't.

It was starting to hit me that these chicks had done this shit before, and they liked it. Passion was still gripping my half-hard dick in her hand, and as old boy fucked Tyra from the back, the two chicks washed my dick with their tongues. I almost laughed as I saw what they were doing. Every now and they they'd come off my dick and tangle their tongues together, kissing each other deep in the mouth, then taking a dive to go back down on me together again.

My dick stayed hard watching them play them little female games, and I wasn't surprised at all when Passion moved her ass around on the bed so Tyra could eat her pussy and get banged from the back at the same time.

Wasn't no fun unless we all got some, so I stood up with my dick sticking straight out in front of me again. I moved until I was standing over Passion and watched as Tyra licked her pussy just like a man would.

I stood there rubbing my dick and digging the scene. Liking what I saw. I took that shit for about five more minutes, then kneeled next to Passion and started rubbing the head of my dick all over her hard nipples.

We switched partners and changed positions after a while, and I was on top of Tyra. Her breasts were just as full and soft as her ass, and instead of sticking my dick in her, I slapped it all over her breasts and nipples, surprised that just that action was making her come.

As she shuddered and moaned, I squeezed her breasts together and slid my dick between them. I fucked her titties with long smooth strokes, playing with her nipples as she held my ass, urging me on.

I need to come inside some pussy, but she wouldn't let me. Instead, I shot my second load all over her breasts, and she came again as Passion crawled over and licked her clean. All I could do was kneel there watching as they pressed their bodies together and rocked, rubbing their pussies on each other and kissing like me and old boy wasn't even in the room.

I messed around with Passion and her crew of freaky girls for the rest of the summer, and by the time we started classes again in the fall I was ready to move on to some new shit. There was this hot little countrified sistah who had caught my eye during the beginning of freshman year, but I just hadn't had a chance to work my way around to her yet.

But a few weeks after I moved back into the dorms somebody knocked on my door in the middle of the night. My roommate was some lame cat in the pre-med program, and he was still up studying, but doing that shit by flashlight.

He answered the door. "Is Thug there?"

It was a female. By the tone of her voice I could tell she had a funky attitude, but I kept my head under the covers and didn't say shit.

"Yo, my man is crashed out."

That jawn went off.

"Well wake that motherfuckah up then!"

The next thing I knew she had knocked Dave's glasses off and was standing over my bed.

"Whassup, niggah? Huh? Where you been?"

I tried to front shit off.

"Damn, Passion!" I sat up, rubbing my eyes. "What the hell is wrong with you, ma? A niggah been in class! We in college, remember?"

"Remember? Remember? Then why the fuck you actin' like you can't remember how to dial my number? I been calling your ass, text-messaging your ass, standing outside the gym looking for your ass . . . your ass ain't been in one damn class this week!" She cut her pretty eyes at me, and them shits looked real evil. "But you *have* been over in the Delta dorm. I heard you been spending all kinds of nights up in there with that skinny black bitch India."

"I'on't even know what you talkin' about. Only thing them girls do for me is keep my braids tight."

This jawn had a real crazy look in her eyes and something told me to move.

I swiveled my legs off the bed and stood up, and that's when she swung on me.

"Liar!" she screamed, swinging her arms back and forth. "Ho! You no-good fuckin' punk!"

I grabbed her wrists and tried to hold her back, and she raised her foot and tried to kick me in the nuts.

I twisted her arm just enough to make her stop kicking, then slung her down on the bed.

"Girl! What the hell is wrong with you? Why you tripping like that?"

She started crying. "Cause," she sniffed, then said real quietly. "I'm pregnant."

I just stared at her psycho ass.

"Uhm, Dre." My roommate opened his damn mouth and cut in. "You need to check your shit, man."

"Man, fuck you!"

I was mad as hell. This funky bitch had told me she was on the pill.

I stared down at her with ice in my heart. "You *what*?"

She sniffed again, then sat up straight and grilled me.

"You heard me, motherfucker. I'm pregnant!"

Dave opened his mouth again. "Dre! You bleeding man! That bitch sliced you!"

And that's when I felt something warm dripping down my leg.

I looked down at myself real slow and saw three long cuts. One across my chest, and the other two across my stomach. They didn't look deep or nothing, but one of the cuts on my stomach crisscrossed over the other one, and that's where most of the blood was coming from.

I looked back at her.

"Bitch . . . you *cut* me?"

She went to stand up, and I saw the razor was still in her hand.

"Get the fuck out my face, Thug. I *scratched* you. You lucky I ain't cut your dick off, fuckin' around on me when I'm about to have your baby!"

I blacked out.

I reached for her and she swung the razor again.

I grabbed both of her wrists and bent them shits back until she screamed and dropped the blade to the floor.

Dave kicked it out of her reach as I dragged her ass over to the door. The only thing stopping me from stomping her out was the fact that she was pregnant. And after all the freaky shit I'd seen her do, wasn't nobody gonna make me believe that baby was really mine, neither.

She cursed and fought me all the way out the room. It took me and Dave to toss her ass out and slam the door before she could jump up and lunge back inside. And even when we got that shit closed she stood out there screaming and trying to kick the door in.

"I'ma get you back, motherfucker!" she hollered up and down the dorm hall. "I'ma tell everybody how you raped me, you punk-ass bitch! *Raped* me! And I'ma tell them how you like to beat women too! Just watch, niggah. Your ass is getting kicked outta school! You'll be lucky if they don't lock your ass up and put you under the goddamn jail!"

Me and Dave just stood there looking at each other. Shaking our fuckin' heads. Dave was one of those low-key brothers who didn't do shit except go to class and study. Every now and then he hit the gym, but he was all about making those grades, and at that moment I wished my life was as drama-free as his.

Passion was still out there kicking the door and beefing.

And the crazy ho said she was pregnant!

Well she sure as hell didn't wanna be pregnant by me. I didn't have shit for her.

Dave nodded toward my stomach. "You gone get that looked at, man?"

I grabbed a towel and wiped at the blood. "Nah. Not tonight." I laid back on my bed and pressed the towel to my stomach. "I might go let them check it out at the infirmary in the morning, but not tonight. It can wait until morning."

Dave laughed. "I don't blame you, man. I wouldn't go out there with that psycho bitch neither." He flipped the light switch off and sat back down at his desk with his flashlight and his notes. "It's good, though. You ain't gonna bleed to death before morning. Stay your ass up in here where it's safe."

Chapter 12

That fool stayed outside kicking the door for about fifteen minutes. I had just dozed off when Dave shook my shoulder.

"Dre. Wake up. Campus security wanna talk to you, man."

I got up. The towel was stuck to my chest.

"What for? Where they at?"

He nodded toward the door. "Out there, man. With that crazy-ass girl."

I went to the door, and three toy cops was standing out there.

"Andre Williams?"

The white cop grilled me. He was tall, but had a stomach like a pregnant woman. The other two were brothers, and they looked like they just didn't wanna be standing there.

Crazy started going off again. "That's him, *awffissah*! Arrest his black ass! That's him!"

I nodded. "Yeah. I'm Andre. Whassup?"

"We've just got an assault complaint. This young lady claims you physically assaulted her out here in the hallway."

"*I* assaulted *her*?"

"Yes you *did,* motherfuckah! Yes you *did*! Look at all these fuckin bruises, *awffissah*! He bent my *awrm* back, and said he was gonna break my wrist!"

They looked at me.

"That tramp is crazy!" I said and ripped the towel off my chest. "Look! Look what the fuck she did to me!"

When they saw my chest and stomach, they all turned around and looked at her ass.

"He had me down on the floor, *awffissah*! I was protecting my damn self. Protecting my baby too. He got me pregnant and now he wanna fight me. I had to cut his ass to get him up offa me!"

All eyes was back on me.

I held up my hands. "Look. Y'all can ask my roommate. I didn't fight this girl out here in no hallway. Ask Dave. He's the one who answered the door and let her in. Matter fact, she was swinging on me so hard I didn't even know I was cut until Dave told me. I don't know what kinda trip she's on, but that's the for-real shit!"

Dave backed my story up. He even got the razor she'd sliced me with and showed them where I'd bled on the floor before he kicked it under the bed.

They made all three of us go down to the security office so they could take a report, but they knew better than to put me and that crazy freak in the same car. I had never fought a woman in my life cause I didn't believe in hurting females, but this was one bitch I was ready to stomp the fuck out.

You know it all got back to my coach. Even though I didn't get charged with nothing, the complaint had to go down on the books.

"Don't fuck yourself up, Williams," he warned me. He was a tough white boy, but he was fair and knew the game coming and going. "This girl is also claiming she wrote papers and did homework for you last semester too. It could mean real eligibility issues for you. I remember having a couple of alcohol-related incidents with you last year, right? You're a great player, Williams, and you have the kind of talent to make a long career out of basketball—that is, if you get serious enough about the game to get your personal life straight. You can't play basketball from a jail cell, so I'll tell you this: If you want to stay on this team you'd better keep your goddamn nose clean. If not, there's a hungry eighteen-year-old freshman we just picked up from Chicago who'll be happy to take your place."

Coach wasn't ragging on me. He was just putting it to me live, and I knew it. I wasn't about to let no skeezer like Passion cost me my scholarship or nothing else. I'd been through too much on the streets to let her and her bullshit drama knock me off track.

"I'm straight, Coach," I said, telling him what I knew he needed to hear. "And you're right. It was a long summer but I trained hard and I'm back now. Ready to focus on my grades and on my game."

For the next few months I did my best to keep that crazy ho as far away from me as I could. And she *was* pregnant too. Passion still looked hot from the back, but there was a for sure 'nuff baby growing in the front. A couple of times I ran into her outta nowhere, and I coulda sworn she was stalking me. But both of us had been warned if we had any more beef our complaints was gonna turn into charges, and as crazy as she was, she wanted to stay in school.

Later that semester I pledged Omega Psi Phi, and the day after I crossed the line I got me a Que brand on my right arm and set about becoming the biggest dog the bruhs had ever seen. I was playing fuck games with two sistahs who'd just pledged Delta, and between running ball and running up in both of them, I was keeping real busy.

I started leaning on a jawn named Isis. She had long legs and clear light skin. She was one of those freaks who played like she was all quiet in public, but get them legs up in the air if you wanna. "Yeah, straight fuck this na-na up, niggah! Lay that gangsta pipe deep in this tunnel, yo!" The girl talked more nasty ghetto shit than a little bit. Isis was studying to be a physical therapist, and I damn sure wanted her to do some therapy on me. She ran track too, and she killed it. Niggahs would be lined up around the fence just to watch that thing she was packing as it switched and jiggled. Her long legs would be stroking like a deer, and we'd be staring at that ass like *we* was caught in some headlights.

Isis had a rep for playing like she was cold, and from what I had heard none of the bruhs had gotten close to getting in them drawers. I set out to change all that, and once a gangsta threw that sweet street game down on her frisky ass she was boxed in with nowhere to go.

The first time I stepped up on her she rolled her eyes and tried to front me off like she had a hard niggah waiting in the bushes somewhere.

"I got a man."

What ya man got to do wit me? I'm not tryin'ta hear that shit.

It didn't take but one fuck to get her nose open. I caught up with her going into the gym one Sunday morning. We rapped for a quick minute, and she let me talk her into going outside to sit and talk instead of working out. Well, outside in the grass turned into going inside to her dorm room, and once I was in there you *know*, Thug was *in* there.

I kept messing with her, sucking all over her neck until I saw big red hickeys popping up. The way she acted you couldn'ta told me this girl wasn't no dick-hound. She flipped the program on me and before I knew it I was stretched out on her bed and she was inching her naked pussy up to my face.

"You like this?" she kept asking me. She used her fingers to spread her pussy lips open wide and damn if her clit wasn't rock hard and sticking straight out like a little dick.

That shit turned me straight the fuck off.

I liked big, soft, juicy clits, but that little mini-joint she had was almost enough to scare a thug niggah for real. But you know how it goes. The girl was shivering and talking all kinds of nasty shit. "Suck this shit!" she hollered. "Lick it! Kiss it! Tongue this little man down! Knock this motherfucker out his boat!" I looked up at her and saw her cute face all squinched up like she was possessed. She flicked that clit back and forth with her fingers, pressing on it and mashing it until her juices was leaking all over my chin.

I wasn't really feeling it, but I went on and ate that thing for her cause I could tell how bad she needed it. That jawn damn near smothered me too. She sat her whole ass on my face. It covered my head like a gas mask. Isis rode my mug like she was on a ten-inch dick, and as soon as she nutted I tossed her ass off a me and flipped her on her back, then fucked the shit outta her cause it was payback time.

Isis sucked some good dick too, and her pussy was real good, which is why I kept messing with her even after I started pushing up on her sorority sister, Lani.

Lani was one of them real religious girls. You know what kind I'm talking about. Her father was a minister, and the girl had never even wore a pair of pants until she got to college and pledged a sorority and started going buck wild.

She strolled around campus with them sturdy legs and thick hips looking scared half the time, like some tall, freaky baller like me was gonna attack that ass and get some of it. Lani was one I had to *ease* outta them drawers. I ate lunch with her every day, hung out in the laundry room and helped her fold her laundry. I let her wear my team jacket, and even went to chapel services with her once. If she wanted us to pray together before we fucked, I was down for that too. I did whatever it took to make Lani comfortable around me, and not just because I wanted to get up inside of her either. She was just different from every girl I'd been with before. Lani had something innocent about her, and even though she wasn't a virgin when I tapped her, she was still fresh and new enough not to have a bit of street in her stride.

But about a month before Passion was supposed to have the baby, Isis threw a crazy brick in my game. I was getting with both her and Lani, taking turns on they asses, and she brought me some news that fucked me up. We were sitting in the student union between classes, and I had just been trying to decide which one of them I was gonna bone first that night.

"I had to go to the doctor today," Isis said with her face all red. She stared at me for a second, then looked down at the floor.

That "doctor" shit scared me. Anytime a female rolled up on

me talking like that it meant I'd shot another baby up in some-body's ass.

"Yeah?" I said, feeling my stomach clench up. "What for?"

She looked up at me. "I got a sore, Thug. On my na-na."

I did a double take. "A sore?" I glanced around, then whis-pered out the corner of my mouth, "On your *pussy?*"

She nodded, then crossed her arms and held her head down. "They tested me for herpes. And you gotta get tested too."

"Girl! You gave me *herpes?*"

"No, motherfucker!" she dropped her arms and beefed. "*You* gave *me* herpes! Know how I know?"

"How the fuck you know?"

"Cause you gave it to Lani too!"

I stood there feeling real stupid for a minute, and I was glad when my cell phone rang. It was Dave.

"What, niggah!?"

"Yo, Dre. I just seen Passion's roommate, man."

"So?"

"So she said Passion started bleeding real bad in class. They had to call the ambulance, man. They took her to the emer-gency room and something might be wrong with the baby."

I closed my eyes and ran my hands over my face. More fe-males, more fuckin' problems. I told Isis to chill and not to worry. I kissed her cheek and promised we'd talk all this shit over later on that night. Then I bounced my ass over to the hos-pital, but by the time I got there everything was all over.

"Are you the father?" a white nurse asked me when I gave her Passion's name.

"Yeah," I said, although I still wasn't ready to be claiming nothing in writing.

She took me in a back room where Passion was sitting up on a bed. Her face was red, and she was still crying.

"She didn't make it, Thug," she whispered, showing me what she was holding in her arms. She let the blanket fall, and I saw a naked baby. It was a girl and she was real small, but she looked perfect.

"Your daughter was stillborn," the nurse said quietly. "Sometimes these things just happen."

My daugher? I thought. The little infant was a funny dead color, and she didn't look nothing much like me or like Passion. But then I reached over and pulled the blanket back some more, and what I saw just about confirmed it.

She had twelve little fingers. Six on each hand. She was my daughter all right. The proof was in the pudding. And at this point there wasn't no use in denying it.

Chapter 13

Carmiesha was almost finished with college, and if it wasn't for all her family drama everything else would have been on track.

Mere'maw was depressed a lot these days. It seemed like tragedy just wouldn't stop dogging her bloodline. The police had found Justice. He'd been beaten and shot, and his body dumped in a drug house somewhere in the Brownsville section of Brooklyn. And just a few months ago Rome had been murdered too. In jail. A dude Carmiesha knew from high school named B-Low had been locked up in Greenhaven with Rome. He told her how Rome had gotten caught out there in the yard by his own boys. He said Rome was exercising, doing chin-ups or something when they bum-rushed his ass, shanking him all in the neck and chest and even in both of his eyes.

"I heard his boy set him up, Muddah," B-Low said. "That niggah wanted him poked in the eyes." B-Low wasn't no snitch, but he liked Muddah and was disgusted by that foul shit. He knew how tight she was with the family of her brother's killer. "They said it was that dark-skinned cat in your building that he used to scramble for. You know who I mean. He put the order out all the way from another joint. But they still heard him loud and clear."

Carmiesha had cried for days after hearing that, hating that deranged niggah even more than she thought possible. She was hoping somebody would take his ass out in jail. If she had the connections and the money she would have ordered it done without blinking her eyes. But she didn't. The most she could do was hate him and try not to talk too bad about him in front of Noojie. She kept the info about Rome's killer and what had been done to him to herself too, because she knew Mere'maw would have only grieved harder if she gave her the horrible details.

Justice had been dead in that building too long to even think about having a real funeral, and they couldn't afford to give Rome one, so she and Mere'maw had agreed to let the state cremate him. She hadn't been real close with her brothers, but they were still her brothers. She felt even more alone and on her own in the world now. Daddy dead, mama dead. Both brothers dead. Mere'maw was really all she had, and for months Carmiesha clung to the old lady, following her around the small apartment afraid of what would happen to her if Mere'maw got sick or died. She walked around worried and biting her nails most of the time.

And to make things worse, Jahlil was acting up as usual. He was getting so much bigger, and so much more temperamental. One day while they were on their way to the Brooklyn Academy of Music he started in with all that "daddy" shit again, and Carmiesha got exasperated because no matter what she told him, he was never satisfied.

"Little boy! I already told you! Your father is in *college*! He's gonna graduate in a couple of years and then he'll probably be playing in the NBA!"

Jahlil's eyes had lit up then, and a rare smile was on his face. "For real? Aw, man! I can't wait until he's on television. What school is he playing for right now? What's his name, Carmiesha. What number is he wearing? Does he know I'm a baller too?"

Carmiesha bit her lip. She had a feeling she'd just made a big mistake. "I can't remember what school he's in right now, Jahlil. I think he got transferred around a few times anyway."

"But you my real mother. Can't you find him if you wanna? Won't schools and stuff tell you where he is since you my mother and he's my father?"

"You know I signed them papers saying I wouldn't try to contact you or tell you anything about us, Jahlil. The only reason I get to see you and spend time with you is because Mr. and Ms. Washington are good people, and they wanted you to know me. They're doing both of us a favor, Jahlil. So please, baby. Please. Can we just hang out together for a while and leave everybody else out of it?"

She felt bad when she saw his cute little chocolate face fall into a frown, but that's the way it had to be. It wasn't doing either one of them a damn bit of good going back and forth over the identity of Jahlil's father. In fact, it was stressing her the hell out. Carmiesha had already sworn she would never tell him about her rape. And since the adoption papers were sealed, he'd never find out whose name she had written on his birth documents.

"That's messed up, Carmiesha," Jahlil said, snatching his hand away. "All I wanna know is where I can find my daddy. Other people know who they daddy is. Even if they don't live with him, at least they know his name. I don't know why everybody keeps hiding him from me. One day I'ma find him all by myself."

"You have a good life, Jahlil!" Carmiesha exclaimed. She was getting exasperated, but she didn't want him to know it. She'd lived her whole life without her murdering-ass father, and it hadn't killed her. Not having a father wasn't what had killed Rome or Justice either. Not having a brain and goals and ambition is what had done them in.

"I wanna know who my father is, Carmiesha," Jahlil said coldly, folding his arms across his chest. "And if you don't tell me that, then you can't tell me nothing else neither."

Carmiesha didn't even answer him. Between school, her part-time job, and taking care of Mere'maw, her head was just too full. She should have told Jahlil his father was dead from the very beginning, she realized. If she had just done that, then she wouldn't have had to keep spinning no tale all these years, and wouldn't be going through all this drama right now.

"Jahlil, don't act ugly like that, baby. You shouldn't let some person you don't even know come between us and mess up what we got. I love you, Jahlil. You know that right?"

Carmiesha almost flinched when she looked at the boy for his answer. He was staring at her with something dangerous and familiar in his eyes, and love didn't have a damn thing to do with it.

Chapter 14

There was a real cool cat who worked in the gym named Sly.

He looked like he mighta been one of them slick hustling brothers back in the day. You know the kinda cat who took time and care with his appearance and his gear, even if it wasn't nothing but a maintenance worker's uniform he was profiling.

Sly had started laying his rap on me right after they tried to bring them gambling charges on me. One of my jawns got jealous over some chick who didn't even mean nothing to me, and snitched like a bitch. I didn't get nothing official, but I did get some restrictions tossed on me off the record, and every damn body seemed to know about it. Coach had me cleaning out the equipment room as part of my punishment, and I was outside hosing down ball bags and disinfecting mildewed nets when Sly came up carrying two dirty mops.

"Whattup, man?"

I looked over at him and nodded. A star athlete like me was already mad as hell cause I had to do some menial shit like clean out a supply closet. Having some janitor all up in my grill while I was doing it would only make it worse.

"You got caught up in some shit again, huh?"

I looked at him again. Harder this time. Niggah sure was pressed out tight for a fuckin' janitor. His uniform was starched with hard creases, and his sneaks was spotless.

I made a get-the-fuck-outta-my-face sound. I didn't know if he was talking about that gambling shit, or the craziness that had gone down with that nut Passion after she bought a hot gat and tried to shoot up the whole gym.

"I'on't know what you talkin' bout, man."

He just nodded and propped the mops up against the door. "I bet that's your answer for a whole lotta shit. Used to be mine too."

I cut off the water, and he turned his back on me and started pulling a big metal bucket from under a sink. "Fuck you," I mumbled. This niggah didn't know who he was dealing with.

"Nah, niggah," he said, turning around. "You the one bout to get fucked. And when they get your ass, make sure you come on back and see me. I'll hook you up with a job, man. With benefits and ere'thang. I'll even throw in one of my uniforms too. It'll fit. Cause you and me, we wear the same size."

Sly tried to get in my head every chance he got. Every time I fucked up he would offer me a hook-up. Remind me that the maintenance department was looking for a few good men.

I noticed he was around at most of the home games too. He would be right down front hyped as fucked, getting in the game from the sidelines.

"Who dat niggah supposed to be?" I asked Blackie Broadwater, one of the senior forwards on our team.

Blackie laughed. "Niggah you don't know who that is? That's Sylvester "Sly" Jones, man. He's an all-around athlete. Football, track, basketball . . . they used to call him the black Victor Hanson. But then that niggah got kicked off the hoop team, ya know? Lost his scholarship and got passed over in the draft. He beat Jordan out for the Naismith in '83 and was the NCAA Player of the Year in '84. He's a bad hooper, man. He just let all kinds of stupid shit fuck his career up, that's all."

I started watching Sly real close after that.

And that niggah was watching me too.

It wasn't long before we was rapping and hitting the weights when he wasn't working. Sly was in good shape for an old head. Something about him reminded me of T.C. though, and sometimes that fucked with my head.

"You oughta leave them chop shops alone, Thug," he told me one day. "That little bit of money you getting from Al ain't shit compared to how you gone be rolling after the draft, man."

"Why you in my business, dog? What the fuck you know about what I got going with Al?"

Sly had laughed real loud. "Man, Al been around since before you was born. I stole enough cars for that fat white boy to open up a fuckin' dealership. What you doin' ain't nothing new. It's stupid as fuck. But it ain't new."

And I felt real stupid too.

Especially after Al got busted and sang like a bitch, snitching out Blackie Broadwater and about five other seniors who'd been fattening his pockets the whole time they'd been in college. I spent the next month sweating like a motherfucker. Wondering if one of those cats was gonna let my name fall out they mouth.

Wondering if I was gonna be the next fool to get snatched up by the po-po and get sent packing by Coach Boyhem.

When a month had passed and I still hadn't gotten knocked, I started breathing a little easier and promised myself I was done with the thug-life for good. At least while I was in college, yo.

But my problems wasn't solved cause that jawn Isis was still tripping on me hard. She was right. I *did* have herpes, but if Lani hadn't had that shit too, I never woulda copped to giving it to Isis.

Lani just cried. That was all she could do.

"I trusted you, Thug. You told me you cared about me, and I really, really, trusted you."

She made a niggah feel real bad. And I guess I deserved it. But I did care about her. Lani was a lot like Muddah to me. Just clean in the spirit, where my shit was black and crusty. I guess that's why I liked her. She was every innocent thing that I had never been.

But a month later she dropped a bomb on me too.

"I'm pregnant. And I'm leaving school. I'm going back to Kentucky to have the baby, and my people are going to help me raise it."

Good thing I was sitting on her bed when she said all that, or my gangsta ass woulda been rolling around on the floor. *Not another baby,* that was all I could think. Damn. Not another one.

And now Lani was staring at me like she hated me and telling me she was carrying my baby too? I didn't know what to say to her. The look on her face told me she wasn't trying to hear nothing anyway.

"Uhm, so when you leaving?"

She stood up. "In a few days."

I nodded. "I'm sorry, Lani."

"Is that right?"

I nodded again. "Yeah, girl. That's right. I shoulda left you alone, ya know? Let some nice square brother in the accounting program come sweep you off your feet."

She smiled a little and smacked my arm. "I'm not into square brothers. But I'll take an accountant, though. But I'm not blaming you for all my sinning. I'm just mad at myself for being stupid enough to sleep with you and not make you use protection. Now I have to live with that."

I didn't say shit.

"You ran that line," she said and chuckled, even though I heard pain all in her, "about not being able to feel it right, and I went for it. It's probably more my fault than yours, cause you don't have to go home and show up at your daddy's church with your stomach poked out in front of you."

"Lani," I said, grabbing her hands and pulling her down on my lap. "I'ma ask you this, just because I wanna know. Not because I'm telling you what to do, cool?"

She waited.

"Since your family is gonna give you drama and you in school and thangs, did you think about maybe not having the baby?"

I saw a tear slip from her eye as she nodded. "I did. I thought about it a lot. But I was raised in the church, you know? My daddy preached against abortion all the time. There's worse things than being pregnant, Thug. I'd rather deal with a baby than go through the rest of my life worried about my soul."

I rubbed her back and held her while she wept, but I couldn't even relate to that stuff she was talking. I had never really thought too much about my soul. I was too busy out there on the streets handling my pockets, cause a niggah had to eat and do his thing. Where I came from, niggahs didn't start worrying about their souls until they were dead.

"Don't cry, Lani," I kept whispering. "Baby please don't cry."

I kept my hands moving on Lani, and she felt real good to me. I kissed her neck and licked the salty tears off her cheeks, then found her soft lips and slipped my tongue between them.

"You got some nerve," she said as I stretched her out on the bed. "First you give me some nasty disease, then you get me pregnant. And now you want to have sex with me on top of all that too?"

"Yeah, baby," I whispered, my teeth tugging gently on her nipple through her shirt. "Thug knows how bad he hurt you, and he's sorry. Now give him a few minutes so he can make you feel good."

Chapter 15

It had taken her three years of working full-time and going to college at the same time, but she'd done it. At the age of twenty-two, Carmiesha was officially a business owner, and as she stood outside of Locks of Love with Ya-Yo she couldn't stop grinning.

"It's all yours," Ya-Yo said, reaching over to give her a kiss. Carmiesha kissed him back and laughed.

"Now all I gotta do is perm enough hair to pay the damn bills!"

Ya-Yo eyed her down. "Oh, you gone make the money, baby. Believe that. You know what you doing when it comes to hair, and you got the business education to back it up. I'm proud of you, Carmiesha. Not a whole lot of sistahs in Harlem got the head or the heart to do what you doing, baby."

Carmiesha felt good with Ya-Yo standing beside her. He was one of them guys that a lot of sistahs overlook as being too nice. But she appreciated that about him. She had some deep feelings for him too. She might not have loved him the way she loved

Dre, but who said she needed to. Ya-Yo brought stability to her life and he was the kinda man who would die before he let his woman or his kids do without. Not that he had any.

Ya-Yo worked for UPS, but since today was the official opening day for Locks of Love, he had taken the morning off to be with her when she set up for the day. Carmiesha had rented chairs out to three excellent stylists who had gotten just as sick of the drama at Flip It and Clip It as she was. Everybody knew as soon as they got up out of a chair in that joint that bitches was gone be checking out their shit and talking about them before they hit the door. Wasn't gonna be none of that kinda negative vibing up in Locks of Love. Carmiesha wasn't gonna tolerate no haters in her place of business. Folks were gonna have to check all that drama at the door or be gone.

Carmiesha knew she had to think up some creative ways to get customers flocking to her door, so she ran specials in all the neighborhood papers and had one of her girls stand outside the shop and pass out flyers and coupons for half-priced services all day long. And it was working too. A week after they opened they had so many customers that they were running back and forth between chairs.

Even though Carmiesha appreciated the business, she promised herself and her customers that she was gonna hire some extra stylists as soon as possible. If it was one thing she knew sistahs hated, it was to go to the shop on time for an appointment just to find the stylist had booked five other heads for the same time slot. A nice little perm-wrap-and-bump that should've taken less than two hours ended up taking almost five. Shit like that was more than bad business. It was plain old trifling.

The next Saturday was her day to get Jahlil, and she decided to surprise him. Carmiesha knew that legally Jahlil wasn't her son, but she had given birth to him, and she loved him. She wanted him to see that things like owning a business were possible for people like them. And if he saw what she was doing, then it might motivate him to sit his bad ass down in class long enough to learn something so that one day he could be successful too.

"Where we going today?" he whined when she picked him up. His tone of voice was weary and sarcastic. Like she'd already dragged him to all kinds of place he hadn't wanted to go and he damn sure wasn't looking forward to wherever she planned to drag him today.

"It's gonna be a surprise," she said. "But it'll be fun too. Just trust me."

Carmiesha had told all of her stylists that she was bringing her nephew to the shop. She wasn't worried about Jahlil telling them anything else because they had agreed a long time ago that they would act like an aunt and a nephew.

All the girls in the shop went crazy over Jahlil. They spoiled him rotten telling him how cute he was, how tall, how pretty his dark brown skin was.

"I swear to God!" a stylist named Xina said. She had Jahlil in her chair, massaging his shoulders. "If this doggone boy was ten years older I would take him home and make him my slave!"

Carmiesha could see that Jahlil was loving all the attention, but she made him get up out of Xina's chair anyway. That girl wasn't all together in the brain and the way she was touching the boy didn't look too correct.

Since the shop was brand-new all the local boosters had to stop in and see if they could get some new customers. Crackheads came in trying to sell shit they had just boosted, and an old lady came in selling tiny sweet potato pies in foil pans. A fly sister rolled in with a suitcase full of hip-hop novels called *The Glamorous Life,* and an African brother with long dreads wanted to sell them some incense and some fake Jacob watches.

Carmiesha didn't really wanna make no enemies, but she didn't want all kinds of people selling no illegal shit in her spot either. She was gonna have to figure out a way to let everybody know they needed to keep it moving down the block with whatever they were carrying.

Everything was going so good in her life that Carmiesha couldn't stop giving thanks. But she had only been open for a couple of months when she found out there were some crazy rules for the businesses on her street.

Every night after the shop had been swept and cleaned, Carmiesha would file her receipts and set out new products for the next day. She didn't worry about nobody robbing her for the day's money, because she always made sure Ya-Yo swung by in his UPS truck before he got off, and took her money bag and dropped it in the bank deposit slot.

The first morning when she came in and found an envelope on the floor she couldn't figure out how it got there. She didn't remember seeing it the night before, but she just shrugged it off and put the envelope in the trash.

That shit got real regular. Once a week, always on a Friday morning, Carmiesha unlocked her shop to find that somebody had slid an envelope under her door at some point in the night.

She was getting a fish sandwich from the shop next door, when she decided to mention it to the owner.

"Mr. Ward. You stay open way later than me. You ever see anybody out there sliding stuff underneath my door?"

The old man froze with his fork in his hand. "Stuff like what?"

Carmiesha shrugged. "Like a damn envelope. An empty one at that. It don't make no sense to me, but every Friday morning there's one in the middle of my floor."

Mr. Ward looked around, then whispered. "The envelope is for the money, baby. You gots to put your protection money in there on Fridays."

"Money? What money? Protection from who?"

The old man sighed. He'd been frying fish on that street for over twenty years and Carmiesha wasn't the first business owner he'd had to explain things to.

"Look, Carmiesha. You ain't just come to Harlem yesterday, honey. You gots to pay to keep your store open around here. Back when I first started we paid a fella by the name of Spoon. He was a terrible niggah, and when somebody shot his ass right out on the sidewalk there, every business owner on the block pulled they shades down and kept right on working. There's been a lot more Spoons over the years. The worst one being Big Sonny. But nowadays Harlem businesses are split by territory. Either you paying G or you paying Hurricane. Don't matter whose list you on, you paying somebody."

Carmiesha felt herself swelling up. "Oh, no the hell I ain't! Why I gotta pay one of them niggahs? I pay my damn *taxes*! I pay my damn *rent*! I pay my damn *employees*! Why the hell should I pay off them niggahs too?"

"Sshhh!" Mr. Ward tried to shush her. "Girl you better watch what you got coming outta ya damn mouth! Now, when that youngster Skeet used to do the collecting he would let me slide every now and then. You know, on a bad week like Easter or Thanksgiving when folks ain't feeling much like eating fish. But now with that evil niggah Pimp outta jail and doing the pick-ups, you betta not be short one brown penny. Cause if you are, he'll make you wish you had robbed your own mama just to get his cash."

Carmiesha was really steaming now. Pimp hadn't been stay-ing at Noojie's much since he came home from jail, and the few times she'd seen him he'd just laughed and licked his lips trying to make her feel dirty, but he kept it moving. She wasn't paying his ass nothing. Not even no attention. He could take that shit to the bank and see how it added up.

"Well I'll just call the damn cops then," Carmiesha said, rolling her eyes. "They get their paychecks outta the taxes we pay, right? Then they should do their damn jobs."

Mr. Ward looked at her and shook his head. He slapped two pieces of fish on her bread and squirted some hot sauce over them. Then he put a small container of tartar sauce in the side of her cardboard plate and wrapped the whole thing up.

"Girl," he said, handing her the food. "You just a baby. You call them damn crooked cops on them boys, and you'll be in worse trouble than you can handle. Take some advice from a wise old man, would ya? Put a hundred dollars aside every night. You got a full house over there every day. Your customers call in orders over here all the time, and I know you can afford it. So be a smart businesswoman and learn the rules. Stick your five hundred dollars in that envelope on Friday nights. It'll be easier on you, and easier on tired old businessmen like me too."

When Carmiesha got home that night she went straight to Noojie's apartment. She wasn't surprised to see Noojie sitting in there trying to stop three babies from hollering and no mamas around.

"Hey Noojie. How you doing with them babies?"

Noojie looked straight at Carmiesha's purse. "You got any money, Muddah? These babies is hungry. Lemme borrow twenty dollars. I'll give it back to you when Pimp comes home."

Without hesitating, Carmiesha took twenty dollars from her bra. "Where's Kathy and them? They didn't bring nothing for you to feed the kids?"

"Hell no," Noojie said. "I told them crazy girls I don't get no food stamps no more. The only thing I got coming in here is the little bit Smoove sends me and what I get from Pimp. And I thank God for that boy every day. He stays here and takes care of me when my own son don't even call to see about me. Pimp is all I got to depend on now."

"Pimp ain't shit," Carmiesha snapped, picking up one of the crying babies. "I can't stand his black ass."

Noojie looked at her like she was crazy. "Girl, that sugar Pimp wouldn't hurt a fly. He's a good boy, Muddah. A real good boy. He's been home for six weeks, and I think he really learned his lesson this time. He got a boys' softball team he's coaching for free, and he's working on doing a neighborhood cleanup. Pimp ain't never did nothing to give you a reason to say something like that."

Carmiesha was about to tell Noojie she had a good damn reason and his name was Jahlil, but the door opened and Pimp walked in.

Noojie was all over him. "Pimp! Damn, I am so glad to see you. Them girls left all these babies here and they hungry. Muddah just let me borrow twenty dollars, but I need you to go out and get these babies something to eat."

Pimp stared at Carmiesha as she sat there rocking one of his cousin's babies. She could feel how much he hated her but was turned on and wanted to fuck her at the same time.

"Oh yeah?" he said, reaching in his pocket. He pulled out a bill and tossed it toward Carmiesha. It fell short and hit the floor by her feet. "Well from now on don't ask Muddah for a goddamn thing. She ain't doing too good of a job paying her own bills as it is."

■ ■ ■

Pimp mighta had Noojie fooled, but Carmiesha knew what that niggah was all about. He was tearing shit up in Harlem. Shaking down poor people just because his criminal ass was too gangsta to get a damn job.

It was a Friday afternoon and she was on her way to the mall to pick up some shop supplies. Usually she got Jahlil on a Saturday, but Ya-Yo was working tonight and she'd left Neicy in charge of the shop. She was feeling good and could spare a couple of hours to take Jahlil to buy a pair of sneakers, and maybe a few pairs of jeans.

But when she got to the Washingtons' house all of the good feelings changed. Mr. Bert was sitting in a big chair in the living room. He looked real sick. His head was slumped to the side and a blanket was covering his legs. Jahlil was sitting across from him on the sofa, and for a brief minute Carmiesha wanted to scream. Just for a moment she had seen something ugly and familiar in Jahlil's face. Something so hard and evil that she wanted to smash it. Ms. Jessie was standing over Jahlil yelling. She was quoting him Bible verses and telling him his soul needed saving.

"Hi, Ms. Jessie. Is everything okay?" Carmiesha asked, being careful not to jump in between them. She turned to the boy. "Jahlil, why don't you go wash your face and change your shirt while I talk to your mother. Maybe she'll let you come to the mall with me."

When Jahlil left the room the older woman snapped her Bible shut and shook her head. "It just doesn't make no sense to us, Carmiesha. We've given Jahlil the best life we could give him. He's had everything we thought he needed and still . . ." She nodded toward her husband. "Bert is sick. He probably needs to be up in the hospital. All I asked Jahlil to do was give him his medicine. Just one pill. I come back here and Bert said Jahlil made him take three! He said that boy yanked his mouth open and made him swallow them damn pills! What's wrong with that child, honey? Do you think he got some unnatural ways? Maybe he gets it from his father's side of the family. You do know who his daddy is, don't you?"

Carmiesha felt so bad standing there in front of this good woman. If they wanted her to take Jahlil back so they could have some peace, she would. She didn't know how she would explain it all to Mere'maw, but she would do it.

"Ms. Jessie . . . I'm so sorry. I hate y'all going through all of this with Jahlil. I know he's your son, but if you want me to take him back, I'll understand. Just tell me what you want me to do."

Ms. Jessie reached out to Carmiesha and hugged her tight.

"Baby, when we accepted that boy from you in the hospital, we accepted all of him. The good and the bad. Nobody knows what kinda child they gonna have, and you don't get to just take children back for a refund when you ain't happy about how they act."

Carmiesha felt so relieved by her words. "But what are y'all gonna do with him?"

Mrs. Washington sighed. "We think Jahlil needs a younger man in his life. Every time I turn around he's in here bugging us about who his real father is. He yearns so bad for somebody he ain't never even known that it's crazy. So I signed him up at the community center a few weeks ago. They got him on a waiting list for a mentor, but he can play at the center as much as he wants while he's waiting. He seems to really like it there, and aside from this thing with Bert and the pills, things have been going really good. I'm hoping when he gets assigned his mentor that it'll help even more."

▬ ▬ ▬

Carmiesha had gotten Jahlil outta there in a hurry. She felt so guilty knowing the Washington's were going into their older years burdened with the problems of the child she had birthed.

"Why you give Mr. Bert all them pills?" she asked Jahlil as they rode the train downtown. She felt like smacking him in the back of his head but she didn't. Instead she just looked at him, not liking what she saw. At ten years old, he was growing up and already he was taller than she was. He was gonna be fine as shit one day, but right now Carmiesha couldn't care less about cute.

She was more worried about what she saw in the depth of the boy's eyes.

"Boy, you hear me talking to you? You better open your damn mouth and answer me. Why you give Mr. Bert all them pills?"

Jahlil hunched his shoulders. "I'on't know."

"What you mean, you don't know? Didn't you hear your mother when she told you to give him just one pill?"

"Yeah."

"And you went ahead and gave him three anyway?"

"Yeah."

"What the hell was you trying to do, Leel? Kill the poor man?"

Jahlil didn't say anything.

Carmiesha sighed and frowned. She didn't know how to deal with this kinda shit. She had only been thirteen when Jahlil was born, and that wasn't old enough for life to show her how to be nobody's mother.

"I'ma get you a pair of sneakers today, cool?"

Jahlil nodded, then looked at her and said, "Thanks, Carmiesha."

Carmiesha sighed again and put her arm around him. She hugged him for a second then kissed the side of his face twice. "I'm sorry you having such a hard time at home, Jahlil, I really am. But I love you, and your mother and father love you too. You just don't know. You have a life a lot of boys your age wish they did have. You've got heat and hot water and plenty of food. You've got your own room and a closet full of clothes and a lot of people who care about you. I can't think of one thing that you need that you don't have, Jahlil. Not one thing."

The look the boy gave Carmiesha damn near broke her heart and she wished she could take her words back. Because in her heart Carmiesha already knew, that no matter how much Jahlil had, it would never be enough because all the boy wanted was his father.

■ ■ ■

They walked around the mall picking up the items Carmiesha had come for. When they were finished getting her stuff she let Jahlil drag her around the mall until he found some sneakers he liked, and then she ended up buying him two pairs instead of just one. They were sitting in the food court eating two big Cinnabons when Carmiesha looked up and immediately got fighting hot.

He was walking his long-legged ass toward them like they was old friends or something. Instinct made Carmiesha reach out and touch Jahlil, who was sitting right beside her. She couldn't believe this niggah was actually gonna approach her, and she stopped chewing her Cinnabon and looked at him like he was a fool for real.

"Whattup, my brother!"

Pimp walked straight up to the table and held out his hand to Jahlil for some dap.

The boy lit up. He stood up so fast he bumped his knee on the table, then tried to rub it on the sly and play it off.

"What's up!" he said all excited. "What you doing up here?"

Carmiesha couldn't believe the smile that covered Jahlil's face. She stared from him to Pimp and wanted to die. It was easy to see where Jahlil's long lanky frame had come from. They were built exactly alike. And their skin tone was exactly the same too. Everybody in Carmiesha's family was either light-skinned or light caramel, but Jahlil had the same pretty ebony skin that Pimp had.

"Sit your ass down, Jahlil," Carmiesha damn near hollered. "What did your mother and father tell you about speaking to strangers?"

The boy laughed and went around to the other side of the table and grinned at Pimp.

"He ain't no stranger. I see him around the community center all the time. You Carl, right?"

Carmiesha almost choked.

"That's right, man," Pimp said, fake punching Jahlil and tapping him all over his head. "I be checking you and your little homeboys out when y'all on them video games. Who this?"

Jahlil laughed and pretended to throw a bunch of punches back at Pimp. Carmiesha wanted to scream when Pimp threw his arms around Jahlil and caught him in a hug, and Jahlil hugged him back.

"This my aunt," the boy said. "Carmiesha. She just bought me some fresh sneakers! You should see 'em, man! They're hot!"

Carmiesha got up and grabbed their bags.

"Aunt, huh?" Pimp looked back and forth between Jahlil and Carmiesha. A big-ass smile came across his face, and he nodded at her and laughed. "You say this your *aunt*?"

"Let's go, Jahlil!" Carmiesha yelled. She grabbed Jahlil's arm and dragged him out of the food court.

"But what about my Cinnabon?" the boy hollered.

Pimp laughed again as he watched them walk away. "Don't worry about it, little man! Your *aunt* got two HOT *cinnabunns*!"

Carmiesha whirled around. *Fuck you,* she mouthed to Pimp. *Fuck your stupid ass!*

"Okay, Auntie!" Pimp said, still laughing his ass off. "I'll meet you in the elevator just like I did before! And we can make that shit go up and down, up and down, up and down. . . ."

Chapter 16

I loved playing ball for Syracuse. Couldn't get enough of doing my thang on that court and showing motherfuckers all my skills. Being a star athlete at a Division I school was everything a Harlem boy like me had ever dreamed of, and for the whole two and a half years I'd been up there I woke up every morning and went to bed every night feening for that noise.

But just like chickenhead girls followed stars around making noise, trouble followed us too. The trouble that almost fucked me up for good caught up with me at the worst possible moment and almost took me out.

It was the middle of my junior year, and aside from the honeys, my shit was way less raggedy than it had been when I got here. I was the team's leading scorer and Coach had named me as assistant team captain. I was getting shit done in most of my classes, and on top of that, I was spending a little more time with Sly. That niggah musta thought he was my daddy for real cause he got a kick outta putting me down on all the crazy shit he'd done. He called his time at Syracuse his "college career to nowhere," and just like T.C. and Miss Lady, Sly cautioned me to keep my focus on graduating first, then getting into the NBA. I was listening too, and my stats was proof of that. My grades were cool, and if I kept scoring and assisting like I was doing, I was almost sure to get a real low number as somebody's draft pick.

It was a Friday night and we'd just waxed North Carolina's ass at a home game. Me and a crew of ballers was drinking and partying at a sorority house and there were more fine-ass honeys up in there than the whole team coulda handled. After all that funky shit with those Delta girls, I'd chilled on all the wild fucking for a few. But tonight was my night. We'd busted some North Carolina ass and I'd been awarded the game MVP, and Coach had let it slip that *Sporting News* had named me as a candidate for the College Player of the Year Award.

I rolled up playing a sweatshirt that said CANDY LICKER on the front. Chicks was pointing at it and covering their mouths, their eyes twinkling with glee. They was giggly and laughing and shit, but every one of them was hoping to be the one to get that candy licked.

My dick was hard and hungry, and I was cracking on this slim sexy sistah. Her name was Breezy and she had a tight little frame with some gapped bowlegs. I knew she was fuckin with one of them thick Nupe niggahs on the football team, but since he wasn't here to block the play on his pussy, I was doing my best to get up in it.

"Damn," I said, moving her long hair to the side so I could get closer to her neck. I licked her collarbone and let my tongue slide up to her ear. "You smell like ice cream, baby girl."

The living room floor was packed with dancing bodies, and I

was sitting in a love seat with Breezy in my lap. I put my arms around her and held her tight, pulling her down to me as I grinded and pushed my dick up against her. "I bet," I told her, moving up and down real slow, "you taste like ice cream too."

She laughed and kissed me. Her tongue was long and slim, just like her body, and I knew right away I was getting me some of that pussy. Some shit was just guaranteed to work. The minute you even hinted around like you was game to eat some pussy, chicks got wet and started feening to hump on your face.

And I didn't disappoint them neither. I liked sucking pussy for the same reason I liked fuckin without a glove. I got off on that stuff. I liked the way it felt. A girl could rub her pussy juice on me seven days a week. All over me. I liked the way that thang smelled on my face. The way it got sticky on my fingers. The way it wet my dick up and coated me with every stroke.

"You hungry?" Breezy asked me, and by the look in her face I knew she wasn't talking about no food.

"Yeah," I said. I slid my hand between her legs and tapped her pussy with two fingers. "For some of this right here." I bit my bottom lip and nodded down at her stuff. "I wanna eat that stuff you got right there."

Breezy took me in one of the small rooms, and we cleared some shit off the bed. I fell on top of her and gripped her ass with both hands. She was a lot slimmer than most girls I usually went for, but she had wide hips and just enough ass to catch my eye.

"Don't do that shit!" she said. She tried to get away from me as I licked and sucked a spot right above her left nipple. I kept right on sucking. I knew what time it was. She wanted this dick, but didn't want that thick-headed niggah of hers to bust her wearing the evidence.

I made sure I gave her a real nice hickey, then let my lips drop down to her nipple. She moaned as I rubbed her pussy through her pants and let my lips and teeth work her nipple into a rock. I wanted to be inside her but I forced myself to slow down.

Breezy was breathing real heavy. She pulled my mouth to her other breast and I took good care of that one too. It didn't take us long to get out our clothes, and when we did I liked what Breezy was holding even more. Her waist was so tiny I could wrap my whole hand around it. And even though she was slim, her hips were round and her butt was soft and full.

"Turn around," I told her. I bent her over a small desk, and she leaned on her elbows, giving me a wide-eye view of her ass. I stood behind her bumping her flesh with my dick as I played with her jiggling breasts.

She moaned as my hands slid down her curved waist and cupped her hips. I nudged her legs a little wider, then swiped my fingers between her wet lips. "Yeah," I whispered as I put them to my mouth and licked them one at a time. "This pussy tastes just like ice cream too."

Her ass cheeks were quivering as I slid two fingers between her lips. "Aggghh," she moaned deep in her throat.

"It's all good," I whispered. I moved my fingers back and forth, sliding them deep inside her hot spot. I pressed her ass-hole with my thumb, and her body jerked.

"Why you do that?" she yelped, turning her head to look at me.

"Shhhh . . . ," I told her, sliding my fingers in and out of her again. "Relax, girl. Thug's about to make that ass feel real good."

I dropped to my knees behind her and finger-fucked her until her knees got weak. She was moaning and bucking her ass back when I took my hand outta her wet pussy and stuck my face up in it. I ate that pussy out from the back, and when sweat started dripping from her butt cheeks I licked that up too.

Her whole body was sweating by the time I laid her on the edge of the bed. I got back on my knees and placed her feet on my shoulders, and went back to work, licking that sweet brown kitty cat and sucking her clit like it was a swollen cherry.

"Thuggggg!" She screeched, digging her heels into my shoulders while raising her ass off the bed. She grabbed her own jiggling titties and screwed her face up in a sex mask. "I'm gonna cummmm!"

I didn't answer her. My mouth was on her pussy, and my finger was in her ass.

She had cried out at first when I touched her asshole, but I ignored her until she was screaming for more. I let her come twice, then I stood up and eased her the long way on the bed. She was whispering my name over and over. Begging me to fuck her. I laid on top of her and felt her soft thighs brush my skin as she wrapped her long legs around my waist. I put my dick inside her and started grinding deep and slow. She rolled her hips to my pace, and I felt myself knocking the shit outta her walls.

"Fuck this pussy," she panted in my ear. Her long hair was all over the bed. "Do it to me, Thug. Slam that fat dick in Jay's stuff. Your dick is so much bigger than his, Thug. You fuck me so much better than he do. . . ."

The more shit she talked the faster I stroked. "This your pussy, niggah! Not Jay's. This shit is wet and thumping for *you*, Thug. You hear me? For *you*!"

I hollered out loud when I exploded inside her. She dug her heels into my butt, sucking my dick as deep inside as it would

go. Her pussy muscles was clamping on me. Squeezing my milk
into her warm inner folds.

I pressed my mouth to hers and tongued her softly. Letting
her taste her own pussy on my lips. Then I got up and left her
laying there. Her legs was wide open, and she was knocked out
sleep with a satisfied smile on her face.

— — —

I had to take a piss real bad. From the sounds coming from the
living room I knew the party was still live. I walked across the
hall and opened a door that coulda been a bathroom, and it was.

"Damn! My bad!" I said when I saw all that stuff I saw.

"W-w-wait!" she hollered, holding up her hand and reaching
for a towel. "Don't go nowhere, boo. I was just getting out. You
good."

I'd caught her coming out of the shower and beads of water
was still on her dark chocolate skin.

She smiled. "I seen you go off with Breezy. She okay?"

I nodded. "She's sleep."

The chick was a little bit on the heavy side, and I was holding my dick hoping she would hurry up and get out so I could
pee.

"Go 'head," she said, nodding toward the toilet. "I got six
brothers, boy. They used to piss in front of me all the time.
Here." She faced the shower. "I'll turn around and give you
some privacy. I gotta put some oil on my skin, but you just go
right ahead and do what you gotta do."

I didn't have no choice. I pulled out my dick and started pissing in a hot whoosh.

"You that rapper guy on the basketball team, right?"

I held my dick and nodded. Fuck facing the shower. She was dead on me.

"Yeah. I be seeing you doing your thang on the court. I'm Dee-Dee." She moved closer and kept drying herself off. "You need to drink more water, boo. Your dick smells like ammonia. Smells like pussy too."

I pushed hard to squeeze out my last few drops.

"Whassup," I said, when I was finished. She'd dropped her towel and was standing naked in front of me. Her stomach was a little heavy, and her nipples were hard.

She turned around and started rubbing baby oil all over her nice plump ass with both hands.

"Ain't nothing up. Can you rub a little oil on my back for me?"

She reached around and poured some in my hand, and I rubbed it on her shoulders.

"So you said Breezy is okay, right?"

"Yeah. She fine."

She laughed. "I know. Skinny girls like her get all the play. If I got half as much attention as she got I'd be happy."

I knew exactly what her problem was. And if she thought just cause she was a little heavy around the middle a star like me was too good to bend her wide black ass over and fuck the shit outta her, she was wrong. Thug liked big girls too.

I was covered in baby oil and smelling like two pussies when I walked outta that bathroom. Dee-Dee was laying on the bathroom floor. Sighing and singing. Another satisfied customer.

A crunk cut was blasting in the living room, and I was on my way in there to get something to drink when one of my boys hollered out for me to come upstairs. I was a little tired from the big game and all that fuckin, but I jogged up the steps and went in a room where about eight or nine of my orange brothers were smoking weed and watching this hot chick dancing up on a dresser.

Somebody passed me a beer, and I sat on the floor with my knees up, watching her move her body. She was real yellow and had small breasts and a big phat ass. She had some thighs that had niggahs going wild.

"Dance wit' me!" A baller we called Hiccup yelled. Hiccup was drunk, and when he tried to snatch the jawn down off the dresser niggahs started beefing and telling him to let her get back up there and shake her ass.

The girl was laughing and tossing her hair and gyrating her hips. She turned around and started clapping her booty cheeks, and somebody slapped her phat banana ass so hard I could see his handprint. I whistled along with everybody else when she opened her legs and started playing in her own pussy, but I was all fucked out and didn't get turned on at all.

"Take all that shit off!" somebody hollered, and the jawn laughed some more and pulled off her shirt. Her titties wasn't no more than a mouthful, and she held a forty up and poured that shit all over her body.

Niggahs was swarming. Tongues out and lips smacking. Trying to drink that beer dripping offa her. I was sitting there laughing when my cell phone rang.

"Dre?"

I stuck my finger in my free ear.

"Who dis?"

"Dre! It's me, goddammit!"

It was Muddah.

Them niggahs was wildin' hard on that girl. I got up and walked out the room so I could hear her better.

"Whassup, baby!"

"Andre."

Just the way she said my name made my heart freeze.

"What's goin on, Muddah?"

She sniffled back tears. "It's Noojie, baby. She got real sick, Dre. And she wouldn't go to the hospital."

"And what you saying? What the fuck you saying, Muddah?"

She was really crying now.

"She's gone, Dre. Noojie's gone."

I didn't say shit. I just held the phone to my ear. Listening to Muddah cry softly.

"Dre? You there? Did you hear what the fuck I just said? Noojie is *gone*! Your mother is DEAD!" It took a long time before I could open my mouth and say a single word.

Finally, "What happened?"

Muddah sniffed some more. "They said it mighta been her heart. She wasn't feeling good, and she fell out in the street. Over there on Lenox Avenue. She was laying in the gutter, Dre. All out in the rain. People walked past her cause they thought she was drunk and passed out, but then some church lady got off the bus and went over to try and get her up. But she was dead, baby. She was already dead."

Guilt snaked all up in my chest, trying to kill me.

I tightened my stomach, reaching for that cold, hard part of my heart. But this time I couldn't find it.

"No . . . ," I whispered and for the first time since Miss Lady had whipped my ass with that house shoe, I broke all the way down. "Don't be telling me no shit like that, Muddah."

"Dre, you gotta come home, you hear? I'ma try to find out who to call to get Smoove here, but the people say they need you to tell 'em what to do with the body."

"I'm coming home," I whispered. I felt the tears running down my face as I stumbled down the steps and pushed through a wall of bodies to get out the door. "I'm outta here right now."

Chapter 17

I didn't tell nobody I was leaving.

Dave was sleeping at his desk when I got to the room. I wrote him a quick note and left it right next to him. I knew where he kept his stash, so I went in his closet and got his winter hat and counted out ten twenty-dollar bills. I grabbed a gym bag, stuck a few pieces of clothing down in it, and bounced.

I got down to the Greyhound station at a little after one. The next bus wasn't leaving until six thirty in the morning, and if I coulda walked my ass back to Harlem I would have. Aside from the dude selling tickets, the bus station was almost empty, and I was the only black person up in there. Two white girls sat across from me and ran their mouths talking a bunch of nonsense, and when I looked at them they both smiled big like they wanted me to say something to them.

I put my head back and closed my eyes. All I could see was Noojie. I felt fucked up behind the way I had talked to her the last time she called me. Somebody had let her use their cell phone, and I was busy and edgy when she called.

"I ain't seen you in so long, baby," Noojie had whined. "And you don't never call. If it wasn't for Muddah I wouldn't know nothing about how you doing."

"I'm in college, Noojie!" I had snapped on her. "I'm good. I just ain't got a lotta time to be on no phone."

"Well when I'ma see you then? When they gone let you come home for a visit?"

I got aggie like a motherfucker.

"I'on't know, Noojie. I guess I'll see you when I see you."

"I'm sick, Dre," she had insisted. "I ain't been feeling too good."

A niggah had actually chuckled. "Leave that crack alone and grab a cheeseburger, ma. You be aiight."

College had gone to my head real bad, and my attitude toward her had been totally fucked up. And it was even more fucked up that my moms had died in the street like a raggedy dog before I could get put on with the NBA and show her what I could do with my life.

Memories tried to push up on me, but I forced myself to stay cold. All I wanted to do was get back to Harlem and bury my moms. Noojie mighta been a crackhead, and yeah, our lives coulda been a lot better. But it coulda been worse too. She'd kept a roof over our heads and put what she could in our stomachs. I had never met my father, and Precious's daddy had gotten smoked before she was even born. Noojie ain't never had nobody to fend for her in this world except her damn self. And still, she'd raised three hardhead boys—two who wasn't even hers—and watched her baby girl get murdered right on her front stoop. When I thought about all the shit Noojie had been through, from drugs and no-good men, to a son who deep down inside had loved her, but still broke her heart over and over again, I was surprised she hadn't dropped dead sooner.

All of this was filling my head by the time the bus rolled up. I got on and walked all the way to the back. I wasn't trying to be nowhere near them two white girls who was still running they mouths.

I kept my bag with me and took a seat near a window, across from the bathroom. I closed my eyes again and minutes later I felt the bus pull off. But we wasn't even out the lot good before I heard the brakes whish and felt us stop again. I opened my eyes. Po-po lights was flashing. A squad car had pulled up right next to us.

My street instincts kicked in hard.

I started to get up and duck into the bathroom, but what the fuck for? I hadn't done shit wrong. Whoever they was looking for, I just wanted them to state their damn business and keep it rolling. I needed to get to Harlem and I didn't have no time to waste.

Two officers got on the bus. They said something to the driver, and that motherfucker turned around and pointed straight toward the back where I was sitting. They moved down the aisle, and when they got far enough in the back where the only passenger left was me, I knew what the fuck was up.

"Andre Williams?"

I couldn't believe that bitch-ass Dave had sent the po-po after me for two hundred fuckin' bills. As many times as I had fed his broke ass offa money I made from stealing cars. All I could do was shake my head.

"Why you wanna know?"

This wasn't no campus security. These was straight state cops. I got the badge flashed at me and all that.

"We have a warrant out for your arrest, Mr. Williams. Put your hands where I can see them, then stand up and turn around."

I knew the drill. I cursed Dave's punk ass again then said. "What's all this about? That motherfuckah cryin' over a little loan?"

"You're being charged with one count of forcible sexual assault, Mr. Williams. You'd probably understand that better as rape."

— — —

But I didn't understand it. Even after they tossed me in the back of a squad car and took me down to the station, I still didn't understand it.

"Who'd I rape?" I kept asking them. "Yo! Who the fuck did I rape?"

"You'll find out everything soon enough."

"Listen, man," I tried to explain at the jailhouse while some rednecked hillbilly cop was fingerprinting me. "I ain't never raped nobody in my life. C'mon, man. I found out tonight that my moms just died. I was on my way home. To the city. I'm her only son and I gotta bury her."

He didn't even look at me. Just kept rolling my fingers around in the ink.

They took me in an interview room, and two detectives came in to question me.

I was so hyped I wouldn't sit down. Them white crackers promised to bust me in my head if I didn't.

"Y'all gotta tell me what's going on here. My moms just died, and I need to go bury her."

One of them glanced at some papers in a folder.

"We received a complaint that you were involved in the gang rape of Kimberly Derrick."

"Kimberly who? Who the fuck is that?"

They ran that shit down on me so I could understand it.

It was crazy. That yellow bitch who was dancing on that dresser had brought a charge on me. And not just on me. On every niggah who was up in that room watching her stick her fingers in her pussy.

"Look, man," I said, shaking my head. "I never touched that girl. I swear to God. I got outta there as soon as I got the call about my mother."

"So that's your story?"

"Hell, yeah! That's the goddamn truth!"

"Well you can tell it to the judge when you and your friends go in front of him on Monday morning."

I yelled. "Monday? I just told you my moms just fuckin' died! I gotta get down to Harlem and handle her business today!"

The old cop nodded, then stood up.

"Harlem, huh?"

"Yeah. Harlem."

"Well, last time I checked they had morgue freezers down in Harlem too. Let 'em put ya mammy on some ice. She'll wait."

— — —

They ended up holding us for over a week.

Me, Blackie, Reg, Lewis, and five other ballers who had been in the room that night. I didn't know what kinda story them other playas was telling, but I straight stuck to mine, cause it was the truth. I didn't rape nobody. I never touched that girl. Yeah, I had boned two females that night, but she wasn't one of them.

I had used my one phone call to call Coach Boyhem. I woke him up outta his sleep, and he sounded mad as fuck about it too cause all the other players had already called him earlier. I explained everything to him the best I could. I even told him about Noojie.

"I know you prolly don't believe me, but I didn't do shit this time. I wasn't even there. I was sitting in the bus station all night long. I don't know how that girl got my name, or why she saying I fucked her, but I swear to God, I didn't."

They kept us locked up two to a cell, and when my boys found out about Noojie, ere last one of them stood up for me. They wrote statements confirming that I had left way before that girl quit dancing and got down off the dresser. None of them said they saw me there when she was getting fucked. Even the ones who was secretly hating on me cause I got mad play time on the court, they told the truth.

I was surprised as hell when big girl showed up. Dee-Dee. The chick I had bent over in the bathroom and whose name I hadn't even remembered. She came down to the jail and gave a written statement in my behalf. She told 'em exactly what time she was with me and what we was doing, and backed my story up when she said she had looked outta her window a few minutes after I left her, and saw me leaving the sorority house and running across the street.

After all that, I saw the judge, and they finally turned my ass loose that next Monday night. Somehow those cracker bastards lost my cell phone, and I ended up having to buy another bus ticket cause technically I had taken a fifteen-foot ride that night, but I didn't care.

I took a late-night bus to 42nd Street, then hopped on the subway and got to Harlem real early Tuesday morning. People was leaving their cribs to go to work, and I saw Muddah coming out of our building as I walked up.

She was walking with her head down, but when she looked up and saw me a look crossed her face like somebody had beat her in the stomach.

"I got locked up," I explained as she put her face in my chest. Her arms was around my waist, and I was holding her too. I couldn't believe how good it felt to be next to her. This girl was like vitamins to me. She fortified me on all levels, and sex didn't have shit to do with it.

"We didn't know where you were," she said. "I kept calling your cell phone, and you didn't pick up."

I just kept holding on to her. She was really the only thing keeping me on my feet, and if she had'a moved I prolly woulda lost my legs.

"I got hit with a charge, but it all worked out. I'm here now. Do Smoove know what happened to my moms? Where's Pimp?"

Muddah had a big handbag hanging off her shoulder, and I took it from her and put it over mine. "What funeral home they got Noojie at? I wanna see her body."

Muddah put her head down for a quick second. When she looked up tears was flowing from her eyes.

"I'm so sorry, Dre. We didn't know what else to do!" She sniffed and pushed her hair back. Then she let go of my waist and held my hands real tight. "We buried Noojie on Saturday, baby. Pimp paid half, and Smoove came up with the rest. He got some kinda emergency loan from the Marine Corps. Your Aunt Dru was here. They brought her down for the funeral cause your mother was her next of kin. They kept her handcuffed, but at least they let her come."

"What?" I yelled. I jerked away from her. "What the fuck you mean she got buried? Y'all had a *funeral,* Muddah? Without *me?* Y'all put my moms in the motherfuckin' ground without waiting for her fuckin *son?*"

Muddah started crying real hard, but I didn't care.

I dropped her bag and started running. Just fuckin' running. I ran for blocks and blocks and blocks, and I didn't see or hear a damn thing. I was deaf, dumb, and blind. The only thing in front of me was the guilty fact that Noojie was really gone, and I would never see her again. I ran across Lenox Avenue and down toward 115th Street. I ran through crowds of people like I was blind. All who didn't get out my way got knocked the fuck down. I don't know how long I kept moving, but I didn't stop until I couldn't control my legs no more. I stumbled into a Spanish store and rushed toward the beverage department in the back, knocking shit off the shelves as I went. I carried three forties of St. Ides up to the counter, then took my purchases outside. I crossed the street and sat on somebody's stoop and started drinking. And I didn't stop until the pain was gone, and I couldn't feel my heart weeping no more.

Chapter 18

It was a week after Noojie's funeral, and Carmiesha had closed the shop down early. It seemed like nobody had realized how big Noojie was in their lives until she was gone, and there was no one there to take her place.

Especially some of them crazy-ass girls who had had babies for Dre. Once she stopped running the streets and smoking crack, Noojie had really been there for her grandbabies, and a lot of times she was the only one their mamas had to depend on.

Kathy and Remy had rolled up on Carmiesha in the funeral parlor at Noojie's wake. They was complaining about not having nobody to help them with the babies now that Noojie was gone. Carmiesha had set up a meeting at the shop and told them all to be there. Those chicks needed to try and figure out what they was gonna do about them babies now that Noojie wasn't gonna be around.

"Look," she told them. They was sitting around in her styling chairs looking at her like she had all the answers. "I don't know exactly what y'all gone do, but I know y'all need to come up with a plan."

Those chicks was staring at their nails, digging all in their high-priced purses, and checking their shit out in the mirror while she was talking.

"Noojie is gone, so the free gravy train ain't rolling through no more. Some of y'all been blowing up my shit asking me to watch your kids when you know I'm running a shop over here and gotta handle my own business. So I'ma tell all of y'all right now. I can't watch no babies all day long, but I can keep helping y'all whenever I have a little extra ends or whenever Dre sends me any money. Which ain't all that often."

Rasheena stood up and smirked. She put her hand on her curved-out hip and started talking shit. "Where's the fuckin' baby you got by Dre, Muddah? Oh, that's right. You ain't got none. That niggah on the mic cutting records for Ruthless and them, why he ain't sending none of that money to us for his kids?"

Kathy jumped in. "Sheena, don't be making no noise up in here. Muddah been helping all a our kids since they was born."

"Nah, nah, nah," Rasheena said, spinning around to put her eye on everybody. Carmiesha just kept quiet. She could see what Dre had seen in this girl. She had a real cute face and a small waist. Her ass was bouncy but her body was tight. Her shit was laid out in all directions. Acrylic nails, blue contacts, blinged-out earrings, butter hair.

"Don't y'all bitches sit around here and front. All a y'all done said the same shit before. To me and to Noojie. Why this bitch so special when she ain't even got no kids by Dre? She got a busi-

ness and living large. I just wanna know why we gotta keep getting our money through her ass."

Remy spoke up for Carmiesha. "We get it through her because she's the only person Dre gives any damn thing to. And
where the fuck was you when we was trying to get some money
outta Dre in court? Your ass didn't even show up. So don't come
blaming Muddah cause the judge said that niggah is in college
and ain't gotta pay no damn child support. She ain't gotta do
shit for you or Duqueesa. But she do it anyway. You oughtta be
thanking her and kissing her ass."

"I don't need nobody to kiss my ass," Carmiesha said, "and I
agree that Dre should be taking care of all his kids. But can't nobody sit around waiting on no niggah to decide to act right.
Y'all need to start helping each other out. Watch each other's
babies. If Noojie did it, y'all should be able to do it too. Pass
them clothes down when they get too small. Hell, ain't nothing
wrong with kids wearing hand-me-downs. They all sisters and
brothers any damn way."

"Still," Rasheena said. She popped her gum and switched her
bubble booty back to her chair. "Thug's ass needs to be deep
checked. What kinda niggah gone miss his own mama's funeral?
Everybody else showed up for Noojie 'cept him. If all of us
hadn't sat up front with Smoove, Pimp, and the kids, that whole
family row woulda been almost empty. That's called cold madness."

"He was locked up," Carmiesha said quietly. "Something
happened up there in Syracuse, and he got locked up for like a
week."

Rasheena laughed. "Good for that motherfucker! He shoulda
got locked up when y'all took him to court! It don't make no

sense for us to be walking around here broke when all these kids got that niggah's DNA."

"But he's gone get his, though," Paula said. "Ballers don't stay up in college forever. Let him get a phat NBA contract and see don't all of us be rolling around here in pimped-out rides!"

Carmiesha agreed with Paula and Rasheena a hundred percent, but she wasn't about to go there with them. She'd been right there in that courtroom when the judge told them Andre's ass was exempt from paying child support as long as he was in school full-time on that scholarship.

But the judge had also ragged his ho-ish ass out for being so damn irresponsible and sticking his naked dick into all kinds of stray pussies. She hadn't said it just like that, but that's basically what she had meant. And Dre's stupid ass had stood up there and acted like he had never heard of safe sex. If he kept going like he was going he was gonna catch something. The way he was running through females he'd probably get up one morning to take a piss and his dick would just fall off and splash in the toilet.

"Y'all talkin' all that shit about Thug," Vikki said, "but let that niggah walk through the door and all a y'all damn pussies gone get wet!"

Even Rasheena bust out laughing on that one, and Carmiesha had to turn her head to hide her smile.

"Girl, you ain't even lying," Kathy agreed. "I ain't *never* been with a man who could lay it on my ass like Thug do. He might not be worth shit when it comes to his kids, but that playa knows how to make a sistah feel good between the legs."

Remy laughed and added, "You mean, feel good everywhere. I was hooked on humping Thug the first time he put his hands on me. The way that boy grabbed my ass and stuck his tongue down my throat . . . I could tell he could eat him up some pussy."

"Damn!" Kathy said. "Just put the niggah's business out there on the street, why don't'cha?"

Vikki waved her hand. "What business? All of us done been with him, and all of us liked it. Thug got a way of making love like ain't nothing in the world is more important to him than making you feel good. Shit, every chick wanna feel like that. I know I still do."

"Me too," Rasheena admitted. "I don't have no problem getting a playa. But getting one who knows how to swerve until ya satisfied . . . that shit ain't easy. I stay my ass in training mode with these so-called hustlers out here. If they worked on hustling that dick the way they hustled their street game they would know how to keep a honey worked and whipped. The last niggah who made me come with his dick was Thug." She looked around at them and laughed. "Damn! Where that niggah at when you need him?"

"Ask Muddah to call him for you," Paula said. "She got his ass in check."

Carmiesha had stayed quiet while they was talking all that shit about what Dre could do in bed, but now she spoke up. "Y'all know me and Dre don't roll together like that no more. I been with Ya-Yo for a good minute, and I'm satisfied with that."

"Girl, stop frontin'," Remy laughed. "Ya-Yo cute and got a real job and all, but you know damn well he ain't holding them legs up in the air and waxing that ass like Thug do."

"Tell the truth, Muddah," Paula teased her. "Just go 'head

and tell the damn truth. That's some good-ass dick, ain't it? If all of us can admit it, why can't you?"

Carmiesha tried to hide her grin, but she couldn't. She was long past hating on Dre for screwing so many females. He was one of those guys who you took one look at and knew he could fuck. He'd given it all up in the sheets for her, doing whatever it took to make sure she was satisfied. That's just the kind of thug lover he was.

"Yeah," she said, remembering Dre's sexy-ass rhythm while his baby mamas grilled her and egged her on. "He aiight. The niggah know what he be doing."

They all laughed with her, and as Carmiesha sat there talking shit with them she realized that even though Dre was a big ho, his babies had brought them all together as sistahs and she liked that.

"Hey, Muddah," Kathy said, changing the subject and breaking the mood. She'd been busy looking around the shop the whole time they were talking. "If I go to beauty school can you hook me up with a job when I graduate?"

Carmiesha nodded. "Hell yeah, I will. And you ain't gotta wait until you graduate to work for me, neither. The day you go downtown and get yourself enrolled in class, that's the day I'll hire you as my shampoo girl. Right on the spot."

Chapter 19

After busting my ass to get to Harlem just to find out my moms had already been buried, I went back to school a few days later. Smoove had cleaned out most of Noojie's apartment while he was there, and Muddah said she would have some young heads take the little bit of furniture down to the curb and give away whatever was left.

Coach acted pretty cool about everything when I got back, but I knew it was only because Noojie had died. If I had brought him that rape shit by itself, he woulda had a lot less mercy on me and mighta even made me forfeit my senior year. Everybody at school was talking about that shit too. They was saying the jawn freaked out and called the cops cause all her sorority sistahs started ragging on her and calling her a stank ho for fucking half the basketball team.

I was the only one who swore up and down that I didn't get no pussy from that girl. Everybody else who was there admitted that they had fucked her, but they said she was down for it the whole time and had set the rules by herself. They said she was the one who had decided who was gonna hit it first and who would be next. And even though the prosecutor tried to say she was too drunk to give permission to get fucked, the school fixed it to where all my boys had to do was go through some bullshit counseling sessions and be done with it. They came out lucky, though, cause nobody got kicked outta school or got their eligibility tapped.

But a few weeks later I had even more drama in my life over that crazy night from hell.

Breezy dropped it on me that she was pregnant. It had happened right before I banged big girl over the tub, then went upstairs and watched that psycho yellow jawn strip so she could holla rape.

I sat there and stared at Breezy as she talked some unrighteous shit about telling that big-headed football player it was his kid, even though she knew it was really mine.

"You could do some shit like that to your man?"

She looked at me like the slicksta she was. "Damn right. Me and my baby can do much better with him than we can do with you."

I fronted her off. "Girl, you don't know who baby that is. Your ass prolly been run through so many times you having a frat baby who looks like every last one of us."

"I don't give a damn who it looks like," she said. "I'm telling you who's gonna marry me and help me raise it."

I dug what she was saying. She had confidence in that other guy's skills. She knew he was destined for the NFL. And she looked at me like I was a stupid little fuckup just waiting to get started. But all a that noise got shushed real quick a few days later when she came crying and whining to me. Talking bout football-head told her to get an abortion cause as soon as he graduated and got in the NFL he was marrying some fat, ugly white girl who lived in the next dorm.

I got a call from Lani a few weeks after she had the baby. She said it was a boy, and she was naming him Dante. She also said not to worry about trying to reach her cause she had sought the Lord and He told her to forget all about me.

Not long after that, Breezy had Malik. He was cute and fat. I had promised to be in the room with her when he was born, but instead I was on the road playing ball. She got mad and would barely even let me see him. She found them a little apartment and tried to juggle things on her own for a quick minute, but when Malik was about two months old she gave it all up and went back home too.

I stayed to myself after that. I wasn't all the way icy. It wasn't like I could just give a girl a baby and forget about them. It fucked with my head, but I tried not to let it cause I couldn't do nothing for nobody until I got on and got paid.

School days went by. I ran across Sly a couple a times, but I wasn't in no mood to talk. He could save all that philosophical bullshit he liked to holla. Didn't nobody need to tell me what was up. When Noojie died, all my bullshit tendencies had died with her. Life was seriouser than a mutha for me now. School was where it was at. I only had a year to go before I graduated and was eligible for the draft. So what else was I gonna do, and where else could I go? Muddah was living her life, and I didn't wanna fuck with that. She told me she was really getting tight with her man, that square from Washington Heights who she said really treated her right.

"Better than I treated you?" I wanted to know. I knew the

lame cat she was talking about. Ya-Yo. Some off-brand niggah with glasses and a big forehead. I didn't even wanna think about his weak ass pumping dick in my Muddah.

"Why you wanna compare shit, Dre?" She had screwed her face up like I was crazy. "I ain't never asked you about none of them girls who got all them babies by you. And you need to be paying some damn child support too. Those sistahs shouldn't have to struggle all by themselves to feed your seed, Andre. Them kids didn't ask to come here."

I acted like I was ignoring her, but I heard her. I was getting lawyer letters out the ass demanding child support. I just kept sending them back. Along with a copy of my college registration.

Even still, I knew Muddah was right. I needed to get my life right, just like she had done. She had her college degree. She had gotten her own shop. She was rolling. She didn't even have no kids to be worrying about, but she always made me feel like shit for not taking care of mine.

"Do good things for yourself, Dre," she had told me before I came back up to school. "Your mother is gone, but me and Mere'maw gone always be here for you. Believe that."

I had nodded. "Smoove is getting stationed in Italy, and Pimp is chillin' lovely. I'ma be cool, girl. Thanks. I luh you, Muddah."

She didn't tell me she loved me back, but I knew she did. I could see it all in her body movements and the way she looked at me.

So once again I fell back on my music and my balling skills. We tore shit up at the Final Four that year, and I landed front and center in mad sports papers, which was real cool since I was gonna be a senior soon and there wouldn't be too many more opportunities to prove myself. I started showing up early for every team practice, and when all those other cats jetted to hit the showers, I put in even more work on the court, eliminating my weaknesses, practicing drills and perfecting my outside shot.

And when I wasn't strengthening my game I wrote mad gangsta lyrics, and I dug up in them books too. I couldn't take a chance on going on academic probation and having Coach yank me off his starting roster. Plus, I had something to prove to that old white motherfucker. He was a good man and knew his shit, but in the back of his eyes I could see exactly how he saw me. Just another talented but ignorant black kid who couldn't shake his hood tendencies long enough to make something out of his life.

And that's basically where Sly had put me too. I was sitting in the caf eating a taco when he sat down across from me.

"You still here, huh?"

He was licking a vanilla ice cream cone and had a look in his eye that I didn't like.

"Where you from, man?" I said quietly.

He shrugged. "Why? Where I come from don't matter. Where my black ass ended up is what it's all about."

I chuckled and took a real big bite of my taco. I crunched that shit down in about three seconds. "You must be from some fuckin' suburb somewhere. Prolly from up here with all these white people." I shook my head and picked up another taco. "You sure ain't from the city, though. A city niggah would know better than to keep fuckin' with me."

Sly grilled me. He bit into that hard ice cream, chomped it fast, then stuck the whole cone in his mouth. "I'm from Chicago, niggah. And we know how to burn a niggah out there too. But I ain't in the Windy City now, and your ass ain't in Harlem. We sitting up in Syracuse, boy. One of us done been somewhere, and the other one is already a junior and still don't know where he wanna go."

I didn't wanna fight. I liked Sly cause he reminded me a lot of T.C. But he was wrong about me. "I know where I'm going, man. Straight to the NBA. I ain't *you*, niggah! Just cause you didn't make it don't throw shit on it for me."

"Andre," Sly stood up and wiped his hands on my napkin. Then he balled it up and tossed it in my plate. "I hope your next rap album blows up, man. You can make it in the music world cause you cold and got lyrical skills like that. But college? And the NBA?" He smirked. "Niggah, you get smashed with one more offense this year and you might as well come downstairs with me and grab a fuckin' broom. Because one more fuckup, and the only thing you gonna be good for around a gym is sweeping up."

I was tired of this drill. So many people seemed to think cause I'd lived the low life I was gonna crawl around blind and deaf forever. I promised myself I'd spend my last year in college working damn hard to prove them wrong.

Chapter 20

Carmiesha got a phone call from Mrs. Washington that made her blood freeze. She sounded nervous and shook up, and Carmiesha knew something was wrong right away.

"Baby, I hate to call you like this, but Bert is sick and I can't leave him here by himself."

"What's wrong, Ms. Jessie? Is something going on with Jahlil?"

The older lady made a noise, and Carmiesha could almost see her shuddering. "I'm so sick of that boy I don't know what to do. I just got a call from the center. Jahlil done hit some poor little girl with a chair and knocked out her tooth. Her mama and daddy is down there cussing and carrying on and threatening to call the police to come arrest him."

Carmiesha's heart banged five times straight. "Dammit! I can't believe that boy!"

Mrs. Washington sucked her teeth loudly. "Well, I can sure believe him. Look like every other day he doing something even more crazy. Last Thursday they kicked him outta school for a day for trying to get some girl to go in a mop closet and pull down her pants. Before that they said he took a bottle of something called Grey Goose to school and was drinking it with some younger boys. There just ain't no end to it, Carmiesha. The boy just can't get right, and with me getting old and Bert being so sick I just can't keep up with him all the time."

"I'll go down to the center, Ms. Jessie," Carmiesha said. "Don't worry. I'll see what's going on and bring Jahlil back home, but I'll probably be done beat his ass real good before we get there."

Carmiesha apologized to the client sitting in her chair and told her stylist Toya to finish the girl's hair. The sistah was getting a perm and cut, and was ready to clown until Carmiesha told her today's service would be free on the house.

She caught a bootleg taxi right outside the shop and was at the youth center in a matter of minutes. She stepped inside with her kick-ass face on, even though there was no way she'd be able to defend Jahlil if he had done what Ms. Washington said he did.

Carmiesha walked into the office and saw a little girl sitting on a chair who had been upset for so long that she was hiccup-crying. She looked about eleven, and had curly red box-braids hanging almost down to her butt. Carmiesha winced when she saw how the little girl's front tooth had been knocked straight out of her mouth, and even though her real cries had stopped long ago, the child still couldn't control herself.

She opened her mouth to say how sorry she was, but a heavy-weight woman jumped up in her face before she could speak. "This your son? Huh? Is this your crazy-ass motherfuckin' son?"

She was holding a bloody washcloth and had big splotches of

blood all over the front of her shirt from where she had held her bleeding child. She was also pointing a big fat finger at Jahlil, who was sitting on the other side of the counter looking guilty in the face.

"I didn't do nothing, Carmiesha!" he said, standing up and beefing as soon as he saw her. "She hit me first! I didn't do nothing to that goddamn girl!"

Carmiesha couldn't hold it in. "Sit your ass back down and shut the hell up! Don't tell me you didn't knock that baby's tooth out when she sitting there with blood all over her—"

Feeling dizzy, Carmiesha stopped in midsentence. She'd been so mad about what Jahlil had done till she didn't realize who he was with.

"What the *hell*?" she screamed on the man, her hands clenching into fists. If she thought she was hot when she walked in the door, her ass was burning up in flames right now. "What the fuck are *you* doing here? Get over here, Jahlil! Right goddamn now!"

She turned to the center director who hadn't had a chance to open his mouth. "I wanna know," Carmiesha said, spitting her words out like little bullets, "why this mothafucker is sitting over there with Jahlil. Ain't nobody gave him permission to be around this boy, and I want his ass outta here right now!"

The director said, "Excuse me, I didn't get your name. You are . . . ?"

Carmiesha rolled her eyes and pointed at Pimp, who just sat there grinning. "Don't worry about who the hell I am. Worry about who this street gangsta is you got up in here around all these damn kids!"

Even the little girl and her parents stopped trippin' and stared at Carmiesha. She knew she was making a big scene, but she didn't give a damn. This crazy motherfucker didn't have no business nowhere near Jahlil, and she was ready to kick his ass all around that office.

"Ma'am," the center director said. "This is Carl Williams, one of our volunteer youth counselors. He's been working with Jahlil for some time and was with your son during the incident. In fact, he was the only person who could get Jahlil to calm down at all."

"Youth counselor!?"

Pimp laughed out loud. "Yo, dis her son?"

The director gave her a questioning look. "Jahlil *is* your son, right?"

"No," she lied quickly. "He's my nephew. I'm Carmiesha Vernoy. I'm on Jahlil's emergency card, and I'm here to pick him up and take his little butt home!"

It took a while, but Carmiesha managed to talk the little girl's parents out of pressing charges on Jahlil. She made Jahlil apologize over and over and then promised to help pay for the child's dental care. She told the mother that she knew what Jahlil had done was wrong, and that she wasn't gonna let him get away with it.

"I can only imagine how your baby girl feels," Carmiesha told her. "And how you and her father feel too. If you need to press charges against Jahlil, then I understand. But his mother is elderly, and his father is really sick. I think the boy is going through some stuff right now, and he needs help more than he needs a juvenile record."

By the time they left the center Carmiesha was totally through. Not only had Jahlil busted that damn child in the mouth with that chair, that asshole Pimp had been right there when he did it and probably didn't try to stop it neither.

"I don't want this motherfucker around my nephew," she'd warned the center director before she left. "Y'all need to do some background checks before you let just any old body get in here around these kids. I know for a fact that that his crazy ass been locked up in jail a few times. He's a bad influence. Keep him away from Jahlil."

— — —

Three days after Jahlil busted the little girl in the mouth with the chair, Carmiesha came into her shop and found a white envelope on the floor. All the other envelopes she had found before had been just plain old blank envelopes, and after a few weeks of ignoring them they had just stopped appearing. But now they were back, and this one had something written on the front. It said DOUBLE.

"Bull*shit*," Carmiesha said out loud. She picked it up and ripped it in half, then tossed it in the garbage can and went on about her business. She didn't give a damn what Mr. Ward said about needing protection. She wasn't taking one penny of her hard-earned cash and giving it to no niggahs running the streets. They could believe that shit.

For the next four weeks straight she found an envelope with the word DOUBLE waiting on her when she opened up on Friday mornings. And every Friday morning she did the same damn thing. Ripped that shit up and threw it away.

But the next Friday morning when Carmiesha came in she was really through. There was another envelope waiting on her. But this time it said TRIPLE.

"That's it!" she screamed into the empty shop. It was still very early and she had a few hours before the shop would be open. She marched her ass over to the phone and dialed the number to the Eighty-third Precinct.

"This is Carmiesha Vernoy. I'm the owner of Locks of Love on 123rd and Frederick Douglas. I got a problem going on with some wannabe street gangstas and I need to file a complaint. . . ."

It wasn't more than ten minutes later when a fly sports car pulled up outside of her shop. Carmiesha was rearranging hair-care products in the display case when she saw two police officers in uniform get out. She couldn't believe they'd gotten there so fast and was glancing at her watch when one of them knocked on the glass door and motioned for her to open up.

"We got a call that you'd like to make a complaint?"

Carmiesha sighed. Both of the cops were brothahs, and one looked old enough to be her father. They wore no-nonsense looks on their faces, and she knew they wasn't gonna be happy about Pimp and his bullshit.

"Yeah. Every Friday morning when I open up my shop I have an empty envelope waiting for me."

"Waiting for you?"

Carmiesha nodded at the older cop. "Yeah. Somebody slides it under my door after I leave on Thursday night, and it's on the floor when I open up on Friday morning."

The cops looked at each other.

"And?"

"And, according to some of the other people on this block who have stores and businesses, I'm supposed to put five hundred dollars a week into that envelope and leave it in the back alley."

The younger cop took off his hat. "You sure about that?"

"Yep," Carmiesha nodded. "I'm positive. I ain't never put no money in it before, but all this month I've been getting an envelope that says *double* on it. Like somebody expects me to give them a thousand dollars a week!"

"The only reason I decided to call today was because this morning when I got here I had an envelope waiting that said *triple*. Now you know that's crazy!"

The older cop stared at some papers on his clipboard, then looked back at her. "Do you have any idea who could be leaving you these envelopes?"

Carmiesha nodded. "Yeah. His name is Carl Williams, but he goes by his street name, Pimp."

"Pimp, huh?" The younger cop said. He moved over to the door and locked it, then started pulling down the blinds.

"Hold up!" Carmiesha moved toward the door. "What the hell is he doing?" she asked the older cop, and for the first time she noticed that he wasn't wearing a name tag and there were no numbers on his shiny silver badge.

The other cop had the blinds down on both windows by now, and his partner looked at Carmiesha and shrugged. "Oh, today is collection day, sweetheart. He's just helping you get ready to pay what you owe."

He swung his clipboard so hard and fast that for a second

Carmiesha didn't know what had happened. She fell back against a display cabinet, and shampoos and gels hit the floor and broken glass and products went flying everywhere.

"W-w-wha—" She pressed her fingers to her temple and felt a stream of blood run down the side of her face.

She stared at her bloody fingers then looked up, and that's when he punched her in the face, cracking her nose.

"Aggh!" Carmiesha screamed and fell to her knees. The old cop kicked her square in the head with his hard black shoe, and Carmiesha found herself laid out on her back.

"No!" she screamed, rolling over and balling up in a knot.

The younger cop was on her now. He came over swinging his nightstick, whacking her on the legs, back, and even on her head.

"Please . . . ," Carmiesha begged through the blood that was dripping from her nose. She tried to crawl up under one of her styling chairs, and one of them grabbed her foot and dragged her back over.

"Help!" Carmiesha cried, screaming as loud as she could. "Somebody help!!"

She kicked her foot so hard her shoe came off in his hand, then grabbed at a bottle of designer spritz off the floor and threw it at him, shattering the glass.

"Stupid bitch!" one of them cursed. And then both of them were on her. They beat her with their sticks and stomped her with their feet. There was no way of dodging their blows. And no way of getting to a pair of her cutting scissors or even a curling iron. Carmiesha twisted and rolled all over the floor bleeding and in deep pain and leaving blood everywhere. At one point she found she'd rolled close to the back of the shop, and she managed to jump up and run through the agony as she tried to get near her office door.

They dragged her back out to the middle of the shop, then whipped out small pistols and started firing at her feet.

"Dance, bitch!" they laughed as she hopped and jumped, slipping and sliding all over the place. She had lost one of her shoes during the struggle, and now broken glass cut deeply into her foot. "Somebody told us to make sure your ass danced!"

Carmiesha was so scared she ran toward her office again, ready to bust through the door without even opening it. The younger cop snatched her by the back of her sweater, catching her bra and ripping it open, freeing her breasts. He kicked the door in and flung her into the small office where she fell and split her forehead on the edge of a file cabinet. Carmiesha screamed even louder as she hit the floor, gushing blood. Her shoulder felt like it went up in flames, and ledgers and sample products rained down on her, battering her some more.

"Next time," the older cop said, unzipping his pants and reaching inside for his dick, "you got a complaint about the collection procedures on this street"—he stood over Carmiesha stroking himself up. "You make sure you call the station again, okay?"

Carmiesha scooted backward as far as she could, and when her back was against the wall all she could do was close her eyes as he bent down next to her. She was moaning and shivering in pain and fear as the sweaty cop rubbed his hard dick all over her sweater, over her breasts, down by her pussy, and over the curves of her hips.

She was in shock, trembling and waiting for him to rip her

clothes off, but to her surprise he just kept fondling her, stroking her legs and nipples and rubbing the head of his dick everywhere he could.

Seconds later his body jerked, then he fell against her breathing hard. Carmiesha kept her eyes closed until she felt the cop rock back on his knees and stand up. She heard his slow footsteps fading as he walked around her desk and headed toward the door.

She laid there crying for what seemed like forever. She had no idea how much time had passed, and when she heard someone banging on her front door her eyes darted around as she looked for a weapon.

"Carmiesha!" she could hear a man's voice calling for her outside. "Carmiesha! It's Mr. Wade, baby! C'mon sweetie. Open the door!"

Carmiesha moaned and forced herself to sit up. There were smears of off-white cum all over her red sweater, and she felt like throwing up.

It took her a long time, but she managed to get through the demolished shop and to the door, mostly on her hands and knees. The moment she got it unlocked Mr. Wade pushed it open and she collapsed at his feet, her whole body hurting and shaking in fear.

"Goddamn those motherfuckers!" he cursed, gathering Carmiesha in his arms and pulling her back into the shop. "You shot, baby? Are you shot?"

Carmiesha couldn't answer. He locked the door behind him and grabbed a stack of towels, cutting on the water and wetting a few of them down in the sink.

He ran back over to Carmiesha and began wiping the blood

from her body. He cried softly right along with her as he cleaned cuts and bruises that would have broken a grown man down.

"You gone be okay," he told her after finding no bullet wounds. He grabbed another towel and wiped her off some more. "You gonna be ok—"

Suddenly Mr. Ward stopped and peered at Carmiesha's chest and stomach. When he realized what the sticky white substance clinging to her sweater was, he cursed out loud in disgust. "Them sick motherfuckers!" he hollered. "Them lousy no-good motherfuckers!!"

Mr. Ward never did open up his business that day. Neither did Carmiesha. He stayed with her throughout the morning, and took her home in a taxi after digging pieces of glass out her foot and making sure she felt strong enough to walk.

"It ain't right," he kept saying over and over, as he helped her get in the building past all the nosey eyes in the windows and on the stoop. "It just ain't right."

Carmiesha agreed with him, but she could only nod. Mere'maw damn near passed out when Carmiesha came dragging into the apartment leaning on Mr. Ward with her forehead cut open and her nose so swollen she had to breathe through her busted mouth.

"Call the ambulance!" Mere'maw screamed. "Call the police!"

Carmiesha stumbled inside and cried out. "NO! Don't . . . Mere'maw. Don't call nobody . . . please."

Word got around real quick on the streets, and it wasn't long before Carmiesha had a roomful of visitors. She'd been sleeping and moaning, feeling every single punch, kick, and blow in her dreams, and when she felt a cool hand on her forehead she opened her eyes ready to scream.

"It's me, Muddah," Kathy said, shaking her head at what had been done to Carmiesha's face. "Remy, Vikki, and Paula are here too. That ho Yasmere been running her mouth up and down the block saying you took a mad beatdown, so we came to see if you needed anything."

Carmiesha felt tears slipping from her eyes and all she could do was moan as the four girls sat on her bed and tried to soothe her. Paula ran down to the Spanish store and got a can of chicken soup, while Kathy and Remy washed the blood off of her that Mr. Ward wasn't able to get. They wrapped ice cubes in a washcloth and put it on her nose, checked the cuts on her foot, and Kathy used her finger to pat some first aid ointment all over her forehead and torn lip.

Mr. Ward had only been able to get her partway on the bed, and she winced and cried as they tried to slide her over and get her under the covers.

"Damn, Muddah," Vikki said. "Why you holding your arm like that? It looks broke like hell. What happened to you, girl? Who fucked you up like this?"

"Girls," Carmiesha whispered around her bubbled-up lip. "Some girls on the train."

"You know them bitches?"

Carmiesha managed to shake her head, although it hurt like hell just to do that.

"No . . . they was from Brooklyn."

Carmiesha stayed in bed for over a week. Kathy and the other baby mamas took turns bringing her and Mere'maw food. Remy took all the dirty clothes in the house down to the Laundromat and washed them, and one afternoon Carmiesha woke up and heard Vikki and Paula in the kitchen laughing over the sound of water running and dishes clanking in the sink.

Two weeks later she was back in her shop. Mr. Ward had hired somebody to get it cleaned up, and Carmiesha was grateful. Her left arm was in a sling and by the end of the day she had to use one of Mr. Ward's canes to walk, but she told everybody, including Ya-Yo, that she'd gotten jumped on the train by a bunch of girls from Brooklyn.

"Them Brooklyn bitches are crazy," Toya said, shaking her head. The shop was full, and she was working overtime trying to handle Carmiesha's clients and her own too.

Carmiesha just nodded and looked down at the floor.

That Friday evening after everybody left and the shop was closed down, Carmiesha took a long white envelope from her desk drawer and stuffed a bunch of bills in it. She licked the flap, and then put some tape on it just to be safe. With tears in her eyes, Carmiesha limped over to the counter and took a pen from a holder. She wrote a single word on the outside of the envelope.

It said TRIPLE.

■ ■ ■

But not everybody bought that bullshit lie Carmiesha told about getting jumped by some girls on the train. Ya-Yo had listened as Carmiesha described her so-called girl-beating and the more she talked, the more she could see Ya-Yo getting swole.

"It's over, baby," Carmiesha insisted after he grilled her with questions for the fifth or sixth time. He was asking her all kinds of shit like, "So what stop did you say they got on the train?"

and "How many of them was it, again? What did them girls look like? How you know they was from Brooklyn if you was riding the train to the Bronx? And how your foot get all cut up and shit, Carmiesha? What? You was on the train fighting with your shoes off or somethin?"

No matter what Carmiesha said he was still suspicious. She knew Ya-Yo was a good man, and he wasn't hard like a lot of these niggahs out on the avenue was. He could hold his own and he wasn't nobody's bitch, but his heart was too big to be gangsta, and he cared about old ladies and respected black women like they was queens.

Pimp and his street soldiers woulda ate Ya-Yo's ass up, Carmiesha knew, and she had to get stank with him to make him stop questioning her.

"Aiight, Meesha," he said after she cursed him out real good and told him to stop making her relive that shit over and over again. "You can tell that story all day long and it still won't come out sounding right. I don't know what the fuck happened to you, but my mind is working to figure that shit out. Everything in due time."

A few weeks passed and Carmiesha's bruises faded and her bones stopped aching so bad. She kept what had happened to her a secret, and even stopped going next door to get fish sandwiches from Mr. Ward. She was just too embarrassed about him seeing her all fucked up with that niggah's cum all over her clothes. Every time she thought about it she got enraged and scared at the same time. Cause if Pimp and his crew had that kinda pull where shiesty-ass cops was covering for him, then there was no need in telling nobody shit. She was born and raised right here in Harlem, and she knew the runnings like the back of her hand. If she opened her mouth again and started making noise there wouldn't be no more ass-kickings and dick-rubbings. The next time they'd find her ass raped and dead in somebody's alley or abandoned lot, and that would be the end of that.

So Carmiesha did the same thing every Friday evening after she closed the shop. She took the money she'd held back during the week and put it in the envelope she'd gotten that morning, then put that shit under the mat in the back alley.

But one night right before the shop closed there was a commotion on the street outside, and one of the female boosters who sold clothes on the corner came busting through the doors of the salon.

"It's about to be on and cracking out there! Them motherfuckers getting ready to get out the gats and spray this whole damn street up!"

Of course everybody ran over to the door instead of running away from it.

Carmiesha looked out the window and was surprised to see Ya-Yo's UPS truck double-parked outside. This was about the time he usually swung by every night to pick up her bank deposit, and she got worried when she realized he wasn't in the truck.

By now people were spilling out on the sidewalk up and down the street. When Carmiesha walked out and saw who was beefing, she damn near panicked. It was Ya-Yo. Up the street beefing and threatening one of them grimy niggahs who rolled with Pimp.

Carmiesha couldn't think of anything worse that could be happening.

But if she went out there and tried to calm Ya-Yo down, she'd punk him in front of Pimp's boy, and that would be catastrophic. If she stood there and watched and didn't do shit, her man might get hurt.

"Don't you worry, Carmiesha." Mr. Ward had come up behind her. "That young brother ain't doing nothing but being a man. He ain't stupid, and he ain't blind. He doing what any man worth his drawers would do if he thought somebody mighta fucked with his woman the way them boys fucked with you."

Carmiesha just stood there looking and feeling worried. "But I never told him nothing, Mr. Ward. I would never put him in no spot where he had to go up against them crazy niggahs over me."

Mr. Ward shook his head. "Some things a man just knows, Carmiesha. You didn't have to tell him the truth. That don't mean he couldn't still smell your lie. Let him do what his manhood is telling him to do. You his woman, and it's only right."

Chapter 21

Carmiesha had never hit Jahlil in his life, but right now she felt like kicking his little ass up and down the street.

"Boy," she told him as she tried to control herself. By now he was taller than her, so she had to look up at him to fuss. "You really need to think about what you just said about Ya-Yo. That man has never done nothing except try to be cool with you. For you to say he ain't nothing but a square bitch just ain't right, Jahlil."

Ya-Yo had swung by to take Jahlil to get a haircut, and instead of being grateful and rolling with him, Jahlil refused to go, saying he wasn't gone walk around Harlem with no square bitch cause playas might think he was a sherm too.

"Come on, Carmiesha! You even said yourself that Ya-Yo ain't down with the streets. The dude drives a big brown UPS truck! How gangsta is that?"

Carmiesha shook her head. "First of all, you need to realize and understand that UPS is a real good business. They pay their people decent salaries, and they don't have to sell no drugs or pimp no women to earn it. Second, I *did* say Ya-Yo wasn't down with the streets, but I meant that shit as a *compliment*! It ain't no diss on him for me to say that. I'm proud to see him rolling down the street in that big-ass truck! It tells me and the rest of the world that here comes a black man who ain't hustling back-wards! He's hustling on the legitimate tip. Working for his! Pay-ing his damn taxes and setting an example for knuckleheads like you, which is a whole lot more than your crazy-ass da—"

Carmiesha bit down but it was too late.

Jahlil looked at her with rage in his eyes. "More than my crazy-ass daddy? Is that what you was getting ready to say, Carmiesha? You was gone say that niggah Ya-Yo is doing more than my crazy-ass daddy is doing? I thought you said my father was in college. Don't that mean he's doing a lot too?"

The boy was smart, Carmiesha had always known that. He could pick up on things and figure shit out far faster than the average twelve-year-old.

"Jahlil," she said gently, "all I want you to do is pay more at-tention to brothahs who are living right, instead of studying hustlers on the streets so hard the way you do. Ya-Yo wanted to take you to get a haircut today, then take both of us out so we could show you a good time. I think you could learn something from a man like him. That's all I'm saying, aiight?"

He just shrugged. "Aiight, Carmiesha. But I'ma find my fa-ther one day, I don't care what you say. I don't see why he don't want nothing to do with me. I ain't never did shit to him."

"Don't curse," Carmiesha said. "And I never said he didn't want nothing to do with you, Jahlil. He's just real busy trying to get his career right. He's trying real hard to get in the NBA, and you know that."

"He got any other kids?"

The question surprised her and she didn't know how to answer it. "Uhm. I don't really know, little man. We don't stay up with each other like that no more, so I just don't know."

Jahlil set his face in a hard, bitter mask. "He better not be having no other kids," he said, "not if he left me back here and forgot about me."

Carmiesha was so unprepared for that kind of quiet fury that she didn't know what to say. So she kept her mouth closed and just walked away.

— — —

Carmiesha was spending the night with Ya-Yo at a nice hotel in Midtown. They could never really chill at his crib because his mother had a shitty attitude toward Carmiesha, and taking him into her bedroom with Mere'maw in the house was out. The only man who had ever been allowed to lay up back there was Andre, and Mere'maw didn't go for that shit too often neither.

Ya-Yo had taken her out for hot wings and fries, and then they walked around Midtown before deciding on a hotel. The room wasn't phat or anything, but it was clean and quiet and it was good to be out of Harlem for a while.

They'd just finished having sex, and Ya-Yo was spooning her in his muscular arms. The sex was kinda boring, but he had tried his best. Still, Carmiesha loved laying up with him. He was sweet and open about everything, and Carmiesha knew she could trust him because he was honest and had truth in his character.

Shit, Carmiesha thought to herself as Ya-Yo's hand moved up and down her bare leg. It was better to have half-assed sex with a guy who wasn't feening under the skirt of every bitch in Harlem than to get her back twisted out by some guy who pushed his dick up in everything that smelled like perfume.

She sighed and enjoyed the way her man's hands felt on her thigh. Ya-Yo was stroking her, but not in a sexual way. He was touching her because he liked to connect with her like that, and Carmiesha appreciated it.

"You feel okay?" he asked, turning Carmiesha toward him and putting small kisses all over her forehead. "You hungry? You want something to drink?"

Carmiesha shook her head and snuggled up against him again. Ya-Yo wasn't one of them hustlers who was scared to be real with his woman. He was always showing his concern for her. He bent over backwards to make sure she was straight and comfortable at all times. She kissed his chest. Ya-Yo had a nice body. He wasn't all that tall, and he wasn't buff like Dre or nothing, but he had hard muscles from lifting boxes in and outta his truck, and his hands were rough the way a working man's hands should be. Carmiesha really liked that about him.

"So, you been thinking on what we talked about? You know, about leaving Harlem?"

Carmiesha breathed deeply. Ya-Yo wanted to take her and their relationship somewhere scary. Lately he'd been pressing her to move outta Harlem with him. To just leave the city and build a new life somewhere else.

"I thought about it a little bit."

"So are you down, or what?"

"I still don't know, boo. It's easy for you to just sky up and bounce, Ya. The only one you have to think about is you. I got Mere'maw and Jahlil. And a business I'm trying to run too. It's just not that simple for me."

"It ain't gonna be simple for me either, baby. You think I wanna live with my moms for the rest of my life? I love her, but I'm willing to do whatever I gotta do to give me and you something better. You know? We gotta be down to do something different if we gonna have something better, baby. That's what's real."

Carmiesha pushed her naked breasts against his chest.

"But what about your job? And what about the shop? What I'm supposed to do? Just walk away from everything I've been building there?"

"I told you. I can put in for a transfer, Meesha. I can get a route in Jersey or Connecticut. My supervisor said he'll give me the hook-up. All I gotta do is ask."

"And what about the shop?"

Ya-Yo hugged her close to him, his hand grazing over the soft hump of her ass.

"We can get you another shop, baby. You can leave Toya in charge here, and we can open you up a second location. Before you know it your ass gone have a franchise going. You'll have Locks of Love shops popping up all over the place. Ain't nothing holding you down and keeping you limited to just one spot. Go for shop number two. Then number three. It's all possible, girl."

Carmiesha closed her eyes and pressed up against Ya-Yo, and she could almost believe him. She could almost see herself with a chain of beauty shops all over New York, New Jersey, Philly, and maybe even Baltimore and D.C.

But when she thought about Mere'maw and Jahlil, she just couldn't see where they fit in the picture, and she said that out loud.

"What about Mere'maw?"

"We'll take her with us. Whatever it takes to make you comfortable and happy, then that's what we'll do."

"Yeah, but I gotta think about my so— I mean, I gotta think about some other stuff too," Carmiesha tried to play it off, mad at herself for almost messing around and admitting that she had a son when she'd already told Ya-Yo that Jahlil was her dead brother's child.

"What else is there, Carmiesha? Shit is getting hotter in Harlem every day. How you think I felt seeing you all fucked up like that? Your face banged up. Bruises every fuckin' where I touched you. Even your feet cut the fuck up? This ain't no way to live, baby girl. Me and you together, we can do better than this."

Carmiesha knew he was right. All of what he was saying was true. Just remembering the fear she'd experienced as she watched him basing on one of Pimp's boys made her start trembling.

"How long you think it'll take before we can leave?"

"Depends on how hard we work to make it happen. They got some lots going on sale in North Jersey. I was down there a few weeks ago, and they already started building some nice three-bedroom houses for working people like us. I already know I can get a decent loan, but we can get more money up front if we do this together."

Carmiesha nodded. She was feeling him. She was getting excited about what could one day be her life. A house? Outside of Harlem? The thought of getting far away from Pimp and his posse brought her immediate relief.

"Okay, Ya. I'm down to do this, but I wanna make sure we discuss everything together. I mean, we gotta agree on every step we take and make all our decisions together."

Ya-Yo smoothed her hair and kissed her again.

"We gone do this shit together, Carmiesha. It ain't me, and it ain't you. It's us, baby. All about us."

Carmiesha closed her eyes, and when she felt his fingers probing between her legs she slid them open for him. Ya-Yo's dick wasn't tiny, but it wasn't big either. It throbbed against her belly, and she knew he was ready again. She couldn't lie as she laid there and faked a few moans. Ya-Yo had a decent tongue and didn't mind eating pussy, but as hard as he tried to please her and as much as he cared about her, he just didn't fuck her as wildly or as passionately as she was used to being fucked. Sexwise, Carmiesha was strung out on one particular dick, and no other man could measure up to that.

But that didn't stop her from riding into Jersey the next weekend with Ya-Yo and visiting the subdivision where they were gonna live. She squealed with excitement as they went into the model homes. They were small, but decorated like palaces compared to the way she'd been living all her life.

Carmiesha held Ya-Yo's hand as they signed the contract and put their first cash payment down on the lot they had chosen.

Ya-Yo was already talking about hooking up the future garage for himself, and giving her a free pass to do whatever she wanted with the rest of the house.

They drove back to Harlem riding high on that excitement, with their paperwork in Ya-Yo's briefcase and the date of their next payment circled on their calendars. And not once while they were laughing and dreaming about the life they were gonna have together did Carmiesha allow herself to think about Andre. She made it her business to keep that niggah outta her head. But that didn't mean he was outta her heart. It just didn't mean that at all.

— — —

Two weeks later the shop was packed. It was Friday, and Carmiesha was looking forward to the next morning, when she and Ya-Yo would be going back to Jersey to take some pictures of their lot. It was just a bunch of graded dirt right now with the property lines marked off, but they wanted to have a record of the whole process, from beginning to end, and planned several picture-taking trips down there over the next few months.

She had transferred her Saturday appointments over to four other stylists, and was just getting ready to sew in some weave tracks for one of her loudmouthed drama-queen clients who didn't trust nobody else's hands in her hair.

"This gone hurt like hell, girl," she told her. "But I gotta catch it tight if you want it to last awhile. Don't worry, though. Your butter's gone be *whipped*! You ready?"

The moment the girl nodded, the sound of shattering glass exploded outside. Once again, Carmiesha's staff and their clients jumped up and ran over, peeping out the door and peering out the windows.

"Oh, shit," Toya said, covering her mouth. "I think it's Ya-Yo, Muddah. In his UPS truck."

Carmiesha dropped the large spool of weave thread she was holding and rushed out the door. The streets were packed and traffic had stopped in both directions.

Ya-Yo musta had an accident, Carmiesha thought with fear rising in her gut. His truck must've careened out of control, because it had jumped the curb, run over a street vendor who'd been selling T-shirts, urban books, and mixtapes, and crashed into the Wong Chi's Chinese restaurant directly across the street.

"No," Carmiesha whispered, and before anyone could stop her she was dashing across the street. She ran so hard and fast her heels kicked up and slapped her ass. Surprise hit her when she saw two guys jump off the back of the big brown truck and run down the street and into an alley, but Carmiesha didn't even slow down. When she reached the truck she jumped in the open door on the passenger side, almost tripping and falling back down the steps as she tried to get to her man Ya-Yo.

"Oh, *baby*!" Carmiesha wailed, her face crumpling as she sank to her knees beside him. Ya-Yo was laying on the floor by his seat wearing his dark brown UPS uniform. The truck had crashed and he'd had an accident all right. But Ya-Yo damn sure hadn't been the one driving. All Carmiesha could do was scream. Scream at the top of her voice as she shook in rage at what they'd done to her man as he lay there with his feet bound with rope and his hands tied behind his back with duct tape.

Ya-Yo had been stabbed.

One time through each of his open eyes. But not before coming under fire from some gangsta niggah's gat, and catching a bad one right in the middle of his forehead.

Chapter 22

Carmiesha moved through the next few months in a haze of grief.

She had a business to run and bills to pay, so she couldn't afford to just lay in bed and cry all day. Ya-Yo had great benefits and insurance through UPS, but she wasn't entitled to a penny of it because they hadn't been married. Instead, his mother got everything, and she made it clear that Carmiesha didn't have no real ties to her son. She blamed Carmiesha for his death, and said that bullet that killed him had been fired in retaliation for Ya-Yo standing up and making noise over that ass-whipping them cops had put on her.

"My baby got blasted behind you and *your* bullshit!" she had screamed on Carmiesha during Ya-Yo's funeral. Carmiesha had just stood there crying in embarrassment as everybody stared at her like it was her fault. She had loved Ya-Yo, and had even made plans for a future with him, but Carmiesha wasn't even listed on Ya-Yo's obituary. Not even as a friend. His mother had pushed her to the end of the funeral line, and wouldn't even let her sit up front in the funeral parlor, or ride to the cemetery in the limo with Ya-Yo's family.

"I don't know nothing about no plans y'all had to buy no house," Ya-Yo's mother snapped a few weeks later when Carmiesha called and told her the next payment was due on their lot. "Ya-Yo never said nothing to me about moving way out to no Jersey with you or nobody else. My son wasn't hardly leaving Harlem. He had a good job here and was living rent-free with me. Why would he want to leave and go somewhere with you? You must be stupid if you think I'm falling for some gold-digging scam to get my dead child's money."

Carmiesha knew she was out of luck. The money she and Ya-Yo had put down on their dream house was gone. If she wanted to get Mere'maw out of that rat-trap building she'd have to find another way to do it on her own, but paying off that niggah Pimp was making all her dreams look like pipe dreams. She just couldn't afford to do every damn thing by herself.

At first she had a lot of nightmares after Ya-Yo's murder. In her dreams at night Ya-Yo would still be alive when she ran up in the truck. He'd be trying to talk and rolling his stabbed eyeballs around in his head, crying that he couldn't see her. Carmiesha would be panicking in her sleep. Begging people as they stared from the crowd to please call 911. Her own cell phone would be right in the pocket of her work smock, but either she wouldn't have any bars for service, or her nail tips would keep slipping off the buttons and she'd hit 811. Or 922. Or 992. Everything except 911, while Ya-Yo lay there moaning and dying right in front of her.

Carmiesha would wake up crying big, loud tears. Missing the way Ya-Yo smelled and the way he felt against her. She missed the way he made her feel when she was in his arms. Like there was no other girl in the world except her. Mere'maw would shuffle into the room and try to comfort her, but there was guilt mixed in with Carmiesha's grief as well.

She had loved her some Ya-Yo. She really did. But the truth was, Ya-Yo was just a second-best love. A good second best, but a second best nonetheless. A small shitty voice inside of her mocked her. The voice told her that if she'd loved Ya-Yo enough, they would have already been long gone from Harlem and he wouldn'ta been beaten and killed like no soft-ass sherm. That voice also blamed her for not taking Pimp out of the picture a long time ago. Carmiesha had never even tried to get him locked up for raping her. She'd taken one good ass-kicking from those cops, then got scared and buckled under the shakedown hustle he had going. Pimp had turned her brothers into lowlifes and gotten both of them killed. He was even fucking around with her son's head, but Carmiesha just didn't have enough gangsta in her to put a stop to it before the boy became twisted just like him.

Carmiesha had almost wanted to kill herself. Somehow, every damn thing she cared about, that crazy niggah found a way to fuck it up. He had a hold on every part of her life and there didn't seem to be a way to escape him unless she killed his ass dead.

After a while Carmiesha started plotting on that shit. She plotted to take his fuckin' ass out and leave the world a better place. She was living between rage and grief every day, and her thoughts were always filled with anger. She stayed focused on getting retaliation on Pimp for the way her life had turned out, and the way Ya-Yo's life had come to an end.

She thought about stealing Mere'maw's gat and shooting him right where he had Ya-Yo shot. In the middle of his ugly-ass forehead. Or maybe, inviting him up on the roof for a quick shot of hot pussy, then stabbing him over and over until there was no more blood left in his body. But she just couldn't. Not she couldn't kill him. She couldn't risk going to jail for it. Ms. Washington depended on her to help out with Jahlil, and Mere'maw depended on her for everything in her life. Killing Pimp might satisfy the anger in her soul, but going to jail would just damn the people in her life to even more misery.

To top things off, over the past several months the situation with Jahlil had gotten even worse. The boy was almost thirteen now, and he looked a lot older. He walked around wearing do-rags and hoodies and had real diamond earrings in both ears. When she asked him where he'd gotten them from all he would tell her was that his man had put him down.

Mrs. Washington had just about given up on him, and Carmiesha didn't blame her. Mr. Bert had died a few months after Ya-Yo's murder, and she was there with the boy all alone. Jahlil was tall and getting real muscular. He was smelling his ass and thought he could get loud when somebody told him to do something he didn't want to do. Twice Carmiesha had gone over to the house and fucked him up with a broomstick for basing on his mother.

"I can take him," she told Mrs. Washington over and over. "I'll take him home with me and put him in that school off of

St. Nick. I'll find a way to explain it to Mere'maw, but I just can't leave him here on you like this no more."

As usual, Mrs. Washington refused to let him go. "I know you gave birth to him, Carmiesha, but he's my boy. Me and Bert raised him up from day one, and whatever he is we had some hand in it. Maybe we spoiled him too much. Or maybe he shoulda been around more kids his age when he was little. I don't know what we did to make Jahlil act the way he do, but I love him and I'm just gone stick it out with him and pray he learns better."

Carmiesha had felt so damn guilty. The Washingtons hadn't done a damn thing wrong. That only thing wrong with Jahlil was them bad-ass genes he was born with. There was no longer any doubt that the child was just as crazy as his father, and even though she still loved him with a full heart, sometimes Carmiesha looked at Jahlil and just didn't like him.

And she sure didn't like the fact that he was still spending a lot of time with Pimp, neither. Carmiesha knew damn well Pimp knew whose son Jahlil really was. When he stood next to Carmiesha you could see a lot of Carmiesha in him. But when he stood next to Pimp you knew for damn sure this child had come outta his balls. She wasn't really worried about Pimp dropping no dimes about it to Thug, cause that would mean he'd have to admit he had fucked her when she was only thirteen, which was way before Dre had even gotten him any.

But Pimp was a crafty niggah. She wasn't sure what kinda poison he was pumping into Jahlil's head, but she knew everything about the boy had gotten much worse since he'd started hanging around him.

One time she'd ran up on them coming out of a McDonald's

by 125th Street in the middle of a school day, and screamed on Jahlil so bad a Jamaican lady threatened to call the cops on her.

"Bitch," Carmiesha said, pointing at the woman as Pimp stood there drinking a strawberry shake and laughing. "You better mind your fuckin' business or the cops gonna need to get over here for real."

She'd pulled Jahlil by his jacket and reached up to smack him upside the back of his head. "Bring your ass on! I'm taking you right up to that school!"

Carmiesha was pulling the boy down the street when Pimp hollered out.

"Hey, Jahlil! I forgot to tell you, man! I found out about that guy for you, and you was right. That niggah is foul, leaving you out like that and taking all them wit' him . . . I think a niggah oughtta get served. . . ."

"Keep moving!" Carmiesha snapped at Jahlil. "And don't even look at that fool!" She didn't know what the hell Pimp was talking about, but there was no doubt in her mind that if anybody needed to get served it was him, because as far as she was concerned he was the foulest piece of shit in Harlem.

⬛ ⬛ ⬛

Carmiesha couldn't keep living with the thoughts she had. She needed something else to focus her attention and energy on, so when Andre started calling sounding serious about his life and wanting to see her when he rolled down to Harlem, she agreed.

"Thug's outside!" one of the street runners would holler in the shop door when he rolled up in whatever whip he had rented for the weekend.

Carmiesha would keep right on doing whatever she was

doing. Even when all the other stylists and female customers were going dope-crazy over the notorious Thug-A-Licious, she played it chill and treated him like the Andre Williams who had been eating her pussy out since she was thirteen.

But secretly, Carmiesha looked forward to the weekends Dre came down from Syracuse. It was the only time she had something to smile about, something other than killing Pimp to completely occupy her mind. Dre had a way of making her forget all her problems and laugh like she didn't have a problem in the world. He was a joker, a silly-ass nut, and he kept her mood up, up, up, whenever they were together.

They hung out just like old times. Sometimes alone, and sometimes they got a few of his kids and took them out too. Dre had some bank, but it wasn't all that long.

"Just wait," he promised. "The NBA draft is coming, Muddah. That's when you and me both gone be set."

Muddah didn't care about no money. She was just glad to be with him, talking and laughing and acting like a carefree young woman her age was supposed to act.

And they weren't even fucking neither.

"Uh-uh," she told him one night as they were stretched out on her bed, grinding and humping through their clothes. "I don't know what kinda freaks you been slinging your dick in up there in that college, Dre."

He laughed and sat up. His dick was so hard the head was sticking outta his waistband and had a big clear drop of pre-cum glistening from the tip. "Muddah, why you always worrying about shit like that? Them girls are just booty calls. Hit and hauls. They don't mean nothing to me, baby. You do. It's always been about you."

"No, niggah. It's always been about *you*. When you gonna start thinking with the big head and not the little one?"

"I'm thinking with the big head now, Muddah. I'm thinking about you. About us. I wanna give you the world, girl. Hand that shit to you with a big red bow on top.

"Check this out, Muddah. This for you, girl.

Honor and respect never gets you no regrets . . . baby
And I'm learning from my own lust
Putting it in check is gonna take a couple steps . . . maybe
Gotta roll to the toll cause
Every project takes a little process to make it
Come together for the better girl
Honor and respect never get you no regrets . . . lady
And I'm learning from my own lust . . .

I ain't with the mind games/giving me migraines
You so special/I respect you/held me down when the
    time came
Damn it musta hurt/when I took you for granted/and ran
    your feelings in the dirt
Couldn't see what you was worth
Playing touch me, tease me/I cussed you/greasy
Didn't go my way then it was fuck you leave me
Always there when I needed a ride/ and though I/cheated
    and lied/how conceited was I?

But now I'm learning from my own lust/feeling you so much
Grown man/with mine that's far from the young crush
From day one ma it's gotta be real/talk to me yo/don't let
    the animosity build

I keep thinking bout how good you on top of me feels
so be cool stay in pocket and chill
Cause I'm all yours . . .

Honor and respect never gets you no regrets . . . lady
And I'm learning from my own lust
Putting it in check is gonna take a couple steps . . . maybe
Gotta roll to the toll cause
Every project/takes a little process to make it
Come together for the better girl
Honor and respect never get you no regrets . . . lady
And I'm learning from my own lust . . .

"I don't know, Dre. You can rap and all, but your ass just can't do right! You been a ho for so long it just comes natural to you now."

"Okay, I'm a ho, Muddah. I know that. But I luh you, girl. Gimme a chance to prove that shit to you. What I gotta do, ma? Huh? What I gotta do?"

Carmiesha had a slick little grin on her face. It had been almost eight months since Ya-Yo's death. Eight months with no dick. Not even a finger in her pussy to give her a quick orgasm.

She stood up and took off her jeans and panties, then smirked as Dre's eyes lit up like a Christmas tree. "Don't get happy, joker," she said laying back on the bed with her legs spread wide. "You still can't get in this pussy until I'm sure you ain't still out there gaming bitches." She gripped his cornrows in her fingers. "But you can bring that sweet tongue over here and give mama a few quick licks."

Chapter 23

Six months later . . .

I had made it through to my senior year of school and life was rolling for me. I had two banging singles climbing the charts so my recording career was hot and my stats were unshakable, and the media was on my dick like mad. And there were even more scouts than usual too. Coming out the ass. My game was so tight I was named the NCAA College Player of the Year for the second year in a row. I lost the Wooden Award that year to a fast kid from North Carolina, but I landed the Naismith, which was even better.

All kinds of talk about the NBA draft was in the air and not only was I almost eligible, I was ready. Coach predicted either L.A. or Houston would snatch me, but I was hoping it would be the Knicks. They had first pick, and I wanted to live in the city. Not in Harlem, but close by, with my peeps. After being upstate around all these white people for so long, I was ready to do the hood thang at least part-time.

I wanted to chill with Muddah a lot more. And my cousin

Pimp too. I'd had four long years to think about what had gone down that night at T.C.'s, and my guilt was just as strong as if it had been last night. I couldn't be sure about that niggah Rome, but Pimp wouldn'ta shot me that night. He knew it, and I knew it too. We was Dawgs-4-Lyfe. Him and Smoove was my only bit of family, and I missed them.

I'd been going down to Harlem a lot to see Muddah, and if she was busy at the shop or had something to do, then I'd go looking for Pimp and we'd drink a little and chill. There was something real different about Pimp, but I couldn't figure out what the fuck it was. Word on the street said he was handling niggahs. Had 'em working for him like sons, collecting rent on businesses and taking in bank from bitches and product. I tried to stay clear of all that. I was too close to reaching my goals to get caught up in the street scene now.

The last few weeks before the draft went by in a blur. I was all about positioning myself and I had signed on with the same agent who hooked up that sweet deal for LeBron. I'd asked Muddah to be by my side so she could help me represent, and she was sitting in Madison Square Garden with me on the night of the draft. We was holding hands like we was kids again, excited like hell at what the next hour or so would bring.

Four of my kids were there too. They were with Mere'maw, who was sitting up higher in the stands where Noojie and Miss Lady shoulda been. Muddah had insisted my kids come with us. She said even though I didn't have no relationship with them they had a right to witness this, so they was chillin' in the stands with the kids of the other players, coaches, and draft hopefuls.

"I can feel it coming for you, Dre," Muddah said. I grinned

and checked her out again. She was the finest thang in the whole damn Garden. My single "Lick and Move" had made it to number four on the Top Ten charts, and I had gotten a nice check from Ruthless Rap. I cashed that shit and took Muddah shopping in Midtown and told her to get any damn thing she wanted. And we was wearing that check too. From my three-thousand-dollar shoes to Muddah's seven thousand-dollar dress. My girl was all the way fly. I'd surprised her with a diamond necklace and earrings that matched, and sitting there next to her made me wanna hurry up and get in the NBA so I could make millions and keep her laced in fine shit for the rest of her life.

I slid my hand down her back to her ass and whispered, "I can feel something coming for you too, baby."

She elbowed me and laughed. "Boy, you need to stop! I just gave you some last night. And hush. Some old white guy is going up to the microphone. . . ."

It was the commissioner. He gave a short welcome speech and all that bullshit, but I wasn't trying to hear nothing except what I came there for. I grinned and laughed when everybody else did, but just like the other college hopefuls and the one or two trying to get picked up straight outta high school, all I could think about was who was gonna make those picks.

The commissioner was finally finished bullshitting. "The lottery was conducted and the New York Knicks," he said loudly, "have the number-one draft pick. The clock is now running."

All eyes was on Coach Larry Brown as he leaned over to say something to his general manager. I knew they already knew who they wanted, and I hoped they wasn't planning to sit up there chitchatting all day. A few minutes later Larry sent a runner up to the mic, and the commissioner accepted a piece of paper and looked at it and smiled. "The New York Knicks have selected . . . ANDRE WILLIAMS as their number-one draft pick!"

The Garden exploded. Niggahs was hugging me and jumping up and down congratulating me like crazy.

"You did it, Dre!" Muddah screamed. "You did it, baby!"

I swooped her up in the air and kissed her, grinning like crazy. Then I waved for Mere'maw to send Lil' Man, T-Roy, Shantay, and Duqueesa down, and headed outta the stands with my kids, dapping fists until we got down to the floor.

Cameras flashed from every angle as they snapped mad photos of me. I took one official photo with just me and the commissioner, and then after he handed me my Knicks cap I stepped over and took some with Larry Brown and the general manager, who handed me my official team jersey.

I held that jersey up in the air and it was the best thing my hands had ever touched.

"Thank you," I said over the noise. Lil' Man and them stood next to me acting shy for the cameras as I looked up in the stands trying to spot Muddah. And even though I couldn't see her little ass I knew she was smiling just like me. "Thank you. Thank you! I wanna say thanks to Coach Brown and the Knicks management team for seeing star quality in me and giving me this chance. New York is my home and I'm gonna wear this jersey with power and pride, cause home is definitely where my heart is. I also wanna send up some special props to T.C., who pushed me toward my dreams and made sure the word *failure* wasn't part of my vocabulary. And last but definitely not least . . . thanks to Miss Lady who loved me better than I loved her, and to my moms, Noojie, who left us too soon to see how bright her baby boy could really shine. I luh you, Miss Lady! I luh you, Ma!"

Chapter 24

A few months after the draft I was hanging out at the House of Homicide in Harlem. Hurricane Jackson had the recording industry on lock in these parts. He'd sent me some props through Pimp for getting picked in the draft, and said he wanted to holla at me about a sweet deal he had to offer with his label, Homicide Hitz.

Like everybody else, Hurricane knew Ruthless Rap was where I was holding, but he didn't give a fuck.

"Fuck them punk motherfuckers," he told me. "I'ma buy you outta that weak-ass contract so we can get you right and take your shit to the next level."

I was ready for that too. I liked the numbers Hurricane was talking and we shook hands on that shit. He knew I was worth every penny of what he was offering me too. I wasn't nothing like them other fake-ass NBA rappers. Shaq, Iverson, Roy Jones, and even Carmelo. Cutting weak albums and crying and shit cause they got banned from wearing they bling. I had actually lived the life I rapped about. Fought, stole, hustled, and came up on those grimy-ass streets, and that's what made my lyrics so powerful and high-post.

The House of Homicide was live, and the music was off the hook. The last time I was up in here I had watched some real fine shawty with red hair and blue eyes do her thang in the pit. Her name was Candy and the girl had hot vibes and mad style. She had a voice on her too, and a body that was phatter than Beyoncé's. Her girl group Scandalous! had come up fast and lovely, and now Candy had a solo thang going that was blowing up too. I had gotten a little disappointed when Hurricane stepped up and claimed her that night cause the jawn was fine as hell and if my man hadn't been blocking I woulda got me some of that for real.

But tonight was another night, and after dropping a few bills shooting C-low in the gambling room, I headed to the VIP lounge with my ex-roomate Dave tagging along to chill with me.

Dave was a deep niggah. I'd just found out that he was one of them closet spitters. All this time he was fronting like a sherm, when his head was deep in the rap game. He had gotten accepted into grad school to study pre-med, and since he was on break he came to see me at the crib and showed me a little bit of what he had. He was nice as hell. I agreed to take him down to Harlem and introduce him to Hurricane and see could he get put on.

My face had been all on TV and in the papers because of the draft, and I was getting noticed left and right with niggahs dapping me out with big props. It wasn't long before I had jawns trying to climb on my lap and aks begging me to spit. I knew Hurricane would appreciate me blowin' it up a little bit for him, so I grabbed a mic and jumped in the pit and started freestyling like a motherfucker.

We get it in/my team pack the club out

Straight to the bar/no crys, yak the cup out

Niggas talk slick/we pull straps and bug out

Step on the kicks/we might black

THE FUCK OUT!

I got the haze/a whole batch to puff out

goons in the back/waitin' for cats to stunt out

Ladies in the dugout/big breasts and butt out

No names needed, that takes the fun out!

Do it like I'm doing it/when I'm doing it big,

Pluck it then I duck it/and boot it outta the crib

Niggah if it's nothing/you niggahs know what it is

You "Thuggin" and you love it?

Then come and roll with the kid!

Let's move!

I'm trying to pop-off with Mami/hit the floor show her how

    we gone pop-off the party.

Let's move!

I'm tryna blow sticky in the back/shawty dancing in the

    front/bouncing with me to the track.

Let's move!

I'm tryna get tips on the liq/sit and watch baby girl strip to

    my hits.

Let's move!

We can blow a whole ounce in this bitch/just make sure my

    squad gets pronounced in this bitch!

Them haters ain't nice and I can smell 'em from here/so tell

    'em I'm here

The niggah wit' the vest on under his gear/Thug of the
    Year/Keep 'em all runnin' in fear

If you ain't down with Homicide get yo' ass outta here/
    so cheer!

The name is Thug-A-Licious/yeah I'm young and
    vicious/when it comes to the Hitz I intend to be the
    biggest

Lemme hear it! So when I say Thugga . . . y'all say *Licious*!

Thugga-*LICIOUS*!

Thugga-*LICIOUS*!

Thugga-*LICOUS*!

I left the pit while they was screaming for more and went
down to the video room to watch a triple X flick, but ten minutes into it Dave started complaining about all the cigarette
smoke fuckin' with his allergies, so we left and bounced over to
a rib joint down the block to get us some grub.

We was in the restaurant working over some barbecue when
a commotion started outside.

"Man, go see what the fuck is happening out there," I told
Dave, digging into my ribs and gulping down some potato salad
with them. The food was good and greasy and I didn't wanna
leave my plate. "Niggahs can't just party and bone a few chicks.
They gotta test each other's manhood up in these parts."

Dave walked outside for a minute, then came running back in.

"Yo, man. Something happened down the street at your boy's
joint. Mad people is tryna get outta that place. They're pressed
up against the exit doors screaming and fighting, but can't nobody get out. People are trying to help 'em, but there's a whole
lotta niggahs up in there and the doors won't open."

I ran outside and down the block, and all I could do was stand outside of the House of Homicide with my mouth open just like everybody else. Just minutes earlier I had been spittin' in the pit and clowning with these peeps, and now they was smashed up against the glass doors like big bugs. There was no way to get 'em out, neither. The doors swung in, not out, and with so many bodies jammed up against the glass, opening them was outta the question.

I watched for as long as I could take it. People inside was piled up on top of each other, banging on the glass and begging for help but everybody on the street was helpless, just like me. I saw about twenty people tryin' to get through to 911 on their cell phones. My chest started hurting real bad, and I was sweating like crazy. Some of my boys was up in there. Cats I had made music with, had chased pussy with, had run the streets of Harlem with my whole life.

"C'mon, Thug," Dave told me. He turned me around and pushed me down the block toward the whip we'd rented. "We gotta slide, man. The ambulance gone be here in a second, and the po-po and the paparazzi too. You don't need your name on none of this, man. Plus, your boy's shit is a wrap. Let's bounce."

— — —

The stampede at the House of Homicide really fucked up my head. So many people had died up in that joint that it was just crazy. And if Dave hadn't been one of them sherms with stupid allergies, both of us woulda been caught in that mob and prolly dead too.

It came out later on the news that Hurricane had been shot and killed in the middle of all the madness, and while my heart went out for my boy and all, I was glad I hadn't signed shit and fucked up on my Ruthless contract like that.

For a minute I stayed away from real crowded places like Big Ben's and even the new Ruthless spot, but I hung out in a few smaller Harlem joints when I wasn't running and lifting weights and getting ready for training camp.

I was chilling with Pimp more too. Right after graduation I had come back to Manhattan and leased a phat crib over on the Upper West Side. It was bigger than every apartment on my old floor put together.

"Yo, son," I told him one night when we was getting ready to go spit at a party. "I got a slick-ass agent, man. My contract is phat, so we gone be paid."

Pimp laughed. "We? Man, you hustled for that shit. It ain't a "we" thang, Thug. Now if you wanna tear a niggah off, you can do that. But you don't owe me shit."

"Whatever, man. You always told me to put you and Smoove down when I finally got paid, man. I'm just trying to do that. I got you on all my paperwork too. You know, my insurance and shit, since Smoove is in Iraq and Noojie is dead, you my next of kin."

I could tell Pimp was feeling that news by the look in his eyes. That niggah had put his shit on the line for me on the streets, and he'd doubted my loyalty a few times too. It felt good to be the one bringing something to the table for once.

But I wanted to hook my girl up lovely too. Living the baller life didn't mean shit if I was living it all by myself.

"You can move into my place uptown," I told Muddah one night right after I signed my lease and got the keys to my nest. I'd gotten her so horny she let me get some pussy on the kitchen floor without wearing a glove, and my naked dick had felt like cream moving up inside her. We had been kickin it on the regular for almost my whole senior year, and it was just like back in the day between us. Nah, things were even better than that cause now a hustler was paid and could give her anything she wanted. "Bring Mere'maw too if you want, cause I got plenty of room."

"Thanks, Dre. But I can't. I have the shop and all . . . you know. I just can't."

I wondered if she was still hurting behind Ya-Yo getting smoked, and even though that niggah was dead and gone their past thang still made me jealous.

"Nah, Muddah. I *don't* know. What's stopping you? They got trains that run downtown every day, all day. So don't use the shop as no excuse. Besides. Ain't you ready to get Mere'maw outta that nasty-ass building? Y'all been there forever, girl. I didn't work my ass off to get where I'm at not to get my peeps out too. I might not can take care of Noojie, but I can damn sure look out for you."

She shook her head. "Dre, please. I know me and you are tight. But trust me. Us living together would never work out."

I kept pushing her. I'd done all kinds of cold-blooded dirty shit to get my life where it was today. Muddah knew how hard I had struggled and how the streets had almost kept me in the gutter.

"Why the fuck not, Miss Carmeshia? Why not?"

She sighed and fidgeted with her sweaty hair.

"Cause, Dre. I'm scared of your ass. I can't believe I let you dig in me raw just now. You be fuckin' with too many females. Ain't no telling what your ass got."

I hit her with it straight. "I got herpes, Muddah. Yeah. I picked that shit up from a jawn in college. But"—I said real quick before she could twist her face up—"that's *all* I got. I had my team physical and everything else came out cool. I'm HIV-negative, my prostrate is good, my asshole is tight and I ain't got no little red bumps on my dick." I looked at her hard. "I'm straight, Muddah. My shit is real straight. I'll even bring you a copy of my HIV results."

She shook her head again. "Still. You got all them kids. . . ."

"Man . . . ," I whined. "And you love them damn kids! You with 'em ten times more than I am. How long you gone hold that shit against me anyway?"

"How long you gone keep getting other bitches knocked up? You know, God has been good to you, Andre. But you keep fuckin' out like you doing. Your ass could get straight cursed."

"No more. I promise. No more, baby. I ain't fuckin' no other women except you. And no more kids either. Unless they're yours and mine."

"How many you got now anyway? More than the six I know about, right? How many? Seven? Eight?"

Shit.

"Nine," I said truthfully. "I've got nine kids, Muddah. I know that's a whole lot, and I'm sorry."

She looked sick. "Damn. Nine fuckin' kids. And if you ain't doing shit for the six you got here, you probably ain't doing shit for the rest of them, right?"

"I haven't done much," I admitted. "But I'm about to do more now. I swear to God. Now that I'm on, I can grind for mine."

"I heard that shit before, Andre. I heard it right outta your mouth. How old are all these damn kids? I ain't talking about Little Precious, Shantay, Duqueesah, Mariah, or the twins. How old are the three you got that I didn't know about?"

"One is dead," I said. "And I think Malik and Dante are both two, maybe almost three."

Muddah made a nasty sound in her throat. "You *think*. What was it? A boy or a girl?"

"Who?"

She narrowed her eyes. "The baby who died, Andre! How did it die and was it a boy or a girl?"

I just went on and told her everything about that crazy-ass Passion. I knew she wouldn't quit dogging me until I did.

That psycho jawn had snuck a pistol into the gym while we was practicing and started shooting shit up like she was some kinda hot female action hero. Niggahs had hit the floor, screaming like bitches and crying for they mamas. A freshman sitting on the bench had gotten popped in the arm before a group of cats tackled Passion and wrestled the gun from that tiger. Nobody except the freshman had ended up getting hurt, but everybody was mad at my ass cause they'd come close to taking a few bullets that had my name on them.

"That's so fucked up, Dre. Somebody coulda been killed. You think maybe losing the baby made her go crazy like that?"

Hell no. Passion was a crazy freak way before she ever met me or had that baby. "Ain't no telling," I said. "I guess it's possible, though."

Muddah got real quiet. She had a big thing for babies, especially mine, and I could only wonder about that shit.

"Get right with your kids first, Dre," she said finally. "Then come talk some shit to me. When you can tell me how old your babies are, when you know their first, middle, and last names and when they was born, then maybe me and you can talk about having something really deep. And I need to see more than one HIV test, Dre. I wanna see one every month, just to be sure. So for now your ass is going back to fuckin' into a glove, and I'ma keep right on resting on St. Nick with Mere'maw."

Chapter 25

The team flew to South Carolina for training camp and that's when I knew I was really in the NBA. That number-one draft pick title didn't mean shit down there. I spent nine days at the College of Charleston catering to the vets. Running around getting towels. Cleaning the locker room, fetching Gatorade, and keeping enough basketballs on the floor.

Some of the rookies had a lot of pride and was pressed out about the gopher treatment, but not me. I thought all that shit was fun. I got to learn from vets like Anfernee Hardaway and Allan Houston and I listened to everything they had to say cause I was planning on blowing up and being around the league for a long time.

We trained hard at John Kresse Arena and by the time we kicked off the pre-season every man on the team was ready to do the damn thang. We traveled to Dallas, Chicago, San Antonio, Milwaukee, Miami, and everywhere we went I shined like a star, putting up impressive numbers that was better than most rookies could dream of.

Coach Brown knew what he had in me. I was still a thug, but I was also his LeBron James and Carmelo Anthony and Allen Iverson wrapped up in one, and the fans loved seeing me clown and put on a show. They gave up the noise and showed me crazy love, and I got high off that shit every time I stepped on the court and illustrated my skills. I'd spent my whole life waiting for this and now that I had it I couldn't get enough of it.

And a niggah was paid real long too. The minute I signed on with the Knicks, companies was blowing up my agent's Black-Berry. I got offers from all kinds of places, and ended up signing on with Nike, Sprite, and Taco Bell. I was lovin' that shit. Me and some of the other players had just spent five days at a baller party on a beach in Anguilla. We'd stayed at Cape Juluca drinking 10 Cane Rum and Moët, boning groupies, and partying to cuts by hot artists like Reem Raw and Ludacris.

No matter what city I found myself in, I worked on Muddah long-distance. I sent her and Mere'maw expensive gifts and jewelry, and wired her money out the ass to spend on whatever she wanted. But as bad as I wanted to be with Muddah, I still partied and got as much ass as I could. I was mad cause Muddah wouldn't give me no raw pussy or make me no promises. She wouldn't even say she loved me, so I did what I felt I had to do. Plus, the groupies stayed on my dick on the regular, giving up that trim and loving what I gave them back. I'd been used to a lot of jawns following me around from when I first got out there on the rap scene. They were usually chickenhead skanks attracted to the gangsta culture who would lick and suck and fuck any and everything you wanted them to. Four and five times, if you told them to.

But the groupies who followed professional athletic teams

from city to city came across a little different. Oh, they were still the biggest hoes on the planet, but these was some gold diggers with a master plan. They looked good, had tight bodies and perfect asses. They dressed right, smiled, and talked like they had some common sense and a little education. And a whole lot of them did. But get one of them bitches behind closed doors and see what happened. She wouldn't fuck both you and your friend at the same time cause that would be too hoochie. Besides, she wasn't in it for the thrill of it, she was in it to get paid. She had to make a niggah think there was a gold mine up in her pussy, and if she could get that thang locked on you she'd have you moving her into your crib and putting a ring on her finger in no time flat.

We were having a hot season and I was the man of the hour. Industry heads were amazed by my versatile skills and calling me the first professional basketball player who could actually spit. They interviewed me for the cover of *Slam* magazine and between my recent number one single, "Just the Head, Please," blowing up, and the magic I was working on the court, the name Thug-A-Licious was coming out of everybody's mouth. I dominated all the hip-hop rags and made the rounds on the talk shows, and my agent was even working on a film deal with New Line Cinema to make a movie about my life.

The regular season just flowed for us, and nobody was surprised when we ended up in the Eastern Conference Championship. We smoked that shit like a big fat blunt, and the next thing I knew we were suiting up for the NBA Championship against the L.A. Lakers.

We played the first three games in L.A. and left California leading the series three to none. I was anxious to get back to

New York. I just knew we was gonna wax L.A.'s ass even harder in front of a home crowd in the Garden, and I couldn't wait to be back in Harlem and be with my girl Muddah too.

I was gonna chill with Pimp for a minute too. I'd gotten him a couple of tickets to the next game, and he said he was gonna bring a few of the young boys he mentored with him so they could see an example of what a street thug from Harlem could become.

As soon as we hit New York I took a limo to my crib. Yeah, it was phat as hell with a doorman and all kinds of finery, but now I was thinking about buying a house somewhere in New Jersey. A crib with a lot of bedrooms and a big backyard. A few weeks earlier I had surprised Muddah's little ass. I'd sat down at my desk and made seven phone calls to seven women. That fuckin' Rasheena started cursing as soon as she heard my voice, and most of the other ones just listened like I was full of shit as I ran down my plan. But all of them gave me the information I needed. And by the time I had finished with the last call I had a full sheet of paper in front of me.

For the first time since they were born, I knew the first, middle, and last names of every last one of my kids. Their names, their birthdates, and how much it cost their mothers to take care of them every week. I e-mailed all of that info to my accountant and told him to set up something so I could start doing right by them with the dollars.

That same day I went over on St. Nick and asked Mere'maw if I could marry Lil' Muddah. By the time I finished slipping that shine on my baby's finger and got up off my knees, both her and her grandmother was crying.

L.A. had been real high-energy, so Coach had given us a day

off before we had to report back for game prep and a short team practice. I unpacked my suitcase and ordered some food from a restaurant downstairs, then took a shower and checked the messages that were waiting for me. Smoove had tried to hit me and left me a message, and so had this chick I used to bone when I was up at Syracuse.

I had something else waiting for me too. An invitation to the G-Spot. Sent by Granite McKay. That niggah G was a Knicks fanatic, and a lot of hot ballers hung out up in his joint. G had reached out to send me some props on my game, and told me to swing by the Spot and check him out if I was up for it. The way his message came across made me wonder if that niggah thought I was some kinda punk. Like maybe I had gotten soft or something cause I was ballin' on a professional level now.

I decided I was gone run up in there for a minute since I was home. G was known for throwin' some lavish parties and showcasing some of the finest strippers to ever slide down a pole. Besides. I wasn't gone let that niggah sit around thinking I was still shook behind that money problem with Smoove.

I watched some television and ate my food. I listened to some music too. My boy Reem Raw had sent me some mixtapes from a street rapper named Beez holding it down in Philly, and I checked it out for a little while then grabbed my remote and turned everything off.

My life was good and I was finally ready and able to walk it the right way. My music was hot, my hoopin' was tight, Lil' Muddah was fine as hell and was ready to become my wife. What more could a niggah want? Some sleep, goddamnit. Some sleep! I slid my tired ass in my big phat bed and got me some winks.

Chapter 26

I caught up with Smoove on the phone later that afternoon and told him to come check me out at the crib. He had just finished serving seven months in Iraq and was about to get sent to Korea. The Marines had put him on leave for a few days first though, and he wanted to see me before he flew out.

"You done good, Thug," Smoove told me, looking around my nest. I got us both a beer while he turned on some music. We were kicked back in my living room chilling, and I didn't realize how much I had missed him.

I nodded. "Your shit is tight too, man. Look at ya. Close shave and a motherfuckin' Caesar! Man, what happened to the braids! I thought we was gone play these babies forever!"

Smoove laughed. "It's the Marine Corps, yo. All that individual stylistic shit goes right out the door. I like it though, man. It can be tough, and Iraq wasn't a whole lotta fun. But the corps helped me climb outta the hole just like college and balling helped you."

"Yep," I said chugging from my forty. "None of us planned to stay broke in that pissy building on St. Nick forever, man. We got ours, man. Now it's time for Pimp to come up."

Smoove shook his head real slow. "I don't know, Thug. That niggah got problems. It's like he still living in that old world where we fourteen and fifteen years old, running around gambling and stealing and raising all kinds of hell. I got away from all that shit and I ain't never regretted it. Noojie was the one who encouraged me to check out the service and hope my criminal record wouldn't keep me out, man. I took her advice and it changed my whole life. I mean, I ain't living in no grand-ass penthouse like you or nothing, but for a little niggah I do aiight."

"Hell yeah," I agreed. "Ain't no way I would wanna still be running them streets from Riverside to the FDR chasing no pussy *or* no papers. I still hang out in Harlem now and then when I can, but not on the regular. Matter fact, guess who I had a message from when I got home today?"

"Who?"

"That niggah, Granite. G McKay."

Smoove put his brew down and looked at me hard. "What that motherfucker want wit' you, Thug?"

I shrugged. "Prolly nothing. You know how his showboating ass is. He see my name up in the papers, hears my sounds rotating on the radio. He want playas like me to be seen lounging up in his Spot. It yeasts up his image. I'ma roll up over there later on tonight, though, just so he don't think a niggah got soft."

Smoove got real quiet for a minute.

"Check this out, Thug. I know what it cost you to help me out that night, but I never really thanked you for what you did. I got sloppy and let Rico and his boys get a drop on G's package." He frowned. "T.C., Miss Lady . . . they got shitted on. Everybody involved got caught up in G's flow just cause my young ass made a bad move."

I shrugged. "It's spilt beer, man. Plus, we Dawgs-4-Lyfe, right? We lived by that shit every day."

"Nah, man." Smoove shook his head real hard. "Nah. See, that's the kinda shit that got us all fucked up from the beginning, man. We gotta let that shit go, baby. You done a whole lotta shit for me, and I've done some shit for you too. Pimp did a lot for both of us. But most of it ain't been to the good, Thug. And you gotta know that by now."

I took a good look at Smoove, and what I saw in his eyes shook me. "Look, man," I said slowly. "What me and Pimp did that night at T.C.'s was the only thing we could think to do at the time. It was wrong, and I regret what it cost all of us, especially the people who practically raised me. But shit was critical. We knew G had you and what woulda happened if he didn't get his package back. And neither one of us coulda lived with that. So it's good, Smoove. We all living with our decisions and our demons, man. It's cool."

Smoove shook his head again. "It ain't always what you do, bruh. It's why you do it."

"What you mean?"

"When Noojie died I got a call from the Red Cross, ya know? Muddah had them contact me and I came home the minute I heard."

I nodded. I was still messed up over not being there.

"I stayed with Pimp over on 114th Street while we waited for you to get here from upstate, but things seemed like they was different between us, man. For the first time in my life Pimp wasn't the bad-ass big brother I looked up to no more because so much about both of us had changed."

I set my forty down on the floor and just listened. There was a shitload of hurt on my cousin's face and I wanted to know why.

"The second night I was there Pimp woke me up real early in the morning. The sun wasn't even up yet. We'd smoked some nice sticky that night and fucked with some Erk and Jerk too, so my head was still cloudy when Pimp came in the room and said get up. He said he needed help carrying something downstairs to this car he had parked in the alley."

"Yeah?"

"Well, I helped him, man. He had rolled something heavy up in blankets, and we carried it down the back stairs and through the alley. Nobody was on the streets that early, so we ran over to a raggedy white station wagon that was parked on the curb and put it in the trunk."

Smoove's jaw was jumping and it sounded like his voice was about to crack.

"What was it, man?"

"It was a girl, Thug. A fuckin' one-toofed little girl. She had real long hair, and that shit was red too. She wasn't much older than Precious was when them niggahs shot her down in the streets. She could have been ten. Maybe eleven. But I can still see her, ak. We tossed her in that trunk and the blanket fell open. She was young and naked. There was some red fuzz on her skinny little pussy and her titties was just starting to grow."

Smoove closed his eyes, and wiped his hand down his face.

"Pimp had fucked that little girl, man. Fucked her real bad. Blood was all dried up around her legs and pussy. She'd been stabbed too. In her chest. Her stomach. That sick motherfucker had even stabbed that little girl in both of her fuckin eyes!"

I pictured Miss Lady and clenched my stomach tight.

"So ya'll just left her there?"

"Nah." Smoove shook his head. "I rode with Pimp down by the East River. He poured gasoline on the car and set that shit on fire, man. With that little girl's body right in the trunk. I swear, bruh. It reminded me of that time me and him fucked that young chick on the roof, and she ended up dead on the ground. But this girl was even younger, bruh. She wasn't no bigger than Precious. Hardly much bigger than that at all."

I couldn't look nowhere but down at the floor.

"The thing is, man, I woulda never got down on no shit like that if it wasn't for Pimp. If any other niggah in the world hadda asked me to do some foul shit like stick some little girl's body in a trunk, I'da killed *him* first. But it's that loyalty thang, man. Them closed lips. That Dawgs-4-Lyfe shit. Everything ain't supposed to go, just for the sake of the family. Some shit you gotta draw the line on, Thug. And when it comes to my brother, neither one of us ain't ever been able to do that."

I nodded. All three of us had blood on our hands, and loyalty had been the way we lived the street life. But I could see how hard this shit had affected Smoove. It was hard just to hear it. And that meant both of us had something Pimp didn't have. A fuckin' soul.

Me and Smoove drank some more and talked a little bit more too. I could tell he felt better getting that shit off his chest. Guilt was a heavy rock to live under, and his load seemed easier once he got all that out. He'd been holding it inside for a long time, cause there was nobody else he was safe telling that shit to but me. I tried to lighten it up by telling him that Pimp was mentoring young boys now. We both hoped that time and prison had chilled his ass out and changed some of that blackness that used to live in his heart.

"Pimp asked me to get him some tickets for the game tomorrow night, man. He's bringing a few kids from the center out with him too. I can get a couple more if you wanna come out. We're leading the series three-jack, and we plan on making it our last game."

I was looking forward to breaking some ankles on our homecourt too. Lani had called and said she would be in town for the game. She was a minister now, married too, and her and her husband were going to some religious conference in Brooklyn. They was bringing my son Dante with them, and I had three tickets waiting at the box office just for them.

Smoove shook his head real quick and stood up. "Thanks, man. But I'ma let that pass me by. I ain't seen or talked to Pimp since right after Noojie's funeral, and right now I'm cool with it like that."

I nodded and gave him some dap.

Later that night I stood in my phat walk-in closet and selected the gear I wanted to play in the G-Spot. A few minutes later I was sitting on the toilet thinking about what Smoove had said. It ain't always about the shitty things you do in life. Sometimes it's the reasons why you do them.

I tucked that thought in my pocket and got ready to hit the streets.

Chapter 27

It had been a long time since I'd chilled in the G-Spot, but the hustle was still the hustle. Other than the faces, nothing much had changed. There was still ass to be had everywhere. Liquor and some dope for your head, and a little touching and sucking in the back rooms or the Jacuzzi if you wanted that too.

Pluto was on the door and I paid my grand to step on the carpet, then walked in the back and hit the cashier with another grand to handle my drinks and any incidentals. G ran a high-powered operation, and I waked through the warehouse-sized joint hollerin' and dappin' some of the old heads and gangstas I'd run with on the streets back in the day.

I noticed that stuttering niggah Cooter was still behind the bar and wondered if anybody had ever found out what happened to his sister, Charlene. She used to fuck with G when we was coming up, and when she went missing and never returned, their moms had bugged out and lost her mind.

"Thug!"

I turned around and saw G.

His old ass was all shine and honey. Tight gear, rocked-up fingers, and beefy muscles.

"Sup," I gave up the dap, and he pulled me to his chest.

G gave me his killer version of a grin. "It's been a long time, son. Come on back in my office and let's holla for a while."

I followed G down a hall that I'd never seen before. We walked past a padlocked door that I knew could only lead down to one place: The Dungeon.

"You know," G said, lighting a cigar as we chilled in his deep office chairs. "T.C. woulda been proud of what you've done for yourself. Real proud."

I just puffed with him and nodded, letting nothing show on my face.

"I seen them two working on you from the time you was just a little boy. Running around here stealing every damn thing you could carry in your pockets. Miss Lady used to whip your ass real good for you too. It's just a shame," he said, and leaned back in his chair, "that they didn't get a chance to see how you turned out."

I nodded again. "Yeah, it is. A damn shame."

G stared at me for a long, long time, and I stared at that niggah right back.

He knew where me and Pimp had gotten all that money. I could see it in his eyes. He knew.

"Well," he chuckled, taking some of the heat out the air. "I just called you down here to tell you I'm proud of you too. I respect a niggah who does whatever it takes to get shit done. Whatever it takes. And you, Andre . . . you done proved to the whole damn world that you that kind of man."

I was glad when Greco knocked on the door and told G he needed him to check out something upstairs. I headed back out to the main lounge and copped me a seat near the stage. I knew I should have been at the crib getting some rest before tomorrow's big game, but instead I sat there watching some fine-ass stripper work the stage.

"Do that shit, Honey Dew! Show these niggahs what you can do with them pliers you got stuck up in your pussy!"

The girl was built with perfect proportions and every dick in the Spot was hard including mine. I put my hand over the rock growing in my lap and sat back to enjoy the show.

The lights went dim, and suddenly a single spotlight flashed over Honey Dew's outrageous body. She gave us a few slow, nasty moves, and niggahs clapped and broke out the dollars as she bent over and spread her fine ass cheeks. She laughed and looked over her shoulder at the audience, then squatted down and sucked a full bottle of Coke off the floor, gripping the neck with nothing but her tight-ass pussy.

"That ain't *shit*! That ain't about *shit*!" some drunk rapper standing beside me with gold fronts on his teeth yelled. "They got that shit beat in the dirty south! I know me a ho down at Club Magic who can puff a cigarette with her pussy. And that pussy be blowing perfect *O*s too!"

I stood up and clapped hard for Honey Dew, then tossed her a bill that fluttered to the floor at her feet. She scooped up all her cash and gyrated her juicy ass off the stage, and I stayed on my feet as the DJ introduced a dancer called Money-Making Monique.

"Goddamn!" I leaned forward so I could see better. This jawn was rocking her hips like a motherfucker. Her long skinny fingers was rubbing and squeezing her firm breasts, and from where I was standing it looked like she mighta had three nipples.

Monique was a true freak. She did some damage to that pole that had my collar choking real tight, and when the music changed and a bunch of big niggahs in tiny drawers came out dancing, I knew it was time for me to bounce. I walked over to the bar and gave a hustler named Moonie some respect. He was tight with G, but he'd been welcome up in T.C.'s Place so I knew he was cool.

"Whattup," Moonie said, showing me love.

I stayed cool. "Handling my shit, man. You know how it be."

"You been balling like a motherfucker, tho'. The Knicks needed you, man. They ain't been this hot in years. Keep 'em lifted, yo."

Jimmy's sister Juicy-Mo walked past and smiled at me real quick like she was scared to speak with her fine self. Cooter's sister Charlene popped in my mind, and I wondered if Juicy knew it was only a matter of time before that niggah G crossed her out.

"Yo, Moonie." I signaled my man. "Lemme get some Moët, ak. A whole bottle."

I took the bottle over to the cashier and got me a chip to room number nine. I'd already scoped out the girl I wanted to get with, and when I got to the room she was ready and waiting.

Her name was Saucy and she was holding a full physical package.

"Whassup," I said and closed the door behind me, ready to show this jawn just how I got down doggie-thug style.

- - -

"**A**ll right now," Saucy joked. She was giving me a lap dance and I told her to turn around so I could watch her from the back. I couldn't believe how she was holding it. She was slim in all the right places and phat where it was needed. She also had one of the biggest, roundest asses I'd ever seen on a slim girl. I couldn't take my eyes off of it. She tossed her hands in the air and jiggled her perfect ass cheeks until my eyes got crossed.

"The Knicks got a big game tomorrow, right? You ain't pumping out none of that supersperm tonight though, are you?"

"Umm," I hummed, gripping her waist and palming her ass like it was a basketball. The way she moved, I knew she had some good pussy. I could just tell. "I don't know what you mean, baby."

She laughed and bent over at the waist. I caught a whiff of her pussy and licked my lips and moaned.

"Oh, I heard all about your ass," she said over her shoulder. "They was talking shit about you the other day on MTV and BET too. Talking about all them damn kids you got. Mama's babies and daddy's maybes! Just don't leave no babies in this room with me tonight, 'kay big boy?"

I laughed. "You ain't gotta worry about that, sweetie. Trust me."

She started laughing so hard she had to stop dancing and turn around to roll her eyes at me. "Trust you? Niggah, please! That's probably what you tell all your baby mamas! But I can see why a bitch would wanna reproduce with you. You fine"—she grabbed my hard dick—"you heavy. And best of all, your bank is long and you paid."

She gave me a "duh" look and slapped herself on the fore-head.

"Then what the hell am I talking about? I must be sleepin'! Who *wouldn't* wanna have your baby! How'd Kanye say it? 'Eighteen years! Eighteen years! Now I ain't sayin' she a gold dig-ger but . . .'"

I laughed with her again, but it messed with my head when people talked shit about my kids. Not because I wasn't proud of having them, but because for the longest time I hadn't done enough to take care of them. Yeah, I had me four little princes and five little princesses. And thanks to my girl, Muddah, I was grinding hard for mine now. I had bank accounts and college funds and ere'thang for my babies. Life insurance too. I'd been a lame-ass niggah before, but my kids were set for life now. And so was Muddah. My whole empire rested at her feet, and if it came down to it I knew she'd take damn good care of mine cause she'd already been doing that for years.

"What else they be saying about me on MTV," I said, chang-ing the subject. I pulled her back into my lap until she was straddling my legs.

"Well"—she grinned, looking hot and sexy—"they say you doing some real nasty shit in the NBA, but on the mic you a lit-tle too competitive. They say you a gaming niggah who likes to keep up all kinds of go-to-war gangsta friction between rappers. That shit must work for you though, huh? You stickin' all over the charts when other artists are fallin' off. They rotating your cuts on the radio like mad too."

Saucy was still straddling my lap and I started licking her big titties like I was a new puppy. Her nipples was rock hard and stood out like little bullets. I swirled my tongue around them and sucked the tips gently between my lips.

She was nibbling on my neck as my hand slipped under her skirt and rubbed her baby-soft ass. I pressed my thumb against her clit and slid my long middle finger between her lips, inserting it deeply. I moved in and out of her tightness. The more I fingered her, the wetter she got. The harder my dick got too.

I got up from the chair without disturbing a damn thing. With my tongue still going to town on her nipples, I carried her over to the bed and lay her down on the thick satin spread. I wanted to eat me some pussy but I knew better. Her shit smelled delicious and looked like caramel candy, but *hell* no. She wasn't my woman. She was a ho.

Saucy started grinding her hips real fast, spiking up the heat. First little circles, and then bigger ones. I felt her insides grabbing and clenching on my probing finger and I slipped another one deep inside of her and fucked her like that. Her eyes was closed tight and she sucked air between her teeth. This wasn't no ho-show, I could tell. Baby girl was feeling this shit and so was I. A minute later she started shaking like she was having spasms. Her slit was so wet her juices were squirting out. Her eyes were closed tight and she pulled her knees up so I could admire her pussy. I massaged her clit gently and she thrust that whole thing into my hand, fucking up on my fingers like they were a dick.

"You like that shit, huh," I asked her when her shaking had finally stopped. "Well wait till I hit you with some of this."

I unbuckled my belt as her manicured fingers went to work on my zipper.

Her lips slid over my joint like wet silk and I started breathing harder. She sucked and slurped me down like a real pro. I clenched my ass cheeks tight and moaned, then cursed because it felt so good. She was giving up the best head I'd ever had in my life. Her throat didn't have no back to it because my dick was pushing all down in her neck. There was a hot pussy down in there, I just knew it. The harder I mouth-fucked her trying to reach it, the longer her neck grew, and the deeper my dick slid down inside her throat.

"You . . ." I shivered, pleasure rolling through me like never before. This was some superhead she was putting on me. Smoking my blunt, trying to steal my nut. Saucy's whole throat was vibrating. She was swallowing my shit so good that if she wasn't a ho I woulda rolled with her all night, based on her neck action alone. "You . . . ," I tried again, "gonna make me . . . bust real quick baby. I'ma have to . . . go out there and get me . . . another chip."

Saucy didn't miss a lick. She reached behind her with one hand and hit the timer button on her nightstand, which bought me some extra time and lightened my pockets by a couple a hundred too.

"Good, then," I said, my joint about to skeet like a water pistol. I was surprised too. I was known for having supreme dick control, and I could usually last a lot longer than this. But Saucy had me captured in her throat-attack, and I promised myself I'd get some redemption on our second go round.

She had me on lip-lock. Her fingers was stroking my ass cheeks and milking my balls at the same time. I opened my eyes and saw her cheeks puffing and collapsing, and my last bit of control went out the window. I screamed like a cherry-popped bitch and grabbed the back of her head, giving her about ten long, hard strokes. Then I busted so hard my knees sagged and I lost my balance. Sucking hard to get every drop, Saucy vibrated that tight neck pussy until I snatched my dick out her mouth and fell across the bed in surrender.

"Damn," I whispered, trying to catch my breath. "That shit was good girl. You a fuckin' professional. I'ma have to leave you a real phat tip."

She laughed and crawled up my body until her wet pussy was resting on my stomach. "You do that, Playa. In fact, hold on to that phat tip until we get through with round number two. I got some new tricks to show you. I'ma freak you out so good I guarantee that you'll be doubling that offer."

But she was wrong.

Just the sight of her stuff sitting up on me reminded me of my promise to Muddah.

No more baby. I ain't fuckin' no other women except you.

Yeah, Saucy had given me some dope neck-pussy, but that wasn't the same as actually sliding no meat up in her. But it was still wrong, I reminded myself. Getting my knob polished was still playing with fire. It was going back on my word and could cause me to get burnt.

God been good to you, Andre. But you keep fuckin' out like you doing. Your ass could get straight cursed.

"Know what?" I told her, pushing her off me gently and setting her on the bed. "You sweet as hell, Saucy, but I'm just wrong for this. Wrong as hell. I promised my girl I wasn't fuckin out on her no more, so I'ma stop right here. Cool?"

She gave me a crazy look, and I dug it. "I already pressed the button, boo. They ain't giving out no refunds, you know."

I stood up and put my shit back in my drawers. I got the rest of my gear on too.

"I know," I said and patted her on the ass. "But it's all good and your tip's still gonna be long. And I'm sure for the right customer you woulda been worth every penny."

Chapter 28

We ran drills on the morning of our big game, and I came back to the crib afterward to find Muddah waiting for me on the couch. I felt real guilty after handling sexy Saucy and her super-lips the night before, but I took a shower and cuddled with Muddah anyway.

It felt so damn good laying next to her that I started playing a little bit. Mouthing her titties through her shirt and rubbing the low part of her belly cause I knew it put her in the mood. Superhead Saucy or no goddamn Saucy, my dick never failed to jump up for Muddah, and I heard her sigh as I unzipped her pants and wiggled them down her hips.

I'd shown my baby three negative HIV tests in a row. And she was satisfied. I'd slid a phat-ass diamond on her finger a few weeks before I left for Los Angeles, and I felt good watching that rock shining on her hand. I was so happy Muddah was gonna marry me that I told her she could plan any kinda wedding ceremony she wanted and invite all of Harlem if that would make her happy.

"Nah," she'd said laughing. "Let's do something kinda small. Just us, Mere'Maw, Smoove, all your baby mamas and their kids . . . hold up. Then that means we bout to do something kinda big!"

I didn't understand it, but Muddah was tight with almost all the mothers of my children. They looked up to her and hung out around her shop. She treated them real good and spent a lot of time with the kids who all called her Auntie.

"They're sistahs just like me, Andre," she told me. "And those kids are yours. That kinda makes them mine too."

I'd shown her my list of names and birthdates, and she was real proud of me for taking that first step.

"Now you gotta get bank accounts for all of them, Dre. For college and shit, you know. They young and you can afford it, so get hot on that right away. Don't forget to put them on your royalty account with Ruthless Rap too. You just never know. You got life insurance, right?"

I'd nodded and decided to fuck with her head a little bit. "I got the bank accounts in trust for them already, but the life insurance and everything else goes to Pimp. I had to put him down on everything since Noojie was gone and Smoove was in Iraq."

That part wasn't really a lie. I *had* put Pimp down on all my shit, NBA policies, Ruthless Rap, the whole nine. But when Muddah agreed to marry me, I called my lawyer and had that shit changed. She didn't know it, but her name was on the first line of everything now.

"But you down on all my shit too," I said real quick before she could beef. "As my secondary, though," I lied. "Pimp is just my primary." I saw the look on her face. "Chill, Muddah," I laughed. "And pull that lip back in, girl. I ain't going nowhere. And even if I did, Pimp knows how a niggah feels about you. He'd break bread with you. As soon as we get married, though, I'll flip that shit."

She put her hands on her hips. "No, Dre. I don't trust that crazy fuckin' cousin of yours. Besides. We might not get married until the end of the summer. You flip that shit now."

I nodded and shrugged, knowing that shit was already done. Then I pulled her into my arms and spooned with her on the wide velvet couch in my living room and whispered in her ear, "I'll flip it as soon as I can."

And that's how we got in the position we were in. All that ass Muddah had on her pressing up into my dick and stomach was just too much to resist. I'd turned her over on her back and ran my lips over her titties through her shirt, and now that I had her pants down past her hips I opened her legs and eased myself between them.

The first taste of her had to be close to crack. I spent the next thirty minutes trying to hit that high spot as much as possible. I slid my tongue in and out of her creamy pussy as her nails dug into my shoulders. Her clit was plump and throbbing, and I rolled it between my lips until she made the sounds I wanted to hear.

I cupped her meaty ass in my hands and moved my mouth up and down her slit until my face was wet and sticky.

"Yeah!" Muddah whispered. She was moving her ass in my hands and pushing my face deeper into her stuff. "Eat it, Dre. Eat it, baby. Yesss . . . eat it, baby . . ."

I felt her stomach clenching tight, and I let her grind that ass anyway she wanted to. I kept licking on that honey bun, sopping up that sugar. I took one hand off her ass and massaged her lower stomach and that's when she brought it and brought it hard.

"Ohhh! Aggh! Dre! I'm cumming baby, oh yeah, lick this pussy, baby. Lick it for me, baby. Aggh!"

My tongue was still moving inside of her, and she was still pumping my face. I waited until she slowed down her movements, then sat up partway and turned her over on her stomach.

I didn't wanna fuck Muddah. I wanted to love her.

I started at the back of her right ankle. I kissed it and let my lips and tongue trail up the toned caramel of her calf until I reached the back of her knee. I sucked her there for a while, my hands massaging her thigh and ass as she squirmed.

My kisses moved up further until I found the curve of her butt where she had that one little stretch mark that looked like lightning had struck her on the ass. I sucked every inch of it, swirling my tongue on it, over it, then parted her cheeks and licked in it too. Muddah was slippery and sweat rolled off her ass-cheeks as they jiggled with pleasure.

I did the left side of her body the same way, loving the way her body smelled as she got hotter and hotter. I took my time and showed her how much I cared as I sucked and licked every bit of her flesh, bite by bite.

She was moaning out loud by the time I spread her ass cheeks open and slid my dick up in her pussy, and I knew I had her. She came as soon as I pushed myself into her, and I held her close to me as she pumped her ass back, giving me access to every inch of her sweet wet pussy.

I waited until she got her another one, and by this time we was doing some serious fucking. Muddah was on her hands and knees and every time I slammed my dick up in her I watched her ass shake and flow like a watery wave, and it freaked me more and more.

I reached under her and grabbed her firm titties, flicking her nipples gently with my fingers and humping her ass even harder.

"Yeah!" I hollered, gripping her hips and yanking her back as I slammed my dick forward. I stroked her deep and hard, throwing my head in the air, and a few seconds later I came, releasing my hot cum as deep inside of her as I could get it.

Muddah collapsed beneath me, laying flat on her stomach. I laid down halfway on top of her and pulled her close to me. "I luh you, Carmiesha," I said, slobber dripping from my mouth.

I felt her inhale real deep, and finally she let me hear the noise I'd been needing to hear so damn bad all my life. "I love you too, Dre. Yeah. I love your crazy ass."

▬ ▬ ▬

Madison Square Garden was live and full of bodies, and even from the locker rooms we could still hear the noise. Game time was still almost two hours away, and Coach Brown was taking care of last-minute details while everybody else just hung around trying to get their heads right for the battle.

Somebody had set up some tables in a big old banquet room where we were supposed to sign souvenir booklets for special ticket holders. I was the only rookie requested to sign, so you know a niggah felt grand being the only youngster sitting in the midst of the vets. My game was just that live.

Thirty minutes later a couple of the older cats were complaining about getting tired of signing, but I was loving it. I liked clowning with fans and seeing that look of awe and respect in their eyes when they realized they were actually talking to somebody they idolized. It was almost as good as the noise, ya know?

A group of kids was coming through the line, and I was surprised when I looked up and saw Pimp standing in front of me.

"Whassup!" I hollered, jumping to my feet to show him some public love.

"Thug," he grinned just like always. "Man, you doing the damn thang, and I love it. You was born for this, yo. You claimed it, and you did it. Now that's some real shit!"

"Who these little ballers, yo?" A group of kids were standing around him looking at me with hope in their eyes. They looked just like me, Pimp, and Smoove used to look back in the day. Gangsta clothes, wannabe stances, and visions of getting paid chinging in their eyes.

"These my little soldiers," Pimp said nodding at them. "My cats from the youth center. I got me my own little groupies."

I sat back down and picked up my pen. "Well let's do it then," I said, taking the booklet that was being held out to me. "Let's get this game rolling!"

I signed about seven booklets for Pimp's Harlem crew, and when I got to the last kid I reached for his booklet but he held it back.

"Whassup?" I looked up at him. "You want your booklet autographed, little bruh?"

His eyes was cold and steady. "Do you know who I am?"

I reached for his booklet again. "Nah, you gotta tell me your name so I can make it out to you, man."

"You don't recognize me?" he said, pleading like he needed me to say yeah.

I glanced at Pimp, then looked at the kid real close. He was a handsome brown-skinned little son, and something about him did look familiar. Real familiar. But I couldn't place him.

Pimp laughed and said, "C'mon, Thug. You don't know who this is? You sure you don't know who this young cat is, man?"

I shrugged. "Nah, I'on't know . . ."

The kid got swole like he didn't believe me. "Oh, so you know everybody else but you don't know me, right?"

I shrugged again. "Nah, man. Can't say that I do. But if you want me to sign your booklet just give it up, yo."

He stared down at me and for a second I could almost place him. But then it passed and he was just another tall, lanky street kid who could have been me, Pimp, or Smoove coming up in Harlem with hoop dreams on the brain.

"Aiight, then," I said when he grilled me hard and then walked away. This little niggah must didn't know how many fans I saw at every game. Wasn't no way possible for me to re-member half of them. I looked at Pimp like, *What the fuck was that about?*

But he just hunched his shoulders and shook his head. "All these l'il niggahs think they got some gansta in 'em, but we was ten times harder than them when we was coming up."

I gave Pimp some more dap and nodded. Then I turned to the next person in line and took his booklet and hit it with my pen.

■ ■ ■

I couldn't think of a whole lotta things in life that were more exciting than being a starter on a winning NBA team. Well, maybe being a chart-topping, havin'-the-number-one-video on 106th and Park, honey-magnet rap artist who was also a starter on a winning NBA team.

I'd recently gotten with an investment-baller-turned-studio-owner, Knowledge Graham and recorded a fly little hook segment to go with my NBA player introduction. They was blasting that shit through the speaker system when it was my turn to run out on the court.

> Listen up
> You're now under the in-flu-ence
> Of the Thug-A-Licous take-it-straight-to-ya-chin music
> Let's do it!
> For the love of the game!
> I'm the best can't you hear the way they calling my name?
>> Know whatt'im sayin?

The Garden was on fire! The fans were screaming and stomping their feet and hollering out the Thug-A-Licious song. And I was lovin it. I was stoked. I was on fire.

>> So when I say, THUGGA . . . Y'all say, LICIOUS!
>> Thugga . . . LICIOUS! Thugga . . . LICIOUS!

I was on like a motherfucker. I was playing the best game of my life.

We got behind in the second quarter, but the third quarter belonged to me. These motherfuckers was in a Thug-zone, and it was all about respecting me up in my house.

The fans was on their feet. My latest cut was blasting outta the speakers. They was stomping and screaming and waving banners that sported my name in big bold letters. They wanted some more of me, yo! They adored me. Pumped a home-grown Harlem niggah up to the sky.

I was running game in triple-double land, the ball like hot velvet in my hand. We were down by three, and I hit a three-pointer and got fouled. *And one!* Yeah, motherfuckers! What y'all know about that? That's how ya get back on top!

Thug-A-LICIOUS! Thug-A-LICIOUS! Thug-A-LICIOUS!

Coach signaled me over and I dapped Marbury on my way to the bench. Somebody passed me a water jug. I swigged a mouthful, pushed my face into a towel, and suddenly blinding heat sliced into the back of my neck and I was falling. Falling. . . . FALLING!

Thug-A-LICIOUS! Thug-A-LICIOUS! Thug-A-LICIOUS!

The crowd was going crazy, and even as I slipped into the blackness I could still hear them screaming my name.

When I say Thugg-A . . . y'all say 'Licious!

"Dre! Yo, Andre! Can you hear me? Open your eyes! Oh, shit! Say something, man!"

Thugg-A-LICIOUS! Thugg-A-LICIOUS! Thugg-A-LICIOUS! Thugg-A-LICIOUS! Thugg-A-LICIOUS!

The noise was fading. I struggled to hear it as I moved into a foggy tunnel.

Some half-naked freak with a killer ass ran over to the bench and threw her sexy black panties in my face. I took a deep sniff then tried to snatch them off.

"It's okay, Mr. Williams," a voice above me said as my hand was restrained at my side. "We're just giving you a little oxygen. Try and settle down, we'll be arriving at the emergency room in less than a minute."

The noise, yo! What happened to the noise? Bring it back, man. Bring it back! Bring it fuckin' back. . . .

Chapter 29

Carmiesha was sitting right by his side when he opened his eyes. The nurses had told her to go home, and said they'd call her when he was conscious, but there was no way in hell she was leaving him. He'd started out in the intensive care unit, but after giving him several MRIs and running a bunch of other tests, they put him in a step-down unit where he was getting critical care.

Every now and then a nurse would come in and ask Carmiesha if she wanted to go home and eat or something, and promise to call her if there was a change in his condition, but it woulda took about five big fat niggahs to drag her outta there by her feet because she wasn't about to leave Dre until he opened his eyes.

"Dre," she whispered when she saw he was awake. "Baby, I'm here with you. I'm right here, boo."

She was holding his hands, squeezing his fingers but if the doctors were right, he probably didn't even know it. Carmiesha rang the nurse's button, her eyes never leaving his. He was confused, she could tell. Maybe scared too. He had to be wondering what the hell had happened to him.

"It's gonna be okay, Andre," she said, hearing footsteps coming down the hall. The doctors had said he couldn't breathe on his own and needed the help of a ventilator. She had wanted to be there when he woke up so that she could be the one to explain what had happened and how their world had gone so crazy and so wrong.

The nursing staff came in and started adjusting some of the tubes running in and out of his body. Carmiesha could only stand there and watch as Dre lay still in the bed. His legs were so long that his feet were almost over the edge of the hospital mattress, and for a second she wondered if he was uncomfortable being like that, and then she remembered the doctors saying he wouldn't be able to move or feel anything from the neck down.

That ice pick had done some major damage. Dre's spinal cord had been cut in a critical spot and he'd never be able to breathe on his own again. He'd never walk again neither. Never rap again. And never play ball again.

The burden of knowing all that almost pressed Carmiesha down to the floor. She couldn't stand knowing it herself and didn't know how she would reveal it all to Dre. But he was her man, and he didn't have nobody but her. She knew she would be there for him for the rest of her life.

The nurses left the room, and it was silent except for the bleeping of the machines. Andre moved his eyes in her direction and Carmiesha smiled, hoping he wouldn't see through her brave mask and worry any more than he already was.

"You've been out of it for three days," she told him after the nurses left. "They had to put you unconscious to run a bunch of tests. Do you remember anything, Dre?"

He moved his lips, trying to talk.

"The game . . . ," he whispered. "We was at the game."

Carmiesha bit her bottom lip and tried not to cry. All kinds of hell had broken loose at Madison Square Garden. One minute Dre was coming off the court to sit on the bench, and the next second security was tackling someone to the ground and Dre was laying motionless on the floor bleeding from his neck.

They had stopped the game and rushed both teams into the locker rooms for security. There hadn't been shit Carmiesha could do as the medical staff surrounded Andre and put him on a stretcher. She'd followed the ambulance by taxi to the hospital and told them she was his wife.

It seemed like hours passed before the doctors came out to talk to her, and she knew by the look on their faces that whatever they were gonna say, it wasn't good.

"He's got a complete spinal cord injury," a black female surgeon said. "I'm sorry, but in most cases like this the patient loses all mobility because those nerves are too badly damaged to rejuvenate."

"Lose all mobility?" Carmiesha had shrieked. She had heard what the sistah was saying, but she wasn't trying to hear it. "You mean he won't be able to walk no more?"

The doctor nodded. "Unfortunately that's correct. The term we use for these patients is *quadriplegic*. It means he'll be unable to move his legs or his arms. I'm sorry. But there is some positive news."

Carmiesha had just stood there looking at her with tears running down her face. What the fuck could be positive about laying up in the bed for the rest of your life and not being able to move?

"With excellent medical care and therapy he should be able to go on to live a relatively long life. I've got some literature for you that will explain his condition more fully and give you an idea of some of the treatment options that are available to him."

Carmiesha had taken those brochures and stuffed them down in the bottom of her purse. There wasn't shit Dre was gonna want to hear about no damn treatment options. She knew her man. She had known him practically all her life. If Dre couldn't ball and do his thing on the mic . . . well, she just didn't even wanna think about it.

And now he was looking at her . . . waiting for her to put his mind at ease.

"Yeah, boo. We was at the game." Carmiesha smiled, hoping he would remember the goodness of that day. He'd been playing an amazing game, and that's how she prayed he would lock things in his mind, elevating the joy over the pain. "You was doing your thang too. Had them all shook with your devastating speed and your amazing skills. But something happened, Dre. One of the kids who came in with Pimp . . . he stabbed you, baby. He ran out the stands and stabbed you with an ice pick."

Thug's eyes never changed. He just looked at her for the longest time, like she was gonna jump up and yell, *Psych! Just kidding! Get your black ass up outta that bed!*

But this was real, and Carmiesha tried to let him see it bit by bit in her eyes.

"He was rolling with Pimp?"

Carmiesha nodded, rubbing his hand. "He hurt you real bad,

baby. I'm sorry, Dre. I'm so damn sorry. As soon as you feeling better I got a lot of shit to tell you. Just give me a chance to explain. I'ma tell you everything. . . ."

Thug's eyes were locked on Carmiesha's hands as they cupped his. He watched her small hands as they squeezed his fingers and rubbed his palms even though he didn't feel a damn thing.

"So . . . I ain't gone never move? I'm paralyzed . . . right?"

Carmiesha didn't even wanna hear the truth of it coming out of his mouth, but she couldn't lie to him. "Yeah, Dre, you are paralyzed. But you're still *you*, baby. And I still love you and wanna be your wife. Okay, Dre? Okay?"

But Thug wasn't even looking at her anymore. He wasn't even listening. He had closed his eyes and gone somewhere inside of himself and wouldn't come back out no matter what Carmiesha said, or how hard she cried.

Chapter 30

I closed my eyes on Muddah. Not cause I didn't wanna look at her no more, but because I couldn't stand the way she was looking at me. I couldn't feel shit except a black spot in the pit of my throat. In a split second everything that I had hustled for was gone. My whole life had changed. And the fucked-up thing was, I couldn't even feel it. I coulda laid there crying like a bitch and blaming everything on Pimp. But like I said, every man gotta hold his own nuts.

I made like I was sleep until Muddah left the room. She was crying so loud and hard the nurses had to come in and make her ass leave, and then she swelled up and got loud on them and they ended up calling security cause my baby just didn't wanna move away from my side.

I opened my eyes later on when a nurse came into the room to check on me. She smiled all cheery and shit like I was gonna smile back.

"Yo, what you doin?" I whispered when she pulled my sheet back.

"You have a tube in your penis, Mr. Williams. It catches your urine and directs it into a plastic bag. I'm just checking to make sure it's working properly."

A fuckin tube? In my dick? Was that how I was gone hafta pee? I couldn't believe it. And I didn't even wanna think about how I was supposed to shit.

Two doctors and a social worker came to see me too. They stood over my bed and moved their lips. Telling me all kinds of shit about how lucky I was that I was gonna live. And with good care, it could be for a long time. And for all of that time I'd be unable to move. The only way I'd be able to breathe was with the help of a ventilator.

Blah, blah, blah, blah, blah. I wanted to laugh. I was gonna live? They called this shit living? Could a niggah handle a ball? Could he jump up on a stage and spit into a mic? Could I jack my own dick or wipe my own ass if I felt like taking a nice shit? No? Then what the fuck did living and breathing mean to a niggah like me?

I could see it now. The whole ball team and half the goddamn league. Standing over my bed. Looking down on me and shaking they heads with pity. Word was prolly all over the streets too. Rappers, hustlers, and gangstas. Them niggahs would all be pushing up in here in a minute. Just to see for themselves. They'd put the word out good too. The Notorious T.H.U.G. was flat on his back. Took down. Niggah's hands was all crooked and curled up, and his legs had turned to hard jelly. Fuck a recording contract. Fuck the NBA too. No more balling and rolling the hottest honeys for old Thug. That niggah can't move shit except his eyeballs and his lips. That infamous gangsta dick got a OUT OF ORDER sign propped up on it. A jawn'll have to sit dead on his face to get her shit off on him now, and he better hope she don't smother his ass. Marrying Muddah was out too. What was she gone do? Roll my crippled ass down the aisle beside her? And then what? She was gonna change my diapers too? Tie a bib around my neck and feed me mashed-up baby food with a cute little spoon? What a fuckin' nightmare. The kind you never wake up from.

The social worker was still talking shit about nursing homes and physical therapy. He offered to get me some brochures on long-term care facilities.

Long-term care? What did that shit have to do with me?

Now the doctors was yapping again but I closed my eyes. I thought about Noojie and for the first time I was glad that she was dead and gone. I was glad Miss Lady was gone too. All a them ass-whippings she had laid on me just to come to this.

I drifted off and saw myself in a hot, bubbly Jacuzzi.

Crazy chicks was chillin' up in there with me, and at one time or another all of them had had some of this thug-loving put on 'em. They was fine as hell too. Some of them slim with big asses, some of them medium-sized with big asses. Some had thick thighs and big asses. They all wanted to be next to me, and they was smiling and rubbing suds all over my arms and legs. Their fingers was playing with my nuts. Their tongues licking all over my earlobes. A bunch a pretty-ass honeys laughing my name. Giving up the noise.

Thug-A-LICIOUS! Thug-A-LICIOUS! Thug-A-LICIOUS!

Yeah! I laughed right along with them as I rubbed me a nice hard nipple. They knew I was a freak. A pussy-hound. A honey knew exactly what time it was when she slid in them sheets with me. I loved females. I loved everything about 'em. The way they walked. The sound of their voices. The way their skin felt. The way they smelled and how they tasted on my tongue. I put the *nasty* on that ass. Hit it until they begged me to stop. I couldn't even bust me a little tiny one until I made her dance two or three times.

I turned to my right and saw my baby. Lil' Muddah Vernoy. She was sitting next to me looking fine as hell. Muddah held a gangsta niggah's heart in her hand! She was my ride-or-die baby and she was gonna be my wife.

Lil' Muddah had a stretch mark on her ass she was all the time trying to hide. On the real, I think I know how she got that shit now. And it didn't make me no difference neither, and that's because I loved her. I blew her a kiss. No matter how she had handled her business, I was Muddah's down-for-whatever niggah and she was my queen.

Thug-A-LICIOUS! Thug-A-LICIOUS! Thug-A-LICIOUS!

I heard giggling and that's when I noticed a bunch of kids was up in the joint with us too. My kids. Precious Monique. Shantay Desiray. Duqeesa Rose. Tyrone "T-Roy" Gabril. Tyreek "Lil' Man" Garelle. Mariah LaChae. Zion Malik. Dante Lamont. They was all up in there rubbing soapy water on me. Their hands worked on my shoulders and arms until my muscles felt like pudding. I had babies on me everywhere, and I took turns holding them. Loving it. Loving them. Damn, I couldn't believe I'd wasted so much fuckin' time! I picked my kids up and hugged their soft little bodies one at a time. They was mine and I loved the way their little bodies felt up against me as those kiddie fingers rubbed and patted me.

But it only took a second for all that shit to change.

Suddenly it wasn't just my arms they was working, but my

whole body that they had feeling good. My chest, legs, neck, back, every damn piece of me was being stroked and adored. Kathy, Remy, Rasheena, Paula . . . even Passion, with her sexy-ass self. She was holding Mariah, our baby girl, and blowing hot kisses at me.

Kiss your crazy-ass daddy! Give your daddy a hug! Go 'head. Pat daddy's back and rub his big head!

Little hands started patting and rubbing on me. And female hands were giving up mad love. My lips got kissed. Somebody stroked me on my neck. Vikki's horny ass tried to sneak and touch my dick.

Yeah! I tried to yell, but Muddah leaned over and stuck her tongue in my mouth, snaking it around in hot circles as she moaned deep in her throat.

They were adoring a niggah big-time. Those jawns was yeasting me up with so much noise it swept my heart up in a cloud.

Y'all sistahs sure know how to bring the fuckin' noise!

I was surrounded by a bunch of fine black women just loving all over me. Calling me baby, and boo-boo, and all kinds of sweet shit.

I nodded and laughed and turned my head, and that's when I saw him.

Trust Chambers. Better known as Harlem's T.C. His eyes was full of pride as he watched me cross that stage and get my college degree. A diploma in my hand, and street dreams on my back. T.C. was pressed out in some deep, expensive gear and had his arm around Miss Lady, who was dressed like a queen-ass diva and had been standing right next to me laughing and clapping on the day I got drafted into the NBA.

I had always known this day would come. What you put out

in the world was what you got the fuck back. But only better. See, this was my reward after coming up on the streets as a hungry ghetto kid. After surviving on nothing but talent and ambition. Skills on the mic and moves on the court. But this was a dream, yo, and the rules of retribution dictated that my black ass had to wake up out of it.

And when I did, I saw my man standing there. My cousin. My Dawg-4-Lyfe. Smoove's brother. Noojie's heart. And Mimi's sugar pimp.

I looked into his black-hearted eyes and saw everything I deserved.

My dawg had shit on me.

His dirty hands had been all over that shank.

Muddah had been smart to warn me to flip my bank. My baby had never trusted his ass. I knew she would die before she let this shiesty niggah get his grimy fingers on a single dime of my money.

"Do it, man," I whispered, and he knew exactly what the fuck I meant. "Do it, Pimp. It's only right."

I saw him hesitate and I understood. After all, I was family and he loved me.

"Do it, man," I whispered louder.

I pulled Pimp toward me using the mental muscle us street nigghas called loyalty. I tossed my monkey on his back and locked him in the cage of a hustler's vow.

"Don't let nobody see me like this," I whispered quietly. "It ain't right. Get my cheese, man. And keep my shawties tight. . . . Keep it in the family, cuz. Anything and *everything* for the motherfuckin family."

Pimp stepped nearer and I closed my eyes.

I don't wanna be here if I can't hear the noise.

He stood over me for a long time, looking down on me.

I opened my eyes again and urged him, "Do it, Pimp." *You greedy, coldhearted motherfucker.* "Do it, man. Dawgs-4-Lyfe, remember?"

I let my eyes fall closed, and when I felt his hands on my face I took a deep breath, then smiled inside and pictured Muddah.

My ride-or-die baby.

Half of a thug niggah's heart.

I'm doin' right, Muddah baby. Check me out, ma. Ya boy is doin' right. . . .

Chapter 31

Carmiesha stepped through the doors of the hospital only hours after she'd left. She didn't give a damn what those nurses and security guards had said. Andre needed her, and she was gonna be by his side as much as she could. It had broken her heart in half to see him laying in that bed. She had rubbed and stroked his fingers but they had felt dead to her touch.

Warm, but dead.

She knew what the doctors had told her, but still she wasn't gonna give up hope. She just wasn't ready to count her man out yet.

"I'm squeezing your fingers, Dre," she'd told him when he first came out from under the drugs they had given him. "Are they numb or can you feel me even just a little bit?"

"Nah," he said slowly. "They ain't numb, Muddah. They just ain't there."

Carmiesha had almost broken down in front of him but she told herself to be strong. She had to be strong for him. She had to be strong for herself. And she had to be strong for their baby.

She got off the elevator and walked past the intensive care unit and down the hall to the unit where they took patients who were no longer in critical condition. After they called security on her, she had gone home and taken a quick shower and made herself eat a banana and a pack of oatmeal cookies, even though she didn't feel hungry.

This time was nothing like the last time. Even though she'd hidden it from him just like before, this time she was happy and looking forward to what the next few months would bring. She had been planning on telling Dre the good news after the championship was over. She figured if the Knicks won the finals, her news would just put the icing on the cake. If they lost, then telling him would give them a reason to celebrate anyway.

But now she'd have to tell him right away. She had never in her life seen Dre's eyes look so damn empty. She'd bent over to kiss him good-bye and almost fell on top of him and hollered. It was like looking into blackness. A big black hole that just didn't have a bottom.

Carmiesha touched her stomach. Them damn doctors didn't know everything. They wasn't God. They didn't know what kinda G niggah they had laying up in that bed. He wasn't just no ordinary homeboy. Dre was strong and had crazy energy. That boy had been fighting his way through life from the day he was born. If anybody had what it took to make a liar outta all them medical books, Andre "Thug-A-Licious" Williams did. And as soon as she got in that room and told him about their baby, he'd have a whole new reason to fight, and fight hard.

Carmiesha rushed down the hallway. She couldn't wait to get up in there and give him the news because this was something she knew he would really wanna hear. She hoped she was carrying a boy. None of Dre's sons had been named after him. Little Andre would have so many sisters and brothers and play aunties that he'd probably be so damn spoiled it wasn't even funny.

But the second the automatic doors swung open Carmiesha blew up with rage.

Pimp.

That dirty motherfucker.

She walked up on him and swung her purse, hard. Catching him by surprise. He grabbed at his face and Carmiesha kicked high, smashing him in his little skinny dick.

"Get the fuck outta here!" she screamed, swinging on him. "This is your fault, you grimy motherfucker! He's laying up in there because of you and your crazy-ass son!"

Carmiesha felt hands grabbing her and she bent over, holding her stomach. "Oh, God," she whispered, trying to calm herself down for the baby's sake. Two nurse's aides were holding her and others were coming over to see what was going on. She prayed Dre hadn't heard her screaming. She didn't want him to know she had broken down and started fighing in front of all these people.

"I'm okay," she said struggling to her feet. She shook the nurses off, ignoring their pleas. "Let me go. I'm sorry for that. Please. Just get out my way. Please! I'm sorry! Oh, God . . ." She stumbled toward Andre's room and stopped at the door.

"W-w-what's going . . . ?"

There were three nurses by Dre's bed.

One of them was taking tubes outta his arms and another one reached up and turned off his monitor.

"What y'all doing to him?"

An older white nurse reached down and yanked the ventilator tube out of Dre's throat and sat it on his chest.

"WHAT THE FUCK ARE Y'ALL DOING TO HIM!?"

One of the nurses spun around. Fluid leaked on the floor from the tubes draped over her shoulder. "I'm sorry," she said. "You're going to have to leave."

Carmiesha almost knocked that bitch down getting over to the bed.

"Dre?"

She covered her mouth, not understanding.

"Dre!" Carmiesha grabbed his arm and shook it hard. "ANDRE!!!!!!!!!!!"

She collapsed on top of his still body, screaming his name. And then the old black nurse was holding her. "Baby, I know," she said, taking Carmiesha in her arms like she was her own grandchild and rocking her against her big breasts.

Carmiesha sobbed into the old woman's neck. Clinging to her like she was Mere'maw.

"I know, baby. I know! It happened so fast. His cousin was visiting him and he just . . . stopped breathing. Sometimes you see that with this type of injury. But look darling . . ." She turned Carmiesha around and made her look at her man laying there motionless. "Look in his face. Don't you see that boy is smiling? He's fine, sugar. He's got the peace. No more worries for him. This child right here got him some peace."

HARLEM HOMECOMING AWAITS SLAIN
NBA RAPPER THUG-A-LICIOUS

NEW YORK (AP)—The body of "gangsta" rapper and NBA rookie Andre "Thug-A-Licious" Williams, whose hip-hop tales of sexual conquest closely mirrored his life, rested in a posh Harlem funeral home on Saturday morning awaiting a widely anticipated funeral procession through the New York streets where he lived.

Nearly a week after he was knifed in a brutal, unprovoked attack during an NBA Finals game at Madison Square Garden, thousands of basketball and rap fans of the 25-year-old star are still numb with disbelief. The rapper's body, outfitted in his signature urban gear along with his official NBA hat, will be driven in a motorcade of stretch limousines from a public service on Harlem's East Side to Washington Heights and then onward for burial in the Bronx.

Posters of the slain rapper and his new album, scheduled to be released next month, are already plastered to storefront windows along the route where fans and police have reportedly had several skirmishes.

Williams's cousin, Carl Williams, aka Pimp-A-Licious, who was one third of the former rap trio known regionally as the 'Licious Lovers, has planned a lavish funeral procession that will travel through the Harlem neighborhood where Williams was born and raised. His mega-hits, "Just the Head, Please," and "How Deep U Want It?" will be playing on loudspeakers during the procession, according to an unnamed source.

In addition to Carl, Williams is survived by a second cousin, Todd Williams, aka Smoove-A-Licious, who is currently serving with the Marine Corps in South Korea, as well as eight children that he allegedly fathered with eight different women.

Five years ago the 'Licious cousins were questioned in a brutal murder/robbery at a gambling hall in Harlem called T.C.'s Place, but formal charges were never filed. Williams was preceded in death by his mother, his infant daughter, and his younger sister. He was rumored to be engaged to wed his childhood sweetheart, who is a small business owner in their old Harlem neighborhood.

On Friday, a public wake was marred by the stampede of a restless crowd who had been gathered outside for hours waiting to view the rap star's body. Later in the day, select mourners attended a small private service in a chapel of Carter's Funeral Home.

A literal Who's Who of the entertainment and sports industries are scheduled to turn out for the funeral inside the Flip T. Carter Funeral Chapel on Convent Avenue. Jay-Z, Reem Raw, Carmelo Anthony, Jermaine Dupree, Beyoncé Knowles, LeBron James, Stephon Marbury, Maurice Taylor, Larry Brown, and Michael Jordan are among the high-profile mourners expected to attend.

Minister Lani McCombs, Williams's former girlfriend and the mother of his son, Dante, will lead the choir at the service, while former college roommate David James will deliver the eulogy. As family and friends grieved, the *Daily News* quoted unidentified police sources as saying a thirteen-year-old boy was arrested immediately after the incident for suspicion of Williams's stabbing. A motive is unknown at this time.

Already hundreds of fans are crowding the blocks where Williams was known as Harlem's black prince. A makeshift memorial shrine consisting of photos, mixtapes, throwback jerseys, flowers, basketballs, CDs, and overturned beer bottles were left at the scene.

Several members of the Knicks Kids youth team stood outside of the funeral home Friday afternoon dressed in Knicks jerseys bearing Williams's number. They were holding up signs that read THE FUTURE NBA STARS OF NEW YORK ARE BEGGING YOU TO STOP THE VIOLENCE.

America seems to agree.

And at the end . . .

The final championship game was being played in Thug's honor.

His teammates had been so shook by his stabbing that they went on to lose that critical game, and tonight they were planning to redeem themselves.

Carmiesha was dressed in dark colors and sitting next to Coach Brown's wife in a VIP seat on the floor, but she knew the real action was gonna be taking place in the skybox overhead.

Her cell phone vibrated, and she pressed it to her ear.

"Everybody set?" she asked calmly.

"And you know that!" Rasheena said. Carmiesha could hear how hyped Rasheena was, and while she looked composed and cool on the outside, inside she felt the same way.

Shit was about to get started, and not just on the court. Dre hadn't been a perfect man, but he had been *her* damn man, and she was gonna see to it that the person responsible for his death got what was coming.

Carmiesha had been so proud of her boo when the commissioner dedicated this game to his memory. Every playa on his team had reached out and touched her with love. They told her how strong and ambitious Dre was, and how much star quality and promise he'd had. He woulda gone straight to the top, Carmiesha knew. On the rap scene and on the basketball court. Her man had dominated everything he touched, and he woulda made it to the top.

But none of that mattered no more. Dre was gone, but he was lucky in a way. At least he'd gotten a chance to taste his dreams. He had reached a lot of his goals and climbed up high to take a seat on his throne. Even if he didn't get to stay there for long.

Carmiesha gazed up at the skybox and nodded to herself. All of the sistahs had come through for Dre and did their part. Remy had helped her convince the other girls that if they wanted their kids to get some of Dre's royalties and insurance money then they had to get down on the program.

"Look, y'all. Muddah is secondary on Dre's shit. They was planning on getting married, but they never got that far. That means all Thug's money is going to that motherfuckin' Pimp unless we do something about it. If you down, stay. If you ain't, step! But don't come asking for shit later on when we all paid."

Nobody had left. They were all down to do what needed to be done.

Paula had made sure the special invitation was printed up and delivered to him by a courier. Vikki knew a guy who drove a limo, and she had arranged to get him picked up and delivered to the Garden on time. Kathy had a fourteen-year-old sister named Pinkie who looked like a baby in the face, but had a vicious body that was stacked with devastating curves.

And Rasheena. Carmiesha almost laughed. However much money they ended up getting, that girl deserved a bonus for real. Rasheena had gotten down on her knees and given the white guy who managed the skybox a def blow job. She'd sucked his dick so good he agreed to let her fill in as the VIP waitress for the night. And now, everybody was set and ready and had done their part to make sure shit went down smooth tonight.

Carmiesha touched her stomach, but her mind wasn't on the baby she was carrying inside of her. Her mind was on that other baby she had carried thirteen years ago. The baby who was sitting up in jail right now. The baby who had cried in jail when he told her exactly why he ran his ass outta the stands and past security and stabbed the Knicks' marquee rookie in the back of his neck.

"He had all a them with him, Carmiesha! All a his kids was with him except *me*! I seent him on TV the day of the draft. Why he wanna be with all them little kids and babies and not wanna be with me? Huh? I'm a baller too, Carmiesha! I'm just like him cause I'm his first son!"

Carmiesha had wanted to spread herself out on the floor and close her eyes.

"No, baby," she said, crying softly as she realized how much damage her lies had caused. "No! He's not your father, Jahlil! He never even knew about you."

"Stop lying!" Jahlil had jumped up and screamed. "His cousin already told me! Carl told me every fuckin' thing about him! Carl said that niggah didn't care *nothing* about me! That's why he left me! And you told me too! You said my father was a rap star and a baller! You said he was in college and that one day he'd be playing in the NBA! You told me that, Carmiesha. Yes you did! You *did*!"

The pain Carmiesha had felt was indescribable. Not even watching her mother get her brains blown out and splattered all over the wall had hurt her this bad. But Jahlil was right. Pimp mighta filled his head up with hate, but she had hinted lies to Jahlil about his father's identity his whole life. All she had ever wanted for him was for him to have a good life. She'd hinted that Dre was his father because she didn't want him to know what kinda rotten-ass tree he had really fallen from.

Right now they were holding Jahlil on Rikers Island, but if her plan worked the way she planned it to, she was gonna get her son a lawyer who could help him get through the legal system and get the help he needed.

And yeah, Carmiesha thought, crossing her legs and smiling at something the coach's wife said. Jahlil was her son, and she was finally ready to admit that shit to the whole damn world. The first person she told was Mere'maw, and it broke her spirit the way that old lady sat there and cried like her heart had been cut.

"That goddamn boy was rapin' you? And you didn't tell me? Don't you trust me even a little bit, Muddah? We got us a baby out there that I ain't never held in my arms? And now he done did something like this, and I can't even help him?"

Carmiesha had dropped to her knees and put her head in Mere'maw's lap and cried.

"Lil' Muddah, you shoulda brung this to me, darling. I'da accepted you and that baby both. God bless Miss Lady, and I hope she restin' in peace, but me and you"—Mere'maw wiped her eyes and stroked Carmiesha's tears—"we coulda raised that baby boy and got through this thing together."

Next she told her sistahs. The mothers of Dre's babies.

"Oh, goddamn!" Kathy had cried. Carmiesha ran it down to them just the way it had happened. She told them all about how Pimp had shit all over her life. How he had made her suck his dick, then fucked her on a pissy elevator floor when she was just a child, how Miss Lady helped her get to a hospital when she went in labor, and about how it felt to give her son up to strangers and not be able to tell anyone about him, especially Thug. She told them about the shakedowns and all the money she'd been paying out, and about those dirty-ass cops who had tried to beat her ass to death. She told them about her brothers, Justice and Rome, both deaded on the word of that grimy-ass bastard. She told her sistahs exactly who had gotten Ya-Yo smoked too, and how his mother blamed her for his death, and how she had wanted to kill herself just to escape the evilness that was Pimp.

To her relief, she found herself wrapped in five pairs of arms. Even Remy was crying when Carmiesha finished talking, and all of her sistahs told her they loved her and would be down for her, Jahlil, and the baby she was carrying, for life.

And now Carmiesha and her sistahs had work to do.

The game was deep in fourth-quarter action when they made their move. Carmiesha sat back and pictured that shit like she was watching a five-star movie, a cold smile spreading across her lips.

She could see it now. Rasheena up there wagging that gangsta booty in Pimp's face as she served him drinks from her secret stash of Thug Passion and St. Ides. Pinkie, switching around the skybox looking young and fresh and hotter than hell. She would know better than to look Pimp in the face or talk to him too much. Nah, that would be acting too grown, and Pimp liked his victims young so he could put fear in them and dominate their baby minds.

Right about now, when there was five minutes left in the third quarter, Pinkie would get up and announce that she had to use the bathroom. She would switch her firm young hips out of the skybox and walk across the hall to the private bathroom where Remy, Paula, Kathy, and Vikki would be waiting in a stall, feet up, standing on the toilet.

That niggah Pimp would be real high offa the scent of all that young pussy, and it wouldn't take him long to follow Pinkie into the bathroom. And when he did, they'd all be waiting to serve him. To give his monster-ass exactly what the fuck he deserved.

A shiver ran through Carmiesha as she pictured him knocking Pinkie to the floor and making her get on her knees. She knew what kinda look would be on his face as he pulled out his dick and leaned against the stall door. She saw him put his head back and laugh right before he pushed himself into her mouth.

He'd make little Pinkie suck that goddamn dick.

He'd yank her by the hair and slam her head down on it over and over.

Pinkie would be called all kinds of bitches and stank-ass hoes as he slammed it into her mouth, swinging his fists and punching her like she was a goddamn man.

Carmiesha shivered again as she pictured Remy. Hiding in the stall. Standing on the toilet, then leaning over the door and slipping the rope around his neck.

Oh, that niggah would put up a good-ass fight.

He would grab at that rope and try to yank Remy's ass straight over that door. But Remy wasn't going nowhere. Because her sistahs had her back.

Paula and Kathy, Vikki, they were crouching on that toilet seat too. Just waiting to reach up and help Remy handle that niggah as he dangled by his scrawny-ass neck.

They'd all get some. Especially little Pinkie. After all, she'd had to take a beatdown *and* suck that niggah's dick, so it was only right.

Together, they'd hang their weight on that rope until that niggah's feet was off the floor and he was pissing on himself. They'd make sure his dick was limp and he was foaming at the mouth before they even thought about easing up. . . .

And when he was stretched out helpless on the floor, hurt but still conscious and struggling to breathe, they'd really fuck him up then. They'd kick the hell outta him. Punch that niggah everywhere. Dent his forehead with the heels of their shoes. They'd take turns stomping that evil motherfucker. Kicking his teeth in until his mouth filled up with blood, and he started choking on that shit. They'd beat that niggah's ass until his eyes rolled up in his head, and he begged those bitches for mercy.

But there wouldn't be a drop of fuckin' mercy in them. They'd beat that niggah until his life was riding on his next breath. And right before he went out for good, Rasheena would step through the door. She'd be carrying an ice bucket. With something special inside.

Carmiesha shuddered in her seat. Her leg jerked as she saw the kicks sinking into his body. Her fists stung with satisfaction as she helped deliver every punch. Her mouth was watering, and she was breathing hard. She listened closely as Rasheena squatted down close to that niggah's face and laughed. "For a shit-talking wanksta who got such a little skinny-ass dick, your breath sure stanks!"

And then Rasheena would take her surprise out the ice bucket and jig him twice. Real quick. Once through each eye. Then she'd grab his pointy dick with two fingers and slide that icepick down deep into his pee-hole. . . .

Maurice Taylor scored a sweet three-pointer, and New York fans roared. The noise was so loud Carmiesha wanted to stick her fingers in her ears. But instead, she jumped up right along with the coach's wife and the rest of the Knicks fans and screamed and clapped her ass off.

"Yes!" she shouted, throwing her fist in the air. "Yes! Yes! YES!"

Thirty seconds later Carmiesha sat back down and waited for her phone to vibrate.

"Hey, Ma-Ma," Rasheena said sounding happy. "The Garden is *live* tonight! All kinds of fine-ass ballers up in the house. They dropping dollas up in this skybox too, but you know some hater aways gotta spit shit in ya' face. I just had to toss some stank-breathed, skinny-dicked niggah a peppermint! Nah, make that two!"

Carmiesha breathed deeply. It was over.

Now the dead could rest, the babies would be taken care of, and she could concentrate on trying to save her son.

She closed the phone and put her hands on her belly. A tear slipped from her eye as she looked up toward heaven and whispered, "Everything for our family, Dre. Everything for *our* family."

A Voice from the Grave. . . .

Thoughts of a Thug

This is just a thug's thoughts
For all my real niggahs it was never love lost
Just get it at all costs
Just tryin to make a dollar turn over again
But when it's over you can never do it over again

I been steppin over stones/runnin reckless with the chrome
going hard in the booth every session when I zone

Bad break, too late/fuck tryin'ta throw a bone
Can't beat it/got defeated/now I'm never coming home

I guess it's what God predicted
Outta sight/outta mind/outta time
Nigga's nonexistent

I was riding to the top/but the tides done shifted
Now I'm rotting in the box/and the grave's my prison

All due to a life full of crime and mischief
lies and bitches
Life in these times is vicious
highly gifted
That's why I grind persistent
So live that even niggas that died can dig it

And I guess the hatas already knew
I'm so thug

And the hood showed me love like I already blew

Son of the slums

Fresh from the heart of the zoo

You get money/they get funny/start targeting you

My crimes/you break 'em down to the simplest fact

And then assemble them back

And you will really know that it's realer than wax

So use your sense/when you pitch

On that strip

Number one rule: Suckers and success don't mix!

This is just a thug's thoughts

For all my real niggahs it was never love lost

Just get it at all costs

Just trying to make a dollar turn over again

But when it's over you can never do it over again . . .

Read an excerpt from Candy Licker by Noire!

Chapter 1

Money, Lust, Fame

It was a little after one on a Friday night and mics were on fire at the House of Homicide. Junius "Hurricane" Jackson was Homicide's CEO, producer, and all-around king niggah in charge. Hurricane commanded mad respect on the streets of New York City, and even the most thugged-out criminals feared him like the badass hustler that he was.

The House of Homicide was located smack in the middle of Harlem, on a block that stayed live twenty-four hours a day. It was originally built as a neighborhood movie theater, but when Hurricane started running things, he converted it into a hot nightclub/recording studio that attracted hundreds of ballers, rappers, and hopeful wannabe artists looking to get on a stage and get paid.

Every superhead in Harlem wanted to be down on Homicide's tip. The crack fiends, the teenage baby mamas. The video hoes who were lost and turned out.

"That Cane niggah is *hard*!" they'd laugh as they lined up half-naked outside the studio, posing and shivering in the cold, just dying to get a spot on his latest video shoot. "Let that rich motherfucka put the camera on me. I'll rock my ass so hard he'll forget his mama's name!"

Yeah, Hurricane was a living legend in Harlem, and he had his House on lock and under total control. He was a genius when it came to recognizing raw street talent, and he dominated the music industry so viciously it made those cats over at Crunk Cuts and Ruthless Rap look weak and broke-down.

Hurricane was in deep with the Mafia too, and they gave him a lot of rope. He strong-armed a bunch of small businesses and laundered Mob money through almost all of them, especially the corner liquor store he owned and his rib joint that was right next door. He played the role of a community leader and all that too. You know, giving out free turkeys during the holidays and sponsoring bookmobiles and things like that for the kids in the hood. He had fat knots in his pockets and was even known to organize street cleanups and pay people's bills when they got too far behind. But nothing went down in Harlem that Hurricane wasn't involved in. No deals got made, no pussy got sold, no dice got tossed. Nobody so much as rolled a blunt unless Hurricane got his cut.

Hurricane had mad pull from coast to coast. In the time that I'd known him he'd signed some of the hottest singers and rap artists from L.A. to Miami and snatched them into his camp. A few artists he straight stole from other labels, and some he actually got honest. But no matter how they got here, the minute they put their name on the dotted line their asses belonged to the House of Homicide, and Hurricane Jackson became their don, their daddy, and their dictator.

This Friday night was starting out just like any other. I was chilling downstairs in one of the recording rooms with two hopeful artists, Jazzy and Danita. Friday nights were fresh-talent night at the House of Homicide. The House was packed, and rappers and video hoes were lined up out the door and around the corner waiting for their chance to jump in the pit and impress Hurricane.

Jazzy had been here once before, but it was Danita's first night in the House. Since we were sitting around waiting for the pit to go live, we decided to kill some time listening to some bootleg mix tapes somebody had brought in off the streets. I'd watched both of these chicks rehearse the tracks they were gonna perform in the pit tonight, and they didn't sound half bad. The problem was they were regular. Didn't nothing stand out about them except they asses. I knew exactly which rooms they would end up in, and it damn sure wasn't gonna be no mic room like they were hoping.

Jazzy was the cutest of the two and she was rocking a pair of Donna Karan shorts that were so tight the V between her legs looked like a camel toe. Danita was just as hot. She sported a fly little Rocawear miniskirt that clung to her thighs and rode up her hips every time she moved. Upstairs, the music was banging and the party was in full charge. The way Danita and Jazzy were flossing I could tell they were ready to rush up the steps, grab a baller, and get crunk in the middle of the mix.

"Damn, Candy," Danita said, winding her hips and slurping from a cold bottle of beer. "I ain't into no bitches, but you one lucky heffah! Booming body, pretty red hair, blue eyes, light chocolate skin . . . I see why that niggah Hurricane got you laced up so lovely. Do you, boo! If I was laying up with Hurricane I'd be iced out and cutting hits left and right too. But just wait till your niggah hears some of *my* rhymes. I'ma press his ass *out*!"

I just nodded and thought about Dominica and Vonzelle, my girls from Scandalous! We was fresh and hot like Jazzy and Danita at one time too, so I understood what kinda cloud their heads were stuck in. Born singing, I'd had visions of being a superstar for as long as I could remember. But hard knocks and cold men had taught me a little somethin' about the music business that Jazzy and Danita must didn't know. These chicks couldn't see past the obvious. The bright lights, iced-out jewels, expensive cars . . . all this shit came with a price on it, a price that sexing Hurricane had taught me I couldn't afford to pay.

◊ ◊ ◊

I'd met some pretty mean niggahs during my travels, but Hurricane Jackson was the first one to show me what real pain was all about. Hurricane held a lease on my life. He'd paid the Mob cash money for my ass, and his word and his protection were the only things keeping me alive.

I got my first taste of Hurricane's cruelty while I was laid up naked in his bed, and the minute I saw what he was working with I knew my shit was fried. The niggah was a bonecrusher. He had a body like Mr. Universe. Mike Tyson didn't have shit on him. Swole chest, twelve-pack stomach. Muscles everywhere. But it was mainly for show. Sex with Hurricane was all about Hurricane, and he got his pleasure by seeing other people in pain. No tonguing me down or licking my neck. That was the last thing on his mind. He didn't even stroke the poon-poon or worry whether or not it was wet. Nope, fucking Hurricane was unlike anything I'd ever known, and I would find out the hard way that his foreplay was even more destructive than his name.

Don't get me wrong. Ain't nobody out here perfect, but there are some brothers who been blessed with gifts that can make a sistah climb the walls. Hurricane, too, had been blessed in a lot of ways. He was powerful, he was rich, he was fine, and everybody knew he had crazy musical talent. But none of that shit made up for what Hurricane was lacking, and a deficiency like the one he had, especially in a such a big, strong, buff-ass man, was enough to turn even the most mellow niggah into a raging maniac. Yeah, Hurricane Jackson had a whole lot of things the average brothah could only dream of, but what he was missing was the one thing all his money and his power couldn't buy him.

A dick.

◆ ◆ ◆

The first time Hurricane took me home to the banging mansion he kept on Long Island, nothing in my life had ever impressed me more. About a thousand niggahs lived up in there with him, but I didn't care.

He was rich.

His place was a palace compared to the holes I'd lived in. The windows were paneless and made of flat dark glass, the ceilings were twenty feet high, and the floors were smoked Italian marble bordered with gold trim. Everything about his crib screamed quality and cash, and as much grief and drama as I had just been through, I figured I was due to lay back and enjoy a few luxuries in my life.

Hurricane took me inside and made sure I met the other wifeys who stayed there, and then later on that night he let me bathe in his $30,000 onyx tub. I damn near melted when I saw his huge custom-built, oversize Hypnos bed. It was sitting up on a raised platform that was down in a sunken area in the middle of the room. The top of the bed had a canopy of black and white silk curtains that were tied back with tiny silver chains. Six carpeted steps led down into the sleeping area, and six more made of smoked black glass led back up to the bed on all four sides. I felt like a queen as he kissed my neck, then held my hand and escorted me all the way up to the top.

"Sweet Candy," Hurricane whispered as he pulled back the thick towel and stared at my naked body. "Soft brown skin and"—he tangled his fingers in my hair—"sexy blue eyes. I've run through some jawns up in here, but you's a keeper."

My nature was always running hot and I couldn't wait to feel him inside of me. My nipples were aching to be kissed, and thick juices were percolating between my legs. I laid there like a fool, grinning and posing all up in those sheets, ready to go all out for the man who was gonna make me a big star.

But I figured out what kind of party it was the minute he pulled down his pants and started grinding me so hard I swore the bed would break down. You ever heard of beating a pussy until you knocked it out? Well that's what Hurricane did to mine. He raised himself up on his hands and knees, slammed his hips down hard enough to crack my pubic bone, then grinded like he was on a mission to kill somebody.

"Slow down, baby," I begged, trying to catch up with his warp-speed rhythm. I wasn't a virgin, but my young ass didn't know shit about shit neither. Yeah, I'd played a little touchy-feely a couple of times, and true, I was a professional masturbator, but nothing I'd experienced had been anything like the express train that was roaring on top of me right now. I wanted to get with him, but all that pounding was drying up my juices, so I grabbed his thick arms, squeezing his muscles, then slid my hands down his back and held tight to his trim waist.

"Wait," I whispered, spreading my legs wider as I tried my best to feel him. "Is it in yet, baby? Is it in?"

He froze.

"What you say?"

Working my hips to get in his groove, I rounded under him and rubbed his ass, letting my hands work the thick muscles of his back. "Put it in *now*," I demanded, arching my back and brushing my nipples against his hard chest, eager to get my pussy stretched out and filled up until it burst. "Go 'head and slide all a' that good dick up inside me baby!"

Hurricane moved fast. He slid his palms under my hips and grabbed one ass cheek in each hand. Then he squeezed my mounds like they were two lemons, balling his hands into tight fists and digging his fingers so deep into my booty muscles he almost paralyzed me.

I screamed.

"I said, what the fuck did you say?"

Sweat broke out all over me and I arched my back and clenched my ass tight, panting against the pain.

"Candy!" he growled in my ear. "What the fuck did you just say?"

I honest-to-God didn't know what the hell I'd said. Whatever it was, I damn sure wasn't about to say it again. He rolled off of me and reached across the huge bed, searching for something under his pillow.

"I'ma put something in your ass," he said in a low voice. "Put something in there that'll shut you right the fuck up."

I almost screamed again when I saw what he had in his hand.

That crazy motherfucker was holding a gun.

And not one of those regular old Saturday night specials either. I'd seen this kind of gun before, it was Seagram's favorite piece. A .44 caliber Magnum with a hair trigger. The kind of shit you roll with when you wanna blow a niggah's brains out through the back of his head.

Hurricane cursed and slapped the barrel across my mouth, busting open my bottom lip. I swallowed blood and panicked when I saw the crazy look in his eyes. My teeth were clenched but he forced me to open them shits, shoving that barrel halfway down my throat, then taking it out and cracking it first against my collarbone and then dead on the tip of my elbow. I yelped and rolled over, balling up in a knot and cradling the black pain that ran from my shoulder all the way down to my fingertips. Suddenly he was on top of me again, and the cold metal was being pushed between my legs. All I could think was that the gun had a hair trigger and was gonna go off and blow me up from the inside out. I screamed and fought, but come on people. You know who had the wins. And then my pussy was being filled up for real. With something so hard and icy it got my whole body to shivering with pain. But as chilly and cold as that revolver was, just take my word for it and believe me when I tell you. It wasn't half as cold as Hurricane's heart.

Jazzy and Danita both did the damn thang in the pit and came out sweating me with a thousand questions, screaming, 'cause Jay-Z and Kanye were both in the house, and feenin' like industry freaks to find out what Hurricane thought about their performance. I tried to tell them to play it chill, that Hurricane knew hot talent when he saw it, and if he thought the opportunity to turn a dime was right there under his roof wasn't no way in hell he was gonna let it slide.

I know I made Hurricane sound like a nine-headed monster, but actually, he wasn't much different than a lot of other entertainment hustlers out there like Suge Knight, Irv Gotti, and even P. Diddy with his crazy self. Cane kept a posse of street-hard soldiers around him ten to twenty deep, and most of them were either bangers or stone criminals who didn't have no artistic talent but were down for whatever. They would take a niggah out real quick and then show you where the bodies were buried.

From what I'd heard, Hurricane had pulled a little bid upstate for killing a drug dealer. It was up there that he made all the connections that helped him launch his record label and finance the hooked-up studio that we were chilling in right now. The real deal was that Hurricane had done something a whole lot of other hustlers wished they could do. He'd gotten in good with the right people and started sticking his fingers in all kinds of pies. Them Italians was the ones who had fronted him the seed money to build his empire, and in return he set his boy Tonk up as Harlem's number one drug distributor and used his Mob connections to make all his buys. Hurricane kept the Mob money fresh and clean by washing it through his label, cooking the books on his artists, and producing underground porno videos and selling them by the thousands as adult entertainment.

Of course I didn't hip Jazzy or Danita to none of this. The fact that I knew about it myself was bad enough, and if Knowledge hadn't been Hurricane's right-hand man and the genius behind his financial empire, a whole lot of things would have caught me blind.

"Do you work anywhere?" I asked Danita as she finger-combed the weave that was hanging down to her ass and long enough for her to sit on. "I mean, you got a job to fall back on if this don't come through, right?"

"Nah." She shook her head. "All I'm working on is my singing career. I got a baby girl and my mama works. I can't find no job that'll pay for day care, so I stay with my daughter during the day and my mama keeps her at night."

I didn't have no babies, but I knew all about working on a career because I'd worked a man's job just so I'd have enough ends to chase one.

I'd signed on as a money mule for the Gabriano family when I was just seventeen, and while the stakes were high, the payoff was lovely. Just like the two girls standing in front of me, I'd been as dumb as they come. Fresh off the corner, I didn't know a damn thing about interstate trafficking. But I was tired of fighting off horny foster fathers and getting my ass felt by a bunch of play-play brothers. Daddy had been dead for years, and Mama was living in a homeless shelter at the time so she wasn't no help. The only other family I had was my baby sister, Caramel, and she was in foster care too, somewhere out in

Queens. I was at one of those frustrated points in my life where anything could have happened. I could have swung to the left or jetted straight to the right. Nicky Gabriano had come along like a life preserver, and getting in with his crew was a stroke of pure luck. The good thing was, I had enough smarts to know it.

◆ ◆ ◆

The first time I heard the name Homicide Hitz, my girl Dominica Santiaga was screaming it in my ear.

"Did you hear what the fuck I just said, Candy?" she shrieked through the telephone, calling me at my crib in L.A. "I got a call from some chick who works at Homicide Hitz! She said they checked out our demo, and they wanna see what else we got! Girl we about to get a contract and make Destiny's Child sit their skinny asses *down*!"

Dominica was a fast-talking Hispanic girl I'd met in foster care. She'd ended up in the system 'cause she snuck out her window one night to go sing in a talent show and got back just in time to catch her house burning down and her whole family going up in the flames.

"Calm down, Dominica!" I said. "And stop talking so damn fast. Who checked out our demo, and how the hell did they get it?"

She sucked her teeth and I could tell she had her hand on her hip. "Hurricane Jackson, stupid. I ran into one of his boys at a show and slipped it to him."

"Hurricane Jackson?"

"Yeah, Hurricane. You know the fine-ass Hurricane who owns the House of Homicide in Harlem? The baddest record label in the nation? You ever heard of Big Joe or that new kid

Dolla Bill? Hennessy? Too Tall? What about Dead Moon, that hot group from Brooklyn that came out this year on his new Homicide Hitz label?"

Dominica was steady talking, but I was so shocked I couldn't answer her. Hell yeah I knew who Hurricane Jackson was. Didn't everybody? He had shit on lock all over New York and way out here in L.A. too. I just never thought we'd get close enough to make a bleep on his radar screen, let alone get him to check out our demo.

We had started singing together in foster care—me, Dominica, and our girl Vonzelle. Dominica was real pretty with big titties and a high ass, and she was also loud and ghetto. Vonzelle was just as bad, but she was sneaky and ten times prettier. She was originally from the Bronx but ended up in foster care after her mother OD'd and her and her baby brother sat locked in a room with the dead body for two days watching it rot and swell. All of us had been through some shit and none of us had had it easy, but Vonnie was the worst in our bunch. She was slick and conniving, and I swear sometimes I'd look in her eyes and see some wild shit lurking there that scared me 'bout to death.

We'd hooked up together and formed a group we called Scandalous! and when I left New York and moved out to L.A. my girls thought I was gonna flake out and leave them hanging, but I didn't. I made sure that every trip I took to the East Coast we got in some studio time, and we'd just finished recording our demo a couple of weeks earlier.

"So what now?" I cut in as Dominica flapped her tongue in about three different languages. "What does he want us to do now?"

She laughed. "He wants us to get our asses down to the House of Homicide for an audition, Candy! Next Friday at ten. The chick on the phone said he was thinking about offering us a little something in writing." Excited, Dominica screeched loud enough to bust my damn eardrum. I wanted to curse her out, but instead I laughed right along with her 'cause I was just as happy as she was. "I gotta call Vonzelle and tell her this shit," she said. "In the meantime get your chocolaty-red ass back to New York real quick so we can get in there and tear Hurricane's muthafuckin' House of Homicide *down*!"

* * *

When I look back on how things went down tears come to my eyes just from thinking about my girl Dominica. She didn't deserve the terrible shit she ended up getting, and my heart twisted up when I remembered our last ride.

I followed Jazzy and Danita upstairs shaking my head. For a hot second I started to sit those two young chicks down and put them up on what was real. Hell, there wasn't no damn recording contract in their future. The most either one of them could hope for was a photo shoot for the porn calendar Hurricane put out every year or maybe a spot in one of them triple-X videos he shot and circulated underground. At best one of them might get picked as an extra ho when Hurricane produced his next video for a hot artist, but a recording contract? They had a better chance of being hit by a speeding train or getting dicked down by a vicious dog.

Something in me really wanted to tell Jazzy and Danita to jet. To warn them that the House of Homicide was really a house of horrors, with young girls like them being nothing but expendable victims. I wanted to tell both of them to head straight toward the door and put as much ground between them and Hurricane Jackson as they could. But? And? Then what? Nobody had bothered to school my ass on the way in, and even if they tried, I'd had industry fever. I was hell-bent on becoming a big-time recording star, and all the schooling in the world wouldn't have mattered.

It had taken me way too long to figure out that it ain't about how high you climb in the music business. It's what you give up in the process. It only takes a split second for things to go bad in this industry, and Hurricane played the game so well his empire was stacked strong and tall. A lot of people ask me how I got here, and others wanna know why I stay. So I'll just give it to you raw and dirty, the same way it was given to me. How 'bout I put you up on square one so you can see for yourself how it all began. Take a look at what went down before Hurricane grabbed hold of my world and spun it around like a tornado, totally out of control. Check out this snapshot of what my life was like before the passion and the pain. Before the money and the madness.

About the Author

NOIRE is an author from the streets of New York whose hip-hop erotic stories pulsate with urban flavor. Visit the author's website at www.asknoire.com or e-mail the author at noire@asknoire.com.